THE SEA GARDEN

Marcia Willett

WINDSOR
PARAGON

First published 2012
by Bantam Press
This Large Print edition published 2013
by AudioGO Ltd
by arrangement with
Transworld Publishers

Hardcover   ISBN: 978 1 4713 3088 9
Softcover   ISBN: 978 1 4713 3089 6

British Library Cataloguing in Publication Data available

Printed and bound in Great Britain by
TJ International Limited

To Regina Hartig

PROLOGUE

Summer

Journeys: all her life she's loved journeys. She climbs onto the train, squeezes her way past other travellers, checking her ticket against the labels on the seats, and swings her small case onto the luggage rack. The middle-aged couple in the opposite seats smile at her as she slides in next to the window, and she smiles back but hopes they won't want to talk to her—not just yet. First she needs to settle into the feel of the journey, waiting for the sudden jolt as the train starts to move, experiencing the sensation that the station, the whole of the city, is slipping away behind her.

As Jess looks out at the people on the platform she remembers riding in the back of the car as a small child, in her little seat, heading out to the seaside and, years later, when she was fetched from boarding school for an exeat or the holidays, being allowed to sit beside the driver—usually Mum, because Daddy was away with his regiment. That childish sense of excitement at the prospect of travelling is just as fresh today.

Outside the window a girl in her early teens is saying goodbye to her parents: her small sweet face shows a mixture of excitement and vulnerability. She is pretending a bravado she does not quite feel: yes, she tells them, she has her ticket; yes, she has her mobile. She displays them again with an exaggerated show of patient resignation that does not for a moment deceive her parents. Her father

1

leans to hug her and Jess sees his expression of love and anxiety, and she is suddenly filled with a familiar sense of desolation.

It is eight years since her own father was killed on deployment in Bosnia but the loss is just as great: she still misses that particular kind of loving anxiety that her lucky friends take for granted. She misses his humour, his directness, the deep-down certainty that he was on her side.

'Your mum is such a strong woman,' people tell her. 'So brave.' And yes, Mum is both strong and brave but, when she married her diplomat lover a year later and moved to Brussels, Jess knew that the first part of her own life was finished: childhood was over. Then started the years of catching the Eurostar to Brussels; of spending holidays at the smart flat near the EU buildings which, even now, doesn't feel remotely like home. Her mother is involved in entertaining, international politics, new friends; it's a world away from the army and married quarters. Slowly Jess has learned that she must forge her own way. She worked hard at school to get a place at Bristol University to study botany, made new friends; but she missed the underpinning security of her father's love, of a sense of support, of family.

Now that she is older she realizes that part of the joy of travelling these days is because journeys allow her to postpone decisions and free her from anxiety about the future. Just for this time she can put life on hold and exist wholly in the moment.

At last the train is pulling out of Temple Meads, gathering speed, and Jess holds her breath; her happy anticipation returns. She feels as if she is embarking on her most important journey so far:

2

leaving university, heading for London and an unrevealed future.

The couple sitting opposite are already unpacking food—cartons and packages and Tupperware boxes—as if they fear they might die of starvation between Bristol and London. Now that she looks at them more closely she sees a resemblance between them: the pouched cheeks and round, solid bodies remind her of Tweedledee and Tweedledum. They spread the feast out on the table between them and the woman looks questioningly at Jess as if she is considering offering her sustenance.

Jess feels much too excited to be hungry. She wants to say: 'I've won an award. A really important one. The David Porteous' Botanical Painting Award for Young Artists. I'm going to London to collect it. Isn't it amazing?'

But she doesn't say it lest they think she's boasting—or a bit mad. Instead she stares out of the window and wonders how well she's done in her finals and what kind of degree she might get. The Award—she can't control a little bounce in her seat at the thought of it—comes with a cheque for ten thousand pounds.

Everyone—even her mother and stepfather— is really impressed with this. She regards it as a breathing space, a chance to see whether she might now pursue a career as an artist rather than her former plan to teach. Her stepfather, however, is still of the opinion that she should get straight on with her teacher training. 'You can paint in your spare time,' he tells her, as if her painting is just a hobby, something she can do on the side. When she tries to explain her passion for it he reminds her how Anthony Trollope wrote all his books after a hard day's work at the Post Office. Her stepfather is prosy and didactic, and she wants to scream at him. Her mother always looks anxious but rather stern at these times of confrontation, which happen more frequently since Jess left school, and Jess knows that she will not be on her side.

'I think you should listen to him, Jess,' she says, irritated by the possibility of argument and the disruption of carefully managed peace in this very controlled environment. 'He hasn't got where he is today . . .'

And Jess listens politely to him—reminded inevitably of the character in that Reggie Perrin TV programme: 'Am I right or am I right!'— and then does her own thing anyway. In this case she's considering taking a year out to build on this amazing achievement.

Even the sight of Tweedledum and Tweedledee munching their way steadily through sandwiches, pies and chocolate snacks doesn't spoil her absolute joy in this moment. Her thoughts rest anxiously upon the new dress packed in the bag on the rack above her head—is it suitable for a presentation?— and on the telephone conversation she had with Kate Porteous, David Porteous' widow. Kate sounded friendly, enthusiastic about the Award, looking forward to meeting her, and Jess is grateful for the phone call.

'Let's meet up before the presentation,' Kate suggested. 'Why don't we? Or will you be too busy with your family?'

'No,' Jess answered, slightly embarrassed. She has no close family on hand to offer support or encouragement or share her joy: no siblings or cousins; her only surviving grandparent lives in Australia. And she doesn't want to go into details about Mum being too busy with some diplomatic function to be able to get over for the presentation. 'But two friends from uni will be at the ceremony.'

'Great. Look, I'll give you my address. David's daughter kept his studio and she lets me use it when I'm in London. I was his second wife, you see. When are you planning to travel? I'm coming up from Cornwall the day before . . .'

They talked for a little longer and so the arrangement was made. Jess would meet Kate at David's studio—his actual studio, where he'd done most of his work—and then they'd go out for supper and talk about what life was like with the great artist. It is the icing on the cake. Jess bites her lip to prevent herself from grinning madly with sheer pleasure at the prospect of it all.

Tweedledum and Tweedledee are now slaking their joint thirsts with fizzy drinks in cans; squeezed together, they perspire and shift uncomfortably. Jess sits back in her corner and watches the countryside sliding past beyond the window. The journey has begun.

*   *   *

At much the same time, Kate's train from Cornwall passes across the Bolitho Viaduct, and she sees a young woman and two small boys in the field below. They are standing in a row, staring upwards, waving furiously at the train. Seized by an impulse, she leans forward and waves back. The small boys jump about, waving with both hands, and she hopes they have seen her and redoubles her efforts.

She sinks back in her seat, aware of the quizzical glance of the man opposite. He takes a newspaper from his briefcase and she is relieved. She doesn't want to get into a conversation, to explain her actions. Instead her mind turns to the past, towards picnics and outings when her twin boys were small: treks over Dartmoor, afternoons on the beach. In these memories it is always just the three of them: she and Guy and Giles. Even in the pre-divorce memories Mark is rarely with them. His submarine would have been at sea, showing the flag abroad. Then after the divorce, years later, when Guy and Giles were at university, there was David with whom she shared fifteen happy years between her house on the edge of Tavistock and David's studio in London. She met artists, photographers, actors, enjoyed first nights, private exhibitions, studio parties: it was a world away from the navy and married quarters.

And now Guy and Giles are married with children of their own, and David is dead—and she is on her way to London to meet Jess Penhaligon, who has won his Botanical Painting Award.

'Not related to the actress?' asked Kate, to whom the name sounds familiar, and Jess, sounding puzzled, said no, there were no actresses in the family so far as she knew.

It's rather sad, thinks Kate, that Jess has no family coming to the ceremony. It was clear that she didn't want to talk about this, although when Kate said she was travelling up from Cornwall Jess said: 'Cornwall? My father's family came from Cornwall. My grandfather was in the navy. Do you live there?'

Kate explained that, after David died, she'd sold the house in Tavistock and had been renting a friend's cottage on the north coast of Cornwall for the last three years. They talked about what it was like to be married to an artist, and how difficult it was to make a living, and Jess said proudly—though rather shyly—that she had a new ambition: to be acknowledged by the Society of Botanical Artists. Kate smiles to herself as the train speeds towards Plymouth. It is a huge aspiration, but Jess might just make it.

As the man opposite turns the pages of his newspaper, and the refreshment trolley comes clattering along, something that Jess has said niggles at the back of Kate's mind. It keeps niggling whilst she asks for coffee and thinks about the cottage she's buying in Tavistock. She has been persuaded that she should get back into the market while the prices are low, and she knows it's sensible, but she's not certain she wants the responsibility of buying to let, and she can't decide whether she wants to move back to Tavistock. She likes living on the north coast, on the sea's doorstep, and within walking distance of the writer Bruno Trevannion— landlord, friend, lover.

Her friendship with Bruno has been very important during these last few years, since David died and Guy moved to Canada with his little family to work with his father in his boatyard. She misses Guy and Gemma and their young boys, worried that their relationship—already shaky when they moved—might have grown worse with Gemma so far from home and depending on two such undemonstrative men for company. Her own marriage foundered on Mark's lack of warmth, his detached indifference and bitter tongue, and though Guy is not exactly like his father there are

7

enough similarities for Kate to fear that history might repeat itself.

She sips the coffee, thinks about Jess again. As the train rumbles its way slowly across Brunel's iron bridge Kate gazes down towards the Hamoaze, where little sails flit to and fro and the ferry plies between Torpoint and Devonport. Turning to look the other way, beyond the road bridge, she sees the familiar imposing façade of Johnnie Trehearne's manor house, set on the banks of the Tamar, and suddenly she makes the connection with the niggling thought in the back of her mind and Jess Penhaligon. Kate remembers Jess saying, 'My father's family came from Cornwall. My grandfather was in the navy,' and she wonders if Jess's grandparents might be Mike and Juliet Penhaligon. Forty years ago Mike was a submariner, like Mark, and a favourite with the Trehearnes. Old Dickie Trehearne was Flag Officer Submarines, back then, and the parties at the elegant old house above the Tamar were legendary.

All the young cadets knew Al and Johnnie Trehearne. For centuries the Trehearnes had been sailors, traders, merchantmen, and Dickie and his sons followed in the tradition by joining the Royal Navy. When he was knighted, Dickie threw a wonderful party that spilled out of the house and into the sea garden. It lasted until the early dawn. Kate sighs, remembering: such an evening it had been. Leaning forward to catch another glimpse of the house, she sees the shadows from her past: young officers in uniform, girls in long dresses. She feels the sharp twisting pain of nostalgia; names echo like a roll call and she murmurs them under her breath: Al and Johnnie Trehearne, Mike

8

Penhaligon, Freddy Grenvile . . .

*   *   *

On that Saturday of the party, all those years ago, she travelled up to Plymouth on this same railway line from Penzance, feeling shy; even awkward. She'd hesitated about accepting the invitation.

'Don't start dithering,' Cass had warned her. 'I know Mark's not invited but that's because he's not part of the Trehearnes' in-crowd. So what? You're not engaged to him yet. Good grief, you only met him a few weeks ago. Come and enjoy yourself. They always need extra girls and it's a really big party. Dickie Trehearne's just been promoted to Flag rank and knighted, and he's invited loads of young officers. You'll adore Johnnie Trehearne. You met him at the Summer Ball. Remember? Well, anyway, Tom and I are going and I know you'll just love it down there on the Tamar.'

Beautiful, blonde, naughty—Cass was her closest friend. Five years together at boarding school on the north Somerset coast had created a strong bond, and both girls were determined that the friendship would survive beyond school. Now Cass had met a young naval officer, Tom Wivenhoe, and was falling in love with him, she was determined that Kate should be part of the naval scene, too. It was because of Cass that Kate had been invited to the Summer Ball at Dartmouth a few weeks earlier—and now to the Trehearnes' party.

As she made that summertime journey from St Just, Kate wondered if Cass was already regretting introducing her to Mark. Tom and Mark were in the same house at the Royal Naval College, they

9

both had ambitions to become submariners, but they weren't very close friends. Mark was reserved, quiet, a bit of a loner; Tom was extrovert, noisy, loved a crowd. It was sheer luck for Kate that Mark's prospective partner had twisted her ankle and Tom—egged on by Cass—persuaded Mark that Cass had a very pretty friend who would be happy to take the poor girl's place at short notice.

The Royal Naval College, set high above the river, the ball gowns, the uniforms, the Royal Marines' Band playing on the quarterdeck at sunset: the Summer Ball had been the most romantic, exciting party Kate had ever been at; she couldn't imagine anything being more glorious. She'd fallen in love at once; with Dartmouth, the river, the navy—and with the tall, handsome Mark, who seemed the embodiment of all these glories.

Perhaps Cass had a point, thought Kate. She and Mark had exchanged telephone numbers and addresses, and a meeting was being planned, but she was still free to go to a party. She was in no way committed to him and it would be crazy to turn down such an opportunity. Mark might even be impressed that she'd been invited to such a popular senior officer's party. Cass was right: it would be fun and she'd regret it if she didn't go.

Yet as she got down from the train, hoping her linen shift dress wasn't too crushed and clutching her overnight case, she was seized again by anxiety. She would know nobody but Cass—and Tom, just a bit but not very well yet—and she would be hopelessly out of her depth. She wished she hadn't come, even contemplated hopping back into the safety of the train, and then two young men appeared out of the bustle of holiday crowds on the

10

platform.

'Kate,' called one of them, a fair-haired, rather stocky young man with a warm smile. 'It is Kate, isn't it? We met at the Summer Ball. Johnnie Trehearne.' She remembered him at once and with huge relief took his outstretched hand. 'And this is my cousin, Fred Grenvile.' He turned to his taller companion. 'You said you'd met Kate at the ball, Fred.'

'You were with Mark Webster,' said Fred, shaking her hand in his turn, giving her an appreciative grin. 'We all agreed that he didn't deserve you.'

She laughed, suddenly feeling delightfully confident, and he took her bag and they all went out into the station car park, where a Hillman Imp waited.

'My mother's car,' Johnnie said rather regretfully, patting the dented nearside bumper tenderly. 'But she's very generous with it. Al pranged it last week and I have to say she was very good about it. But then Al can do no wrong. Did you meet my big brother, Al?'

He opened the passenger door and Kate slid in; sitting in the sun-warmed seat, she wondered if she'd met Al. There had been so many young men, alike in their uniforms, full of vitality and confidence.

'Doesn't matter if you didn't,' said Fred, climbing in behind her, leaning forward. 'You'll have your chance in a minute. He wanted to come to meet you but Johnnie and I won the toss.'

Instinctively Kate knew that this wasn't true, that these two young ones had been detailed off to meet a fairly unimportant guest coming by train, and her

11

heart was warmed by his courtesy.

'I'm glad,' she said. 'I remember you and Johnnie but I don't remember Al.'

'A-ha,' crowed Fred triumphantly, hitting Johnnie's shoulder. 'We've scored, Johnnie, my boy. She remembers us but she doesn't remember Al. It's a first. You must be sure to tell him, Kate, when you meet him. You will, won't you? I can't wait to see his face.'

Kate glanced at Johnnie as he drove out of the car park and saw that he was smiling too, and she was filled with an irrational and overwhelming affection for these two; for Johnnie and Fred.

*   *   *

The train rattles off the bridge and Kate sits back reluctantly in her seat. The man sitting opposite is watching her rather anxiously. He raises his newspaper a little higher, screening himself, and Kate is left to her memories: the ghosts of her youth and that first party at the Trehearnes' house on the Tamar.

*   *   *

As the forty-foot yawl *Alice* sails through the busy waters towards the two bridges Sophie, sitting in the cockpit, glances up to watch the train rumbling off the bridge. Two children are standing at a carriage window, waving, and quickly, instinctively, Sophie waves back. Johnnie Trehearne, standing at the helm, smiles.

'Friends of yours?' he asks idly.

She laughs. 'Don't you remember doing that

when you were little? Waving at trains and lorry drivers and passing cars? It was always such a thrill if anyone waved back.'

'If you say so,' he says agreeably.

They're heading upriver under power, avoiding a little group of racing Laser dinghies and a couple of Sunday sailors who take their boats out only at the weekend or at holiday time. Johnnie feels the sense of contentment that he always has out on the river or at sea. That moment when the anchor is hauled up, the mooring is dropped, or as the distance widens between boat and quayside, is when he is happiest. Perhaps, having spent his young years in the shadow of his older brother—glamorous, brilliant Al—it was his own way, back then, of experiencing independence and pride in his abilities. As a child, being alone in the dinghy—skimming over the water, testing his skills against the wind and the tide—expanded his self-esteem and confidence in a way that was never possible if Al was near.

Today, as they motor up with the tide, Sophie's presence adds to his contentment. She is housekeeper, gardener, chief cook and bottle-washer, companion and ally. A close friend of his younger daughter, Sophie has been with them since both girls left university, and now, twenty years on, she is as dear to him as any other member of his family.

'One of Johnnie's lame ducks': this is how his mother referred to her in those early years, when he insisted that Sophie must be paid a salary for all the work she did. Yet Johnnie knows how much they owe to Sophie who has seen them through deaths and births and daily joys and traumas, with her own off-beat common sense and philanthropic cheerfulness. She came to them to recover from an abortion and a broken relationship, and simply stayed on. It's a bonus that she loves sailing and is a very competent sailor. After his darling Meg died, and when his girls and their families moved abroad—Louisa to Geneva, Sarah to Germany—he would have been very lonely without Sophie.

Johnnie wonders if even Sophie knows just how much he misses his girls and their children. He knows he's lucky that they return at regular intervals to invade the house, sail his boats, and have parties in the sea garden. And here again, he knows that part of their readiness to travel from Geneva and Germany is due to the fact that Sophie is here to plan and organize, and make things comfortable and easy for them. They often bring friends and their children, and they continue to celebrate birthdays and Christmases together here on the Tamar. His throat constricts a little as he thinks of his sweet, loving Meg; how much she has missed, and how happy her pretty, clever daughters and their boisterous, fun-loving children would have made her.

The tide is sweeping in, carrying them up the wide reaches of the river where the gulls abandon their feeding grounds and the tawny rustling marshes are threaded and crisscrossed with blue rivulets as the water pours into deep muddy channels.

Sophie glances at her watch. 'We'll be in good time for lunch,' she says. 'Rowena will be pleased.' And a quick humorous glance goes between them, acknowledging the tyranny of the older generation.

Johnnie's mother—Rowena, Lady T, the granny-

14

monster, depending on who speaks—continues to live with him. Frail, dominant, ungrateful, she is still a presence to be reckoned with, but he loves her—as far as she allows any show of emotion—much as he has always done.

The house, with its spare elegant lines, can be seen clearly now, set amongst lawns and shrubberies that slope to the sea garden and the river. The sea garden, created by one of Johnnie's ancestors, is built on the foundations of a quay. Its grassy spaces curl out into the river, bounded by lavender hedges and, on the seaward edge, by a stone balustrade. Guarding it, gazing downriver towards the sea, stands the imposing figurehead of Circe, taken from an old sailing ship.

Between Circe and The Spaniards, the pub on the western bank of the Tamar in Cargreen, stretches an imaginary line. This is the finishing line for many a race during childhood days: Al and Mike in the Heron, he and Fred in *The Sieve*. Johnnie suddenly remembers that particularly glorious day when, for the first and last time, he and Fred crossed the line ahead of the Heron, and briefly he is a boy again, laughing with Fred as they paddle *The Sieve* into the boathouse.

*　　　*　　　*

In the end it was Al who gave *The Sieve* its name. Fred discovered the boat—an old National 12 lying neglected behind a shed in Cargreen—while he was helping in the garden to earn extra pocket money. Its owner had gone to war in 1942, never to return, and his widow was only too pleased to allow Fred to take the boat away for nothing. He consulted with

15

Johnnie, who asked his father for permission to put the National 12 in their boathouse so that he and Fred could rebuild it.

It was clear that his father was delighted with their initiative. He drove them round the head of the river to Cargreen, loaded the boat onto his trailer, brought it back and installed it in the boathouse.

It took more than a year to restore her. The boys earned money where they could, saved their pennies, bought the timber and other things they needed, and spent all their spare time working on her. They loved their boat and as they worked on her they tried out names for her: nothing seemed quite right.

'*Avocet*?'

'Boring.'

'*Queen of the Tamar*?'

'Pretentious.'

'*Al's Doom*?'

'You must be kidding.'

One afternoon at tea-time, after a few hours' work in the boathouse, Johnnie and Fred wandered up to the sea garden. Al was there with Mike, and Johnnie called out: 'She'll be ready to launch tomorrow. We'll be taking you on any time now.'

His father strolled to meet them, carrying his teacup, smiling at the two younger boys.

'Good work,' he said approvingly. 'We'll do the job properly and Mother shall break a bottle of champagne against the bow in the approved manner.'

Johnnie beamed at him, thrilled at the prospect of an official launch to honour the hard work he and Fred had put in. He knew that his

16

father did not quite approve of the way that Al commandeered the Heron so that nobody else got a look-in, but this fellow feeling was unspoken between them, not to be acknowledged. Yet Johnnie was comforted by their complicity.

'And after the launch we'll do sea trials,' said Fred, unable to contain his excitement. 'Just to check her out.'

'Don't forget to have the coastguard on standby.' Al's voice was amused, not quite jeering. He lounged on the grass near his mother, confident of her approval, and she smiled at his remark. Mike leaned against the balustrade, grinning. 'A couple of Jumblies,' Al continued more contemptuously, encouraged by his mother's partisanship, 'going to sea in a sieve.'

And the name stuck.

'We beat the old *Sieve* again today, Mother.'

'How many times now has *The Sieve* capsized, Freddy? Shouldn't it be in *The Guinness Book of Records*?'

So Al and Mike teased and mocked the two younger boys and continue to win their races. This was usually because they were more focused, more determined—they were competitive even with each other—whilst Johnnie and Fred were content simply to enjoy themselves.

And then, on that particularly magic afternoon, *The Sieve* beat the Heron; sailing inboard around the windward buoy, and on to cross that invisible line stretched between Circe and The Spaniards, ahead of Mike and Al. Johnnie cheered and saluted Circe as they skimmed past the sea garden, heading for the boathouse. They dropped the sails and paddled her in through the big doorway, joyfully

17

reliving every moment of the race, comparing notes.

They were too busy at first, furling the mainsail, to notice the grim faces of Al and Mike as they paddled the Heron into the boathouse behind them. Not for these two the gracefulness in defeat expected—even demanded—of Johnnie and Fred. Al snarled at Mike, who snapped back; they blamed each other, and so bitter were their recriminations that the pleasure of success was almost done away with; almost but not quite. Johnnie and Fred remained quietly exultant, tasting the first sweets of triumph, and it was then that Johnnie realized the friendship between Al and Mike was not of the same depth as the bond that existed between him and Fred. Perhaps it was then he ceased to envy his older brother.

*   *   *

And now, remembering, Johnnie sees the foreshadowing of the dangerous quality of that deep rivalry between Al and Mike, usually masked by their apparently close-knit friendship. Here the seeds were sown that flowered so disastrously years later, when Mike won the beautiful Juliet, whom Al desired. Johnnie remembers the four of them—he and Fred, Al and Mike—sailing home from another race; the raised voices, the sudden gybe of the boat and then Mike's frantic voice: 'Man overboard!' and he and Fred scrambling from their bunks below. They searched all night but Al's body was never found.

As he slows the engine and circles the buoy, Johnnie salutes Circe as he always does, and Sophie goes forward to pick up the mooring. They are home.

TAVISTOCK

Autumn

'I've been seeing ghosts,' Kate says, twirling the claret in her glass and setting it down on the table. 'Up on the moor. Down in the town. D'you know what I mean?' She glances at him. 'No, of course you don't. You're too young.'

Oliver sits with his long legs stretched out beneath the kitchen table, one hand in the pocket of his jeans, the other cradling his own glass. 'The ghosts of Christmases past?' he suggests. 'Or perhaps the ghosts of Christmases yet to come?'

She shakes her head quickly, makes a face. 'Definitely not this Christmas yet to come. You know Cass has invited me?'

'You'll accept, won't you? You mustn't let this talk about divorce get you down. You're acting as if you're responsible. Guy and Gemma are grown-up people.'

'Oh, come on, Oliver,' she says impatiently. 'You know it isn't that simple. Cass and I have been very close friends for most of our lives, since we were children. Guy is my son and Gemma's her daughter. How can either of us pretend to be unaffected if they divorce? In her heart Cass blames Guy . . .'

The retriever, lying beside the Aga, raises her head, watching them, then comes to settle at their feet beneath the table. Warm early autumn sunshine floods in suddenly through the tall windows and washes across the table: it glints on Kate's mobile, two empty coffee mugs and the bottle of Château Brisson.

'And in your heart,' Oliver says into the silence, 'you blame Gemma.'

'No,' Kate says quickly. 'Well, yes. Sort of. Oh hell.'

'I know my little sister very well,' he reminds her. 'I know why Guy insisted that they should move to Canada, leaving Gemma's tiresome ex-lover behind her.'

She looks at him affectionately; Oliver has always been her favourite of Cass's children. Behind him she sees a succession of Olivers: the engaging, manipulative toddler with his mop of blond hair; the mischievous, quick-witted schoolboy home for the holidays, teasing his younger brother and sister; the tall, elegant Cambridge graduate, an expert at winding up his father.

'And there are upsides so far as Ma is concerned,' he adds softly, unaware of these ghosts at his elbow. 'She misses Gemma and the twins. She hasn't much liked them being so far away. Now Gemma is coming home and bringing the twins with her.'

'But . . . divorce. And what about Guy?'

'Ah, well.' Oliver shrugs. 'Just between you and me, Kate, I'm not sure Ma is too bothered about Guy.'

'Well, I am,' she says indignantly. 'He's my son. I want him to be happy.'

He looks at her shrewdly. 'And is he happy? I've known Guy all my life and he doesn't strike me as someone who "does" happy. Brief spells of jollity

20

here and there; the odd moment of exaltation, most probably when he's had a drink or two, but do you truly believe Guy is someone who can be ordinarily bog-standard, day-to-day happy?'

She stares at him; his observation echoes a private fear hidden deep in her heart. 'How d'you mean?'

'You know what I mean.'

She nods reluctantly, sadly. 'But that doesn't stop me wanting it for him.'

His look is compassionate, but before he can speak the kitchen door opens and Cass and Tom surge in, laden with bags and parcels, speaking in unison, startling the sleeping dog at Kate's feet.

Kate leaps up to hug Cass and receive Tom's kiss. And even here the ghosts are present. A youthful tough submarine captain lurks at Tom's shoulder, brown eyes twinkling, one closing in an appreciative wink behind Cass's back. Cass's ghost is slender and sexy, tying up her long blond hair as she leans to whisper a naughty remark in Kate's ear. Oliver doesn't see the ghosts. He is moving his glass out of the reach of the toppling shopping bags, reassuring the dog, smiling lazily at his parents.

'What kept you?' he asks brightly, beaming at his father. 'Have you been enjoying a morning of retail therapy, Pa? Did you remember to buy a newspaper?'

'Just don't get him started,' warns Cass. 'Pour us a drink. Sorry to be so late, lovey.' She gives Kate another quick hug. 'You know what Fridays are like. Tavistock was heaving. Lunch won't take a minute.'

'Shopping,' says Tom, dragging out a chair and sitting down. 'I hate shopping.' He eyes the nearly

21

half-empty bottle of wine. 'I was keeping that for supper.'

'Kate's been enjoying it.' Oliver's voice is gently reproachful, chiding his father for being un-hostly. He leans forward, takes the bottle and tops up Kate's glass. 'Haven't you, Kate?'

As usual, when Oliver baits Tom, Kate wants to burst out laughing. Tom's expression is a mixture of frustration, fury and apology as he protests that he's very glad that she's enjoying it; of course he is.

'And anyway,' says Oliver, 'I bet you've got plenty more of it. What's for lunch, Ma?'

Kate gets to her feet. 'D'you want some help, Cass? Or would you rather Oliver and I take Flossie for a walk while you get organized?'

'Well, I would,' says Cass gratefully, 'if that's OK. It's been a bit hectic and I want to put this lot away. I'm running rather late . . .'

'And I was early,' says Kate. 'Come on, Ollie.'

He rises gracefully; reaches for a glass from the dresser and puts the glass with the bottle in front of his father.

'Help yourself,' he says kindly. 'You look like you could do with a drink.'

*   *   *

'Why do you do it?' asks Kate, as they pass through the hall and pause on the Rectory steps to pull on jackets. 'Why do you like to wind Tom up?'

Oliver shrugs. 'Because I can. He responds so beautifully. Always has.'

This is true. From childhood Oliver has had the knack of outwitting his father and—to Tom's immense irritation—Oliver has never yet suffered

22

a comeuppance. The First from Cambridge, the success of the business he and old Uncle Eustace ran together making media products and, when old Unk died leaving Oliver the bulk of his shares, the clever way Oliver sold the business just at the right moment and made a very great deal more money: all these have contributed to Tom's jealousy of his elder son.

Kate chuckles. 'Poor Tom. It must be very difficult for him to watch you going from strength to strength with apparently very little effort on your part. Come on, let's walk up to the moor.'

The Old Rectory, across the lane from the small granite church, stands at the edge of the village only a short distance from the high moorland road, but the climb is a steep one. A few sheep scatter before them into tall thickets of gorse, but Flossie ignores them: she's been trained well.

'I wish Ma still had a dog,' says Oliver. 'Did she tell you that they're planning to sell the Rectory and move into Tavistock?'

'What?' Kate stands still, staring at him. 'Are you serious? Cass loves the Rectory. And if Gemma and the twins are coming home . . .'

She turns away and stares out across towards Burrator. Sheepstor is a distant scribble of grey lines above the reservoir and dying bracken is rusting on the hills.

'Gemma will need somewhere to go if she comes back from Canada,' Oliver agrees. 'But Pa says that if she is going to leave Guy then she must learn to manage on her own. He says that the Rectory is costing a fortune to run and he can't afford it any more. He wants to buy a small house in Tavistock where they can walk to the shops. And to the pub.'

'And what does Cass say?'

'Ah. Well, Ma prevaricates and says, "Oh, but how will the children fit into a small house in Tavistock when they come for the holidays?" and then Pa says that he isn't running a hotel and they can stay near by in a B & B or a self-catering cottage, and Ma says that that wouldn't be the same at all.'

Kate smiles reluctantly: she can imagine those conversations. Tom will grow more irritable, he will shout, and Cass will continue calmly to state her case—and they will remain at the Rectory.

'The trouble is,' she says, almost talking to herself, 'I haven't a leg to stand on, really. I left Mark for probably much the same reasons that Gemma now wants to leave Guy. That is what Cass says to me. She remembers how it was for me and she says, probably quite rightly, that if I couldn't hack it with Mark why should Gemma be expected to with Guy. And I don't have an answer.'

Oliver slips his arm in hers again and it is a comforting, companionable gesture.

'Except,' he says, 'that Guy isn't Mark.'

She is almost overwhelmed with gratitude. This is why she loves Oliver: he is quick to see and understand and go straight to the heart of things.

'No,' she agrees quickly. 'No, he isn't, is he? Guy adores his children and he's tried hard to understand Gemma's need to flirt with every available male, and even when she had that affair he accepted that it was because he'd been away so much delivering and collecting boats, and she got so lonely.'

'It was a pity that Guy insisted on them going out to Canada. I know it sounded good, to make a new

24

start and all that, but I think it was too optimistic to hope that Gemma would settle in contentedly with two rather strong but silent men so far from her friends and family.'

'Mark would have found Gemma difficult,' agrees Kate. 'She's so like Cass, and he could never get on with your mother. He was frightened of her sexuality and he thought she was far too affected and silly. He simply couldn't cope with her exuberance.'

'But Guy can,' he reminds her. 'Guy rather likes Gemma's exuberance, except when it involves other men.'

She clutches his arm tightly. 'Whatever shall I do? How can I help but be on Guy's side? He's my son. I love him. And his children love him. I hate to think of all the disruption and sadness. How will they ever see him if he is in Canada and they are here with Gemma?'

They've crossed the narrow road that winds across the open moorland and pause to look down on the reservoir: a slice of gleaming water edged about with trees, deep in the valley.

'I think,' he says quietly, 'that Gemma's right to come back.' Kate looks up at him quickly, anxiously, but he nods, still staring down into the valley. 'Yes. Let her come home and then we'll wait.'

'You think she'll miss Guy?'

'I think that Guy will miss Gemma and the twins much more than he realizes he will, and I don't think his relationship with Mark, or the job, will be enough compensation for his wife and children. If I know anything about Guy, he's a one-woman man and he loves his boys. I think he'll come after them.'

Kate is seized with a longing to believe him. 'But what about Gemma? Suppose she doesn't love him any more?'

'We'll have to chance that one. It doesn't sound like that to me but we'll have to wait and see. But if she stays out there it will go beyond the point of no return.'

They stand for a moment longer, then Kate glances at her watch and whistles to Flossie.

'We should be getting back. So can I expect arguments about downsizing during lunch?'

'Oh, yes,' says Oliver confidently. 'I've decided to side with Pa. The shock of it will throw him completely off his stride and make him question his judgement.'

Kate laughs. 'In that case I'll need another drink,' she says.

*   *   *

'I simply cannot understand,' Tom is saying, 'why Kate doesn't move back to Tavistock. She's got a lovely cottage in Chapel Street but she goes on renting that little place miles from nowhere down in Cornwall. It's crazy.'

'St Meriadoc might be a bit remote,' answers Cass, assembling the ingredients for lunch: ciabatta bread, couscous salad with apricots, ham, and a goat's cheese flan, 'but it's got one important asset as far as Kate's concerned. It's got Bruno.'

'Oh, I know that's your theory.' Tom is dismissive. 'She doesn't move in with him, though, does she? He stays in that weird house of his stuck out on the cliff and she stays in the little row of cottages down by the boatyard.'

26

'Bruno's a writer,' Cass says impatiently. She is weary of these conversations which Tom returns to like a dog digging up an unsavoury old bone. 'He spends hours closeted on his own but they also spend a great deal of time together. I think it's a very good plan for them each to have their own space. And Kate's used to that with her men. First Mark, always away at sea, and then David spending half his time painting in his studio in London while she stayed down here. She's used to semi-detached relationships. They suit her.'

Tom shrugs. 'I'm damned if I'd want to live stuck out there if I had a smashing little house in Tavistock. The agents did a damned good deal for her with that cottage. I popped in to see them this morning while you were in Crebers and told them that we're considering selling this place.'

Briefly, Cass's hands are stilled. She experiences several emotions: fear, anger, and a desire not to start a row just before Oliver and Kate return.

'What did they say?'

There is a little silence; Tom dribbles more wine into his glass.

'Said it couldn't be a worse time,' he answers reluctantly.

Cass heaves a silent breath of relief. 'Hardly a surprise, is it? It would be crazy to try to sell this type of property at the moment.'

'The point is, though,' protests Tom, 'whatever we bought would also be a lot cheaper. If it's a buyers' market we can cash in on it. Surely it works both ways?'

This too is becoming a familiar argument and Cass is relieved to hear Oliver and Kate in the hall.

'Please don't go on at Kate about moving back,'

27

she says quickly. 'She's so pleased at the thought of Jess coming to stay and I want her to enjoy it. She doesn't need our input at the moment.'

*   *   *

Determined to steer the conversation away from divorce or downsizing, Kate talks about Jess at lunch.

'It was such a shock,' she says, 'to see how like Juliet she is. Of course, Jess is about the same age as Juliet was when I first met her. It took me way back. I lost touch after Mike and Juliet went out to Australia but Jess was so thrilled to think that I'd known them. What an amazing coincidence.'

'I can't wait to meet her,' says Tom. 'Especially now you've told us she's just like her grandmother. Juliet was a real looker. We all lusted after her. Sad about poor old Mike, though. I wonder if Juliet will come back home now he's dead.'

'Hardly likely,' says Cass. 'They must've been out there for forty years. Why should she come back? Especially if Jess's father is dead, too. What a tragedy. Poor Jess.'

'She told me that her father and Mike didn't get on,' says Kate. 'That's why her father came back to England as soon as he left school to join the army. I have to say she's a quite brilliant artist and a really sweet girl.'

'I'm looking forward to meeting her,' says Oliver.

'We'll have a thrash,' says Tom. 'Introduce her to old Johnnie and show her where it all happened back in the day. She can meet Lady T and Sophie.'

'She used to terrify me,' says Kate. 'Lady T, I mean. After Mark and I divorced she'd cut me if

28

she saw me in the town, but Johnnie was always the same.'

'Johnnie's an absolute darling,' says Cass quickly, trying to pretend that Kate hasn't used the 'd' word. Now Tom will get moody and distracted, thinking about Gemma and Guy, and Oliver will probably wind him up just for the fun of it.

'Anyway,' Kate is hurrying on, aware of the same danger, 'I can't wait to introduce you to Jess. It'll be fun for her to meet some of her grandparents' friends.'

'So when is she arriving?' asks Oliver. He is intrigued by Kate's description of Jess and her rather bleak little history. 'I think I'll hang around so that she has some younger company. Oh, I know you were a bunch of swingers "back in the day"—' he beams at his father—'but even so . . .'

'Next week, I hope. She really likes the idea of spending some time down here so I'm getting Chapel Street ready for her. I'm hoping to be staying there myself from Tuesday, once the furniture turns up. Then I can leave you in peace.'

'You can stay here for as long as you like,' says Cass. 'You know that.'

Kate smiles at her, and between them is a lifetime of friendship and love, shared terrors and silly jokes, and an underlying continuum of mutual support.

Surely, Cass thinks, even Guy and Gemma's divorce couldn't alter this relationship—could it? And why, she asks herself crossly, did it have to be Mark? All those years ago Kate could have had her pick. She could have chosen Johnnie or Freddy; at the Trehearnes' party, where everything started, Kate, Johnnie and Fred had been inseparable. Why

29

had she chosen Mark?

Cass gets up to make coffee. She fills the kettle, pushes it onto the hotplate and, as she waits for the kettle to boil, she can see in her mind's eye the groups of people having tea in the sea garden, Kate arriving flanked by Johnnie and Fred, and she can feel Tom's hand gripping her elbow as he leans close to whisper: 'Kate's scored.'

*　　　*　　　*

The first thing Cass noticed was that Kate looked very much at ease. Johnnie piloted her between the small groups of people, introducing her, whilst Fred wandered off in search of tea. Old Dickie Trehearne and his wife greeted Kate—Dickie with great warmth, Rowena with cool graciousness—and Fred returned carefully carrying a cup and saucer, which Kate took gratefully.

Watching, Cass felt a little surge of warmth towards Dickie as he bent towards Kate, chatting easily, whilst Fred and Johnnie joined in. After a moment or two, Rowena's glance strayed aside; with a brief polite smile towards Kate she drifted away. Cass saw that she joined the group that included Al and Mike and two very pretty girls, slipping a hand into the crook of Al's elbow as though regaining possession of him. He smiled down at his mother, made a remark that made them all laugh, though the two girls seemed a little less assured in the presence of Rowena.

Leaning against the balustrade whilst Tom exchanged civilities with an older couple, Cass continued to watch the scene. There was no doubt that Al was the most glamorous of the little

30

group of young men: as he stood there, beside his mother, it was clear that he'd inherited his elegant, predatory good looks from her. Whereas Mike, stepping aside now to fetch Rowena a cup of tea, looked a typical Englishman of his class: fair, slightly sandy, curly hair—which would presently begin to thin on top—and a ruddy complexion that spoke of outdoor pursuits: the sporting man. As he gave Rowena her tea his expression was an odd mix of the charming deference and confident familiarity that goes with the knowledge of being a favourite: he was part of the family. Rowena took the cup and saucer, smiling into his eyes—he was no taller than she—and murmured something that resulted in another burst of laughter. The two girls looked even more uncomfortable, smiling sycophantically before they began to edge away.

Now Fred and Johnnie, keeping Kate between them, were joining the group, and Cass watched Kate being introduced to Al, shaking her head slightly as if denying any knowledge of meeting him before, whilst Johnnie and Fred looked on, grinning delightedly. Kate shook hands with Mike, who was laughing, ruffling Fred's hair as if he were a child, putting him in his place.

Young Fred, little Freddy; that's what they called him: long-legged, thick brown hair, hazel eyes that always seemed on the edge of a smile. He was littlest, least and last; nearly a year younger than Johnnie, who was two years younger than Al and Mike. Nevertheless, thought Cass, Freddy had something: a secret, exciting quality missing in the other three. There was a faintly bullying, patronizing air about both Al and Mike, whilst fair-haired Johnnie was sweet-tempered and lovable, but give Fred another year or two and he might surprise them all. Meanwhile he was laughing off Al's bantering comments, ducking away from Mike's—slightly rougher now—hair tousling, submitting amiably to his role as the youngest member of the group.

Even at this distance Cass could see that Kate disliked the way that Al and Mike were openly bullying Fred now, with the tacit consent of Rowena who laughed at their antics, but it was Johnnie who took Kate by the arm and steered her away across the grass to where Cass was waiting.

'Glad you came?' murmured Cass, hugging her, and Kate said, 'It's fab,' and Johnnie beamed delightedly. As Tom stepped forward to embrace Kate, Fred appeared at his elbow.

'No poaching,' he said. 'We saw her first. No pulling rank,' and they laughed with the simple uncomplicated joy of being young and beautiful and strong.

*   *   *

Now, Cass brings the coffee, puts the pot on the table.

'Funny, isn't it,' she says to Kate, interrupting Tom, 'to think that you might have married Johnnie?'

There is a little silence as they stare at her in surprise, and she laughs and shakes her head. 'Sorry,' she says. 'I was just thinking back. Sorry. So what were you saying?'

*   *   *

32

As Kate drives towards Tavistock on Saturday morning she remembers Cass's odd remark: 'You might have married Johnnie.'

It is true that she was drawn towards Johnnie but not in any kind of sexual way; there was no magnetism between them, no exciting chemistry. She'd felt the same kind of comfort in his presence that she experienced with her brother. There was an easiness between her and Johnnie, free of any tension, and she valued it. She understands Cass's subtext, though: why did you have to marry the difficult, uncommunicative Mark when you could have had the sweet-tempered Johnnie? And perhaps the answer to that question is simple. To a girl of nineteen, a strong, silent, twenty-two-year-old man just made up to sublieutenant is always going to seem more exciting than a friendly boy of her own age just finishing his first year at naval college.

How young we were, thinks Kate. How confident and sure in our judgements.

As she passes over Plaster Down she sees a Volvo parked where she usually stops to walk Flossie. Two small boys of eight or nine are playing football with a man she guesses is their father since they all look so alike. A golden retriever bounds around them, getting in the way, trying to seize the ball, and the boys shout and the man attempts to distract the dog by flinging a broken branch for it to fetch.

Kate slows the car, engine dawdling, watching whilst the ghosts crowd in again. She feels quite certain that the boys will be boarders at Mount House School, out on exeat, and the lean, tough young man will be a naval officer, also on leave and

33

taking some time with his children. The dog comes back with the branch and he grabs it at each end, tugs it, turning in a circle in an attempt to take it from the dog: but the dog hangs on until it is carried right off its feet and is swung in circles still grimly holding onto the branch while the boys laugh and cheer.

She drives on across the familiar moorland roads, unsettled by these strong emotions, wondering if she is right to be considering moving back to this place where she lived for thirty years: two marriages—one ending in divorce and the other with bereavement—bringing up Guy and Giles, working in the bookshop in Tavistock, breeding golden retrievers. Already, on this short journey, she has passed three very different houses in which she has lived: the colonial-style bungalow in Dousland, a delightful old cottage in Walkhampton and the Victorian house on the edge of the town in Whitechurch. Will the cottage in Chapel Street be the place where she decides finally to settle?

She thinks of the narrow valley on the north coast, and the cottage at the end of the row, on the sea's doorstep. The cottage might belong to Bruno but it's full of her own things, and he is a short walk away in his strange stone house—The Lookout—halfway up the cliff, so that she never need feel lonely. She's been very happy for these last few years—a magical time, as if real life has been put on hold—no responsibilities to speak of and a part of the small, close-knit community that lives at St Meriadoc. If she hadn't been persuaded that she should buy back into the market she wouldn't now be faced with this decision: should she continue to rent Bruno's cottage or move back to Tavistock?

Seized by a sense of panic, she does what she has done so many times before: she drives through Tavistock and into the car park of the Bedford Hotel. With Flossie on her lead, they go together up the front steps and into the bar.

She looks around at the familiar surroundings, at the people drinking coffee and reading newspapers, and there in the corner by the window is Johnnie Trehearne, already hailing her, getting to his feet. Kate sees with a sinking heart that his mother is sitting with her back to the window, crabbed and suspicious as she watches them hug. Johnnie forestalls any of the past prejudices with his natural warmth and friendliness.

'You remember Kate, Mother,' he says firmly—it is an instruction not a question—and Kate, hiding her instinctive reaction to behave like a junior naval wife, smiles at the imperious elderly lady, who inclines her head. The small terrier, almost concealed on her lap, gives a sharp warning bark, and Kate jumps back a little and tightens her hold on Flossie's lead.

'Shut up, Popps,' says Johnnie affably to the terrier. 'Haven't seen you around for a while, Kate. Can I get you some coffee?'

'Thank you,' she says, sitting down, pulling Flossie close to her chair. 'This is really so odd. I'm staying with Cass and Tom and we were talking about you. Well, not just you but remembering times past.'

'Dangerous,' he says cheerfully, pausing to stroke Flossie as he goes to the bar.

Kate turns to Lady T, trying to think of some topic of conversation that might melt thirty years of ice. She must be at least ninety but the old woman's eyes are still bright and sharp, and Kate's heart sinks: no chance that she will have forgotten the past.

'I've bought a cottage in Chapel Street,' she begins—nothing contentious about this, surely—'and I'm moving some furniture in next week. I've been living down on the north coast of Cornwall since my husband died.'

'Died? I thought you were divorced.'

Kate almost laughs: Lady T still doesn't take prisoners. 'My second husband,' she explains. 'David Porteous. He was an artist. An RA. The granddaughter of old friends has just won his Award. I think you know them too.'

Johnnie is back and she turns to him. 'You remember the Penhaligons, don't you? Juliet and Mike? I've met their granddaughter, Jess. She's coming to stay with me.'

There is an odd little silence, then Johnnie sits down, bending to pat Flossie, again.

'They went out to Australia, didn't they?' he says. 'He transferred to the Australian Navy. We remember Mike Penhaligon, don't we, Mother?'

'I remember him very well.' Her voice is thin and cool.

'Jess is really looking forward to meeting any friends of Mike and Juliet's. Tom thought it might be fun if she were to meet you, too.'

'You must bring her over,' Johnnie says. 'What's her name? Jess? How amazing. I think Juliet and Mike met at one of our parties. What fun.'

His voice lacks its usual warmth and when Kate looks at his mother she sees that the elderly woman's expression is an odd one: bleak and remote. She looks beyond the walls of the bar to a

36

scene only she can remember; hearing other voices in another time.

Kate suddenly recalls that Al died in a tragic sailing accident when he was still young, and she is seized by a sense of foreboding.

'I wouldn't want to be a nuisance,' she says quickly. 'And I don't know how long she can stay . . .'

'Of course you must both come to lunch,' says old Lady T. 'Johnnie will arrange it. Kate is moving into Chapel Street, Johnnie. Write down her telephone number. I've got a pen here somewhere.'

The coffee arrives as she scrabbles in a capacious handbag, and Kate is able to hide her surprise at such a positive invitation from her old detractor. They talk of Jess, and Kate explains again the girl's history, wondering why she still feels so uneasy, and presently they part.

TAMAR

Sophie stands by the balustrade in the sea garden watching Freddy Grenvile rowing across the river from Cargreen. It is typical of Freddy, she thinks, to row across rather than to use the outboard motor. Even now, in his sixties, he is strong and fit; he loves to sail, to ski, to play tennis. Behind his small terraced cottage the courtyard will be full of bits and pieces in various stages of repair. He is always mending, building, and he and Johnnie are at present restoring an old naval cutter down in the boathouse. Below her, Sophie can see *Alice* moored against the stone wall of the old quay, so that she can be leaned against the wall as the tide drops, ready to be scrubbed down. Freddy is on his way to join the scrubbing party.

He pulls strongly, heading against the tide, which is on the ebb. As he glances over his shoulder Sophie raises a hand to him and he pauses to return the salute before he settles again to his stroke. She rests her elbows on the balustrade, relaxing in the sun. Between them, she and Johnnie and Freddy— with a bit of help from a couple in the village—keep the whole place together and a strong bond of trust and affection has grown between the three of them.

Way back, right at the beginning, she imagined herself in love with Freddy. She didn't care that he was twenty years older than she was, in his early forties; he was tall and lean and very good-looking, and he and Johnnie always had great times together. She crewed for both of them, went to the pub with them, and they were such good company that the pain of being so brutally dismissed by her ex-lover slowly eased and her self-esteem gradually reasserted itself. Nothing had come of that early infatuation. Freddy had been posted to the Far East and for the next two years he'd spent only a few weeks of leave at his little cottage across the river in Cargreen. When he got back from Hong Kong he gave her one of his beautifully detailed little sketches; this time it was of a three-masted junk. It was a warm gesture that implied affection, that she was one of the family, but nothing more.

Just as well, Sophie thinks now, that her infatuation was nipped firmly in the bud. Much better to have this easygoing relationship with both men than the emotional muddle that goes with being in love. Apart from the disadvantage of the twenty-year age gap, Freddy probably wasn't good husband material either. His marriage to a divorcee with two children failed and she returned to her first husband taking the children with her, but, according to Johnnie, Freddy wasn't overly distressed by it.

'I don't think he's particularly home and hearth, our Fred,' he said. 'He's the original free spirit and I think he's quite happy the way he is.'

And Sophie is happy with it, too. She strolls across the lawn to the boathouse and waits for Freddy to haul the dinghy up onto the slip.

'Johnnie and Rowena have gone into Tavistock,' she says. 'They won't be long. The library has got some books Johnnie ordered, to do with his research on the Tamar. Rowena took a sudden whim to go with him. Come and have some coffee.'

They wander companionably across the lawn, round to the back of the house and into the kitchen. Freddy leans against the sink, hands in the pockets of his old shorts. He wears an ancient, faded Aertex shirt and a pair of plimsolls: his scrubbing-down rig. It's rather typical of Fred, thinks Sophie, that he still manages to look elegant in a rakish, sexy kind of way.

'Johnnie's chosen the perfect weekend,' he says. 'It'll be a good afternoon for it. The tide's just right.'

'I'll come and give a hand after lunch,' she offers. 'And Will's got a Sunday out tomorrow so he can help too. He'll like that.'

Young Will, Louisa's eldest, is now at Mount House, the prep school just outside Tavistock. It is his turn to be cherished on Sundays out and exeats when he can't get back home to Geneva. He

39

misses his parents and his three little sisters, but his grandfather—'Grando', as Will calls Johnnie—and Sophie do their best to keep him busy and happy. They go to the school plays and concerts, to rugby and cricket matches, and Sophie encourages him to bring his school friends down to the Tamar with him at weekends.

Freddy smiles at her approvingly. He's very fond of Sophie. He likes her directness, her sense of humour. He'd guessed at the infatuation, was flattered by it, but relieved that nothing came of it and that Sophie was clearly unscathed. His one attempt at marriage had shown that he hadn't the temperament for it and he had no intention of risking it again.

'Will's very much like Johnnie was at that age,' he says. 'Rather serious and mad about boats. I wonder if he'll follow the family tradition and join the navy.'

Sophie edges Freddy along so that she can get to the sink and he moves aside and picks up his mug.

'It's his ambition at the moment, but he's only ten,' she says.

Freddy thinks about it. By the time he was ten his father had been killed in the war and his mother had gratefully accepted her cousin Dickie's offer of the cottage in Cargreen. Dickie had generously taken responsibility for young Fred's education so that he and Johnnie and Al had grown up more like brothers than second cousins. It had been taken for granted that all three of them would join the navy as a matter of course. And so they had. When they passed out from Dartmouth, Al and Johnnie had joined the submarine service like their father before them, but Fred had been unable to face being shut

40

in a metal tube under the water, all packed together like sardines, and he'd joined the surface fleet.

'A skimmer,' Al had said derisively. 'Poor little Fred. Always littlest, least and last, but never mind. I suppose someone's got to do it.'

Al considered himself to be one of the élite: first, best, special—but Al had died. For a brief moment, Freddy is transported back to the past; he recalls the sound of the wind and the snap of the sail, raised voices and then the cry in the darkness of 'Man overboard!'

'Are you OK?' asks Sophie. 'You look like you've seen a ghost.'

And so he has. 'I'm fine,' he says. 'Is that the car?'

Johnnie comes into the kitchen and drops a pile of books on the table. He looks at Fred, an odd, warning look, as if he is preparing him for something.

'Hi,' says Sophie. 'The tide should have dropped enough. I think we'll be able to start any time now. Go and change, Johnnie. Shorts and gumboots rig. It's quite hot out there.'

'Yes,' he says abstractedly. 'Yes, of course. I'll just go and have a quick look at her. Coming, Fred?'

He goes out and Fred, raising his eyebrows at Sophie, follows him. Sophie stands for a moment, puzzled, and then shrugs. She'll change too, into her shorts and a halter top, but first she'll just check on Rowena.

She finds the older woman in the morning room; Rowena's favourite place. She stands by the table, staring at nothing in particular, her whole concentration inward as if she is seeing other scenes

41

and hearing other voices. Sophie sees that she is holding a silver-framed photograph and, even at this angle, Sophie recognizes the frame and knows that it is a photograph of Al: Rowena's first-born, her favourite.

Sophie comes closer and Rowena glances up, startled out of her preoccupation.

'What is it?' she asks sharply, as if Sophie is a servant—but Sophie is used to Rowena and merely smiles at her.

'I'm going to help the boys scrub down *Alice*,' she says. 'I wondered if you need anything before I go.'

Rowena shakes her head. 'We had coffee in the Bedford,' she says. It seems as if she might say something else, something that is causing some kind of excitement, but decides against it. She nods to Sophie, as if to dismiss her, and then adds, 'Thank you,' as an afterthought.

Sophie grins as she goes out.

'Grandmother is simply the end,' Louisa has said on numerous occasions. 'No wonder the children call her the granny-monster. I'm really sorry, Sophes.'

But Sophie doesn't mind. The Trehearnes are as dear to her now as her own family. From those early days, coming here from university with Louisa, her best and dearest friend, and the strange yet simple way in which that last holiday after her abortion morphed into a job, she adopted this family: Old Dickie, a bit confused mentally by then and crippled with arthritis, and Rowena, sharp as a tack, autocratic and demanding; Johnnie, kind and warm and generous, with a wife just as sweet . . .

As she climbs the elegant curving staircase Sophie sighs, remembering poor Meg's long battle

42

with cancer; a battle that had already started when she, Sophie, first came to stay at the house on the Tamar. Very quickly she'd seen how she could be useful, to repay some of the kindness they'd shown her.

Perhaps, thinks Sophie now, as she drags off her jeans and looks for her shorts, perhaps it is easier to be patient, willing, less judgemental, with those who are not related to us; they are not as critical as our own kin; they value us more highly and, when we are very young, we can show off a little to them and try out roles so as to see ourselves more clearly without being mocked or humiliated. She'd done her serious growing up with the Trehearnes.

'I don't mind you telling your mum about the abortion,' she said to Louisa; somehow she knew even then that Louisa's parents wouldn't condemn her.

Meg was sympathetic and warm, whereas her own mother was shocked and angry. It was a relief to stay here, on the Tamar; to be cherished, and to cherish in her turn. When Johnnie was posted to the Ministry of Defence in London she was glad to stay with the frail Meg whilst keeping a watching brief on the still fiercely independent Rowena and dear old Dickie. Then Dickie died, followed not long afterwards by Meg, and Johnnie was glad to have her support and company and strength.

And all the while she was growing; discovering that she was very happy to nurture and support this family, that she valued her freedom and independence and that she had no wish to become inextricably linked with one single man. She was not particularly romantic or maternal. Slowly she understood that, while the care of

43

the Trehearnes fulfilled her nurturing needs and gave her companionship, there were young men who were quite ready to minister to any physical requirements. Perhaps that early disastrous relationship, culminating in betrayal and abortion, had cured her of any desire for a long-term intimate relationship.

Sophie pulls on a halter top, ties a spotted handkerchief over her short fair hair and goes down to join Johnnie and Fred.

*   *   *

Rowena continues to stand, holding the photograph of Al, staring into the past at long-vanished scenes. She sees him dancing with Juliet at the Christmas Ball on HMS *Drake*. They are dancing to 'California Dreaming', a slow smooch, circling in the shadows at the edge of the floor. Al's eyes are closed and he's holding her much too tightly; the silky chiffon skirt of Juliet's long, pale ball gown floats and clings to her partner's dark uniform. Mike's at the bar, getting the drinks in, but he turns to watch them and his rather foolish, half-drunken expression hardens into watchfulness.

She hears Juliet's voice, strained and desperate, whispering just outside these morning-room windows during a party one warm spring evening. 'I should never have married him, I know that now. I thought I was in love with him. I really did. How was I to know? What shall we do?' and the low, murmuring response: 'We must be very careful.'

She remembers Juliet as a house guest, staying for a week whilst Mike is at sea.

'You don't want to stay in that poky flat in

Plymouth in this wonderful weather,' Rowena says. 'Come and spend a few days with us. Johnnie's at sea but Al's got a few days' leave . . .'

Juliet, slipping away to the sail loft, along the river bank, and, after a while, the shadowy figure of Al following her.

The last scene is the most important: the Midsummer's Eve party. The sea garden is strung about with fairy lights, the table in the summerhouse laid with delicious food and wine, and Johnnie and Fred are put in charge of the record player. The sail loft has been turned into a dormitory for the young single men—only a very few of the couples are married—and the girls stay in the house, sharing bedrooms.

The sea garden is a magical place. Reflections jitter and dance on the smooth black surface of the water; shadowy figures dance or lean against the balustrade beneath Circe's imposing figure. The tall lavender hedges are pale, cloudy shapes, their scent still lingering on the warm air.

As she approaches the summerhouse with a tray of cream jellies, Rowena becomes aware of the whispering. The first voice is urgent, demanding; the other is frightened.

Rowena steps back into the shadows, watching the two people behind the summerhouse. Juliet's dress is in disarray, her hair loosened. Al's face is buried against her throat but her face is twisted away from his, her hands on his shoulders.

'Listen,' she is saying, still in that desperate whisper. 'Please just listen to me. I'm pregnant, Al. Just for God's sake, listen . . .'

And then Dickie comes across the lawn from the house, calling out cheerfully, carrying some bottles, and Rowena sees Al's head turn sharply, and both figures freeze into immobility and silence. She slips quickly away, joining Dickie a few moments later, and then Juliet appears alone, pinning up her hair and smiling—but there is no sign of Al.

Now, standing in the morning room, holding Al's photograph, Rowena remembers how she waited during the weeks that followed; waited for some word from Al: an explanation of Juliet's failed marriage, perhaps, or of how much he loved her. She was so certain that Juliet would leave Mike; so sure that the child was Al's. She desperately wanted them for him: Juliet and the baby. She was sorry for Mike, of course she was, but she could see how Juliet had been carried away by all the glamour of their early meetings and it wasn't until she'd come to know Al that she realized that she'd married the wrong man. They were too young, she and Mike, and all those ladies nights' and parties and summer balls had been too romantic.

Perhaps it was wrong of her to invite Juliet that spring, knowing that the girl was regretting her marriage, falling in love—but no . . . Rowena shakes her head. She sees again Juliet slipping away from the house, disappearing towards the sail loft or the river bank, and then, a short while later, Al following her to the trysting place. How can she regret that joy they shared when a few months later Al had died in a tragic sailing accident?

Or had it been an accident? She'd never be certain; never be absolutely sure that Mike hadn't knocked Al overboard. Perhaps they'd quarrelled and Al had told him the truth and Mike had simply lashed out. Perhaps Mike guessed and had accused Al. Either way, even in the first fresh agony of grief, she wasn't able to blame or accuse Mike. He'd described how a squall hit the boat and Al was knocked over by the swinging of the boom; and both Johnnie and Fred asserted that Mike searched and searched, shouting Al's name in the darkness, refusing to give up until the dawn broke and they stared at the empty sea.

Mike was posted to a nuclear submarine running out of Faslane and Juliet went with him. The baby boy, Patrick, was born and Rowena's heart yearned for a sight of him but Juliet stayed away. Johnnie saw Mike occasionally, Dickie ran into him at Northwood, and then they heard that they'd gone to Australia. From a distance Rowena managed to keep a watching brief for a short while but there was little news: Mike's promotions, no more babies.

'It seems,' her confidante in Australia wrote, 'that poor old Mike's been firing blanks. That's what nuclear submarines do for you, apparently. Lucky he managed Pat . . .'

And so the years passed and, though she never recovered from Al's death, she believed that at least she'd come to terms with it until earlier, in the Bedford, when Kate had said: 'You remember the Penhaligons, don't you?' and all the longing and hope and pain had returned, fresh and vivid.

Now, Rowena gently places the photograph back in its place. It was odd that Johnnie was so quiet driving home in the car, slightly edgy when she'd pressed him about inviting Jess to lunch: not like him at all. After all, Johnnie is very hospitable; he loves a party. However, he has promised to telephone Kate at the weekend and make a date. Rowena checks that she has the piece of paper with the telephone number safe in her bag. She will remind him to make the call—and if he is dilatory she will do it herself.

TAVISTOCK

On Tuesday morning the cottage in Chapel Street is filled with sunlight: clean, newly painted, empty, it waits now for new life. Kate stands for a moment in the narrow, well-fitted kitchen that looks onto the garden where a path leads towards the shady pergola at its far end. She passes through the hall into the sitting-room with its glass-fronted alcoves on each side of the charming Victorian fireplace. Across the passage is a room with two walls lined with bookshelves, which will make a useful living-room. She will put the big table in here—the kitchen is too small to eat in—and make it all very comfortable and welcoming. Upstairs she pauses on the landing to look down over the garden. Tall, pale Japanese anemones grow in the long border under the garden wall, and nasturtiums sprawl across the winding path. The Rambling Rector has covered the pergola and its rosehips glow orange and scarlet in the October sunshine.

Three bedrooms, one no bigger than a boxroom, and the bathroom are set about the small square landing. Kate comes downstairs and sits on the bottom step. Even here, it seems, ghosts wait. This cottage has been owned or rented by other naval couples—people whom she knows—and she sees them passing through these rooms, calling to each other on the landing above, eager with plans, excited about the future, waiting—as she

48

waits now—for the removal van to bring her furniture out of store. She remembers other naval quarters, hirings; tiresome married quarters' officers and helpful removal men. Jess, with her army background, will be familiar with all this.

Kate wonders what Jess will think of the cottage, of Johnnie and Lady T, and Cass and Tom, and feels again a strong sense of misgiving. Well, it is too late now: she glances at her watch and gets up. The removal men will be here very soon and the hard work will begin, but she has remembered the essentials for a happy move: the kettle, mugs, teaspoons, milk, tea, coffee and sugar are all waiting in the kitchen to be unpacked.

*　　*　　*

'You know we love it when you come home,' says Cass to Oliver, as they drive together into Tavistock, 'but I have the oddest feeling that this time you have an ulterior motive for being here. Are you going to tell me what it is?'

Oliver shrugs, looks blank as he negotiates the narrow bridge over the River Meavy. He remembers how, years ago, he scraped his father's car on these unforgiving stones when he was learning to drive—and the row that followed.

'I like to see for myself how you're both doing,' he says, 'that's all. I'm being filial. It's not new.'

'Mmm.' Cass is sceptical. 'But you usually dash off after a day or two of being filial to put another iron in a fire somewhere. This time it's like you're waiting for something. Or someone.'

'Oh, I am,' says Oliver quickly. 'I'm waiting to meet Jess. She's arriving on Friday so I thought I'd

49

stay on to see this Infant Phenomenon who's won David's highly prized Award. No harm in that, is there?'

'No,' says Cass, but she's not convinced. She is unsettled, on edge. 'Only I'd be grateful if you'd stop winding your father up while you're waiting. It doesn't help. He's very upset about Gemma's threats to leave Guy and your levity isn't helping.'

'Sorry, Ma,' he says. 'I was trying to lighten him up a bit, that's all. You usually say it helps to keep things cheerful.'

'I know I do.' It's quite true, but just at the moment she doesn't know what she wants. Nothing is right. 'I'm all jangly, Ollie, as if something cataclysmic is about to happen.' She laughs. 'I sound like Kate. She's always the one with the signs and portents, isn't she? I used to say that it was she who should have been called Cassandra, not me.'

'Do you want to drop in and see her?'

Cass thinks about it. She is very pleased that Kate might be coming back to Tavistock after three years: she's missed their close relationship, the impromptu dropping in and meeting up. St Meriadoc is only an hour and a half away but to have Kate near by again would be very good news. Tom has become more grumpy of late: he's wearying of the hard work that is required to keep the Rectory and its grounds in good shape, and it's an effort to keep jollying him along. The prospect of Kate close at hand, supporting and encouraging, is wonderful. Or, at least, it was until the subject of divorce between Gemma and Guy loomed. Now she and Kate are skating warily round this subject. It is the elephant in the room, and effort is required to avoid outright comment about who is to blame.

Each of them is sensitive, ready to protect her own child, and Cass doesn't feel up to the stress of the cut and thrust of it this morning. She wants to shop, to buy something elegant to wear from Brigid Foley and browse in Crebers for a delicious treat to eat for lunch; she simply longs to relax and be happy.

'Kate will be busy,' she says, 'getting the cottage right and all that stuff. Moving in is such hell, isn't it? Especially if Jess is arriving on Friday.' A pause. 'How did you know she's arriving on Friday?'

'Kate texted,' he answers.

'Oh.' Cass feels slightly hurt. 'She didn't phone me. I wonder why not.'

'Perhaps,' suggests Oliver, 'for the same reason you're not dropping in to see her this morning.'

Cass is silent.

'I'm going to Book Stop,' says Oliver, 'so we'll park at the Bedford and meet up for coffee or a drink when you've finished shopping. Does that sound OK?'

'Yes.' She glances sideways at him. 'Shall you go and see Kate?'

She doesn't want him to visit Kate. She feels it will put her in a bad light if Kate knows she's in town and isn't popping in to see how she's managing. She feels guilty and restless and cross.

'No,' says Oliver. 'We'll leave Kate to her settling-in today and phone later to see if she'd like any help tomorrow. I'll text her. Stop worrying, Ma. We've come to have some fun, remember? That's what you said to Pa, anyway.'

'Yes,' Cass says at once. 'We have. And that's a good idea about texting Kate. We can come over again tomorrow if she wants us to. Do that, Ollie. Give me an hour and then I'll buy you a pint.'

'Sounds OK to me,' he says.

*　　　*　　　*

Jess is heading west; driving across the motorway bridge spanning the River Exe. She glances quickly at the sheet of paper on the seat beside her, pulls into the inside lane and takes the turning off the M5 onto the A30.

'The quickest way to Tavistock,' Kate told her, 'is to come down the A30 and turn off at Sourton. It's much more dramatic to drive over the moor but this is quicker and we can explore the moor later if you want to.'

She'd liked Kate at once: they hit it off straight away. There was a direct simplicity about the older woman that appealed and they'd laughed together about how they hated having to dress up.

'At least you scrub up well,' Kate commented. 'My default mode is bag lady. I can't wait to get back into my jeans.'

Jess grins, remembering. And it's really weird that Kate should have known her grandparents way back. They'd talked about service life, the moving around and the separation, and it was like they were old friends who hadn't seen each other for ages.

It's good to be this happy, she thinks: to have won this really prestigious Award, to have a good Honours degree, and to have a whole year off to think about what direction she should take for her future. The Award money has bought her some space—just as it's bought her this little old car and real independence. Jess can feel her face positively beaming but she can't help herself: life just hasn't been this good since Daddy died—and part of it is because she's going to the place where he was born, where her grandparents met, to chill out for a few months.

Kate, in one of her emails, suggested Jess should come down and explore, meet some of her grandparents' friends, and offered her this cottage in Tavistock so that she'd have somewhere to stay.

'You can be alone if you need to be, but I can show you around and introduce you to some people,' Kate said—which is really cool because she can't quite decide what she'll want or how it will be. Sometimes she needs to be alone, have her own space, but it's good, too, to have a few friends nearby. Meanwhile the sun is shining and she's in her little car, listening to Jamie Cullum, with nearly all her belongings packed into the boot because at heart she's a minimalist. And all the while, at some deeper level, she's noticing the shapes and patterns and colours of the green, rounded hills and small, square fields; the crimson, crumbly earth being turned by a rackety old plough and the grey and white cloud of gulls streaming behind it; tall trees and boxy hedges, their leaves scorching with autumnal fire.

So here she is, on the journey to the west, feeling good.

*   *   *

Kate waits nervously: she prowls, checking the rooms, wondering what Jess will think and if she will approve. Last evening she phoned Bruno. He answered straight away and she knew he'd been expecting her call.

53

'What am I doing?' she asked. 'Am I mad or what? I don't know this girl and now she's coming to stay. Why did I do it?'

'Because you felt it was right. Forget what you feel like now. That's just nerves. What you felt then is what really counts.'

For three years she and Bruno have been friends in the best possible way; they've spent hours talking about the messy muddles that have been their lives, trying to make sense of things, admitting failures and fears, laughing and weeping alternately, giving each other courage. She's missing him now, wishing she'd stayed at St Meriadoc and simply let out the cottage in Chapel Street.

'It was crazy,' she said, 'to bring the rest of the furniture out of store. It's best to let the place unfurnished. I should have waited until I'd really decided where I want to be.'

'It needed to come out and be used again,' Bruno answered calmly. 'Jess may decide to stay there and be your tenant. Stop panicking, Kate. Leaving the place unfurnished wouldn't have helped you make up your mind. You've got the cottage here—I shan't evict you in your absence—and being at Chapel Street, actually living there, will help you make your decision properly.'

She pictured him, Celt-dark, wandering about the kitchen in his usual jersey and jeans, preparing his supper; carrying it into that amazing central room with its out-flung window that seems to hang right over the sea. The sofa would be piled with books and newspapers and his collie bitch, Nellie, curled up at one end of it in front of the fire.

'I miss you,' she said. She said it quite lightly, feeling a bit of a fool.

54

'Missing people is good,' he answered. 'Makes you realize how much you love them.' And then, before she could think of an appropriate answer, he asked: 'How's Flossie liking Chapel Street?'

She stared at Flossie, who was curled in her basket beside the radiator. 'She's OK. I left her with Cass when the removal men came but she's settled very well this last couple of days. Cass and Oliver were brilliant yesterday, helping to get the place into shape. I hope Jess likes it.'

'It'll be fine, Kate,' he said gently. 'Stop worrying.'

He hadn't said, 'Move in with me. Let's be together,' and, even if he had, how would she have answered him? She was used to having her own space, privacy when she needed it, when her family visited her—and so was he. Being together might ruin everything. They'd been to bed a few times, usually after a long, late supper when the deep level of their shared emotional intimacy required some kind of physical expression, and it had been good. Yet they both held back from the ultimate commitment.

Now, waiting for Jess, Kate sees that he is right; she must trust the instinct that has resulted in inviting Jess here and turning Chapel Street into a home. She doesn't need to make a decision just yet. Even as she heaves a great sighing breath of relief, and puts her anxieties aside, there is a knock at the kitchen door. Flossie barks and Kate glances at her watch—too early for Jess yet—and then she hears Oliver's voice and she hurries out to meet him.

'Shall I be in the way?' he asks. 'I wondered if you might be needing a bit of moral support. I can go away if you'd rather.'

55

'Absolutely not,' she says. She is suddenly excited again, delighted to see him. 'This is just perfect. Much easier for Jess if you're here too.'

'It's a nice little house, Kate.'

He looks in through the sitting-room door at the alcoves full of pretty things and at the comfortable armchairs; and then he crosses the hallway and wanders into the bigger room, which now has the big table under the window and a variety of chairs around it. There are books on the shelves, and paintings hanging, and a long sofa against one wall.

'It is, isn't it?' Her confidence is restored. 'Why don't I make some coffee? Jess texted at Exeter so we've got another half an hour, I'd say.'

'Shall I open the front door?' he asks. 'It's so much more welcoming, isn't it, than having to knock and wait? The sun's simply pouring in and Flossie can sit outside and watch for her.'

*   *   *

So it is that Jess, driving slowly along the street checking house numbers, first sees a retriever standing eagerly at the gate and the front door flung wide in welcome. As she stops the car, leaning from the open window, the dog's feathery tail begins to wave and a tall, blond man wanders casually out into the small paved front garden.

She assesses him: is this one of Kate's sons? He's very good-looking. Very cool. Mid-thirties, perhaps a bit older? They look at each other, and she feels an odd desire to laugh, to leap out of the car, as if she is coming home to people she knows and loves.

'Jess,' he says: not a question, just a statement. And he opens the gate.

The dog is at the car door, tail wagging madly, and Jess gets out, the laugh really bubbling up now, and here is Kate, dashing out of the cottage to welcome her.

'This is Oliver. He's the son of friends of mine who knew Juliet and Mike,' she is saying. 'And Flossie. Are you going to offer your paw, Flossie? Gosh! It's great to see you again, Jess.'

And Jess shakes hands with Oliver, hugs Kate and strokes Flossie's shining, feathery coat, and then they all bundle into the house together.

At once she knows she's going to like it here. Always, she knows straight off with people and places whether they will be right for her. Even as a child she's had this strange gift: a kind of second sight, which warns or encourages, and she's learned to take it on trust.

This cottage, for instance, has good vibes. It's a home and a place in which to feel relaxed. The dog has climbed back into her basket, Kate is pouring coffee, Oliver perches on the end of the table and asks about the journey.

She likes him; she likes the way he looks at her as if she is Jess, first and foremost, and a female after. It's as if he sees the important things about her and she intuits that she can trust him. This strange gift has grown more and more crucial since her life was smashed apart, first by her father's death and then by her mother's new relationship and her move to Brussels.

Kate passes her a mug of coffee and Jess looks around her. She's been happy enough at school and at uni but she's learned to toughen up, to fight her corner. For three years the little house in Bristol, which she shared with her student friends, was home—not the smart flat in Brussels—and since all that finished she's felt rather rootless and a bit scared. Now here she is, sitting in this sun-filled, comfortable room with two new friends and the dog. Everyone is very relaxed; there is no formality here, no third-degree questioning to discover what she's been doing or what plans she might have; they've simply accepted her into their lives and are giving her space.

Kate is unwrapping a small parcel. She shows the contents to Oliver, and Jess sees that it is a painting.

'I brought this with me. I thought you might like to see it,' Kate says, passing it to her. 'David painted it nearly twenty years ago. He was staying on Dartmoor with a friend of mine and when she died she left it to me. I hadn't met him then but he told me that it was the first time he'd really taken an interest in the botanical aspect of painting and that's when he began to study it properly.'

Jess takes the painting: it is a sketch of an old stone bridge over a river, and a part of the bank beneath it where a group of foxgloves grow against the sun-warmed stone. It has been lightly colour-washed, and sunlight glimmers on the water, which seems to flow and splash even as she looks at it. Deft, tender strokes reproduce the foxgloves, the texture of the crumbling stone and the tiny springing cushions of moss that cling to it.

'It's wonderful,' she murmurs, tilting it, examining it. 'It's so accurate and yet so imaginative. How did he do that?'

'I thought you might see it as a sign,' says Kate. 'Or a portent. I mean, it being the one that started him off along the botanical painting path. And the

58

fact that he was around here when he did it.'

'Do you do signs and portents?' asks Oliver. 'Or are you more practical?'

'I don't know.' Jess stares up at them, still holding the painting. 'Yes, I think I *do* do signs and portents, actually. But now I'm on my own I have to be careful.'

She feels a fool, wishes she hadn't said it: it sounds childish. She bends her head over the painting, studying it. To her relief, neither of them reacts: they don't say: 'Oh, but you're not on your own now,' or other embarrassing things, they just leave her alone.

Oliver is saying, 'Ma's talking about lunch tomorrow, if you both feel up for it,' and Kate says, 'That might be good. Will you thank her and tell her I'll phone later on? Flossie will need a walk soon so I thought Jess and I would take her up on the moor when she's settled in a bit.'

While they talk, Jess turns the painting slightly and reads the words scrawled across the corner: 'Bless you for everything. It's been perfect. Love D.'

She feels an odd little twinge of sadness and wonders who the woman was and what happened to her.

Oliver is going and she gets up to see him off. He kisses Kate, smiles at Jess and walks away down Chapel Street.

'Come on,' says Kate. 'I'll show you your bedroom and you can unpack.'

*   *   *

Oliver drives out of the town, through Horrabridge and Dousland and up on to the moor. He thinks

59

about his reaction to Jess—apart from the normal physical response to a young and very attractive girl. He's picked up on the complications of her character: strength and vulnerability; determination and fear; an openness to outside influences and a strong sense of self. He ponders on the fact that everyone is shaped by external events, and wonders what Jess might have been like if her father hadn't been killed in Bosnia and her mother hadn't remarried and gone abroad.

'Now I'm on my own I have to be careful,' she said revealingly: careful how she responds to signs and portents now that she has nobody to catch her if she misreads them and crashes. She has no margin for error, no safety net, she's saying, and he's rather taken aback by his strong reaction to protect her. Luckily he has too much experience to verbalize it, and a great deal of practice in hiding his feelings. He's let the moment pass. The age gap between them is a big one and he mustn't make a fool of himself: he's done that before.

And now he, too, sees the ghosts of past years: beloved Phyllida, for whom he'd cherished an agonizingly romantic infatuation but who preferred to remain happily married: beautiful Claudia, with whom he had a brief but very physical and passionate affair; and sweet Chrissie, who adored him, but was too young for him to take seriously enough for a long-term relationship.

As he turns in between the gates of the Old Rectory he sees Tom cutting the grass on his sit-on mower and feels relief that there won't be an immediate third degree on Jess. He knows that Tom's questions will embarrass him.

The minute he sees Cass, however, he realizes

that something much more important has happened and Jess is no longer the hot topic. His mother is looking excited but anxious and she glances past him as if she fears that Tom might have followed him into the house.

'Oh, darling,' she says at once, 'Gemma phoned. She's coming home next week with the twins. She says she's fed up with discussing the question of divorce with Guy, who simply pretends it isn't happening, and she's had a terrific row with Mark.' Cass drags Oliver into the kitchen and shuts the door. 'Your father is furious,' she says, speaking quickly, still holding his arm, one eye on the door. 'He thinks we are sanctioning the separation by allowing them to come here. But what else can she do? She's made no real friends there and we have to think of the twins. Deep down Tom didn't believe she would actually leave Guy. He thought it was just one of those blips and that she'd get over it. He says it's absolutely wrong of her to behave like this with no plans or arrangements made.'

He releases himself gently. 'And what do you think?'

Suddenly she looks frightened. 'I don't know any more. Of course I want Gemma and the twins nearer than they are in Canada, and I want her to be happy, but I don't *want* her marriage to break up. Guy's not really my type—he's too much like his father—but he's been good with Gemma and the twins. Your sister hasn't been exactly . . .' she hesitates, searching for a word that isn't too blunt, '. . . easy,' she says at last.

Oliver laughs. 'I thought that was rather what my dear sister *has* been. Isn't that how the trouble began?'

61

Cass stares at him for a moment. He sees that she doesn't quite know whether to be outraged on Gemma's behalf or amused—and then she laughs too.

'Honestly, though,' she says, 'what on earth shall I do?'

'You'll welcome them home and give her breathing space,' he says. 'Don't get heavy about this. What has she said to the twins?'

'She hasn't told them the absolute truth. She's said that they will be coming back to live here and Daddy will come when he can. Meanwhile they think they're having an extended holiday from school.'

'Fine. So let them go on thinking that.'

'But what about Tom? You know what he can be like.'

Oliver thinks about it. 'It's a pity that Jess has turned up at this precise moment,' he says thoughtfully. 'Gemma and the twins could have stayed in Chapel Street.'

'But I want them here,' protests Cass. 'We haven't seen them for months. What's she like, by the way?'

'Jess? She's lovely. Rather boho. Definite personality. Look, I still think that this whole Gemma thing needs to be regarded as a time for getting things into perspective. Don't turn a drama into a crisis.'

There is a telling little pause.

'Great,' says Cass. 'And shall you tell your father that or shall I?'

*   *   *

As she sits on the edge of the bed, brushing her hair, thinking about the day, Jess sees that Kate has put the painting on a specially made, small wooden lectern and placed it on the little chest beside the bed.

A sign or a portent. *Bless you for everything. It's been perfect.*

Jess gazes at the painting; she feels on the brink of something very mysterious and important. She is touched by the warm welcome she's been given. It's as if Kate and Oliver have always known her, accepting her and making her feel easy in an almost casual way while, at the same time, cherishing her as someone special. She's already texted her two closest friends, who are travelling together in Thailand, to say that she's arrived. Now she picks up her mobile and stares at it, wondering whether to try to explain to them how great everything is.

How, she wonders, could she describe the space and silence of the moors where she and Kate walked whilst Flossie ran ahead, tail waving with the joy of it all? In that space and silence there was a sense of peace and healing and, as she sits there on the edge of the bed, Jess remembers how deeply she breathed, drawing in great gasps of the clean moorland air. The cold grip of loneliness that has curled around her heart for so long was eased as she took those deep breaths. When Kate pointed to a sinuous, dazzling glint of water away in the west and said, 'Look, that's the Tamar,' Jess's heart, freed from that chill, habitual constriction, suddenly bumped with an odd sensation of recognition. Her roots were here: here, in this part of the West Country, her father's family once lived. Just for a brief moment she experienced a feeling of closeness to him, as if he were beside her, encouraging her, approving her journey.

Jess puts her mobile on the little chest beside her bed: there is simply too much happening to condense it into text-speak. She looks again at the little painting and, seized with a confusing mixture of excitement, happiness and terror, she switches off the light, slips quickly beneath the duvet, curls into a ball and prepares to sleep.

*   *   *

'I can't get over it,' Tom says for the third or fourth time. 'She's Juliet to the life. She's gorgeous.'

Kate has brought Jess over for lunch and he is absolutely captivated by her. Now, after supper, he sits with Cass in the drawing-room, remembering the parties down on the Tamar and the lovely Juliet.

'You're salivating, darling,' Cass says, leaning forward to switch channels. 'Not very attractive.'

Tom makes a little face behind her back. Meeting Jess has made him feel young again: strong and virile.

'Well, you've got to admit that it's true,' he says. 'It's an extraordinary likeness. Wait till Johnnie sees her, and old Fred. We really must have a thrash to celebrate. Who else do we know who'd remember Mike and Juliet? What about the Mortlakes? Stephen always lusted after Juliet. He got quite serious about her, actually, way back before he was married.'

There's an odd little silence. Cass seems to be engrossed in *River Cottage*, her head slightly turned away from him towards the television, and Tom

64

remembers that Stephen was also very attracted to Cass, much later on after they were all married and settled with children. He'd been a bit of a pest—but then Stephen had always been a chancer.

Anyway, that was a long time ago, water under the bridge; Tom makes another little face and finishes his glass of wine. Funny how Jess has really jollied him up. Oh, he'd been aware of Oliver's sardonic eye on him through lunch, but that hadn't stopped him. He'd been on form; a bit of a devil. Jess likes him, he can tell. He settles back to watch Hugh—'Sod it, where's the corkscrew'—Whittingstall and, glancing sideways, Cass can see that he is now totally engrossed.

But Cass is wrong. Tom is staring at the television screen but the pictures he sees are quite different from Hugh doing clever things with ducks in his kitchen. He has slipped back forty years in time and is seeing the ballroom on HMS *Drake*; Juliet twirling in Mike's arms, laughing across his shoulder, her long skirts floating and clinging to his smart uniform.

*   *   *

Tom stood at the edge of the floor, waiting for Cass to come back from the heads, watching Juliet and Mike. Juliet's beauty was not ethereal, though she was graceful and slender; her hair and eyes were a strange mix of red and brown, the colour of a vixen's coat. She was of the earth, earthy. The long thick hair was piled up high tonight, but long shining strands fell around her throat, and Tom imagined himself taking the hairpins out, one by one, and watching that heavy shining mass fall down around

65

her shoulders and over her bare breasts.

Cass tiptoed up behind him. 'Keep your eyes in the boat, darling,' she whispered, and he jumped and turned quickly, a self-defensive denial ready in his mouth. But Cass, as usual, forestalled him.

'Ah,' she said, 'the lovely Juliet. Well, she *is* lovely. Oh, look. Al has cut in. Doesn't Mike look grim?'

And Mike did indeed look grim though he tried to laugh it off, to pretend that he didn't care if his best friend and oppo was making up to his wife. He shrugged, headed for the bar, but even Tom, who wasn't particularly analytical, could see that Mike was cross.

'Al's the limit,' Cass was saying. 'He's holding her too tight. He will do that. Lots of my chums say the same. It's damned annoying. He knows we daren't slap his face or make a fuss, especially with his father sitting over in the corner looking on. No girl wants to get her husband into Dickie's bad books. Al trades on our good manners.'

Tom muttered something about it not being that bad. He felt uncomfortable. He thought it was a fuss about nothing but Cass was right about one thing: none of these young men was going to be pleased if his wife showed herself up in front of a senior officer. After all, nothing much could happen on a dance floor. He said so to Cass, who asked sharply how he'd feel about being touched up every time he danced with a woman.

'Chance would be a fine thing,' he said, laughing it off. 'I certainly wouldn't mind if it was Juliet, I can tell you.'

He glanced at Cass, wondering if he'd gone too far, but she was laughing again and he felt a great surge of gratitude: God, he was lucky to have her. She was so ready to laugh, to enjoy life, and his friends lusted after her almost as much as they lusted after the divine Juliet. He was damned lucky. And here came Stephen Mortlake, wanting a dance, taking Cass away, and Tom waved them off good-naturedly and went to join Mike in the bar.

'That's the penalty,' he said, ordering a Horse's Neck, grinning at Mike, 'for having a beautiful wife. You and me both.'

But Mike wasn't in joshing mood. He looked glum as he downed his drink and his eyes were fixed on Al and Juliet as they slowly circled the floor. And then Johnnie and Fred arrived with the usual brace of pretty girls they always produced for a ladies' night or a party. Tom made a little face, jerked his chin towards Mike so as to warn them, but Johnnie and Fred weren't likely to pander to Mike's mood. They'd suffered too much from his bullying in the past.

'Been stood up?' asked Johnnie genially, and Fred asked, 'Would you like me to go and cut him out for you?' and Mike snarled at him, 'When you're big enough you'll be too old,' and took another pull at his drink.

Johnnie and Fred made comical faces and, grinning at Tom, ushered their girls out onto the floor. Stephen Mortlake brought Cass back.

'Says she's had enough,' he told Tom.

'Of course she has,' said Tom. 'That's why I married her. She's got such good taste.'

And he took Cass in his arms and they moved away onto the floor as the band began to play 'California Dreaming'.

Tom's thoughts return to the present; he reaches for Cass's hand, smiles at her. Cass takes a tiny breath of relief and relaxes a little. Stephen Mortlake's name has raised old ghosts, reminding her of a younger, naughtier Cass, who took chances, got caught out. Clearly, Tom hasn't made quite the same connections but she doesn't want to pursue the topic of conversation just now. Let him think she's jealous; that will do nicely. It will massage his ego and put him in a happier frame of mind. She squeezes his hand in return and they settle more comfortably together on the sofa.

'Who was the woman who owned the little painting?' Jess asks. Her first few days in Tavistock have been very busy—meeting Cass and Tom, exploring the moor—but even with all these new experiences it is the painting that continues to fascinate her. It is the first thing she sees when she wakes in the morning and the last thing before she switches out her light.

'Felicity,' says Kate. Her voice is thoughtful, rather sad. 'Felicity was a naval wife too, like me and Cass and Juliet. She had a cottage up on the moor over near Mary Tavy. Anyway, when Felicity was in her forties her husband died of cancer. It was very quick and unexpected . . .'

'Did she have children?' Jess feels that a little prompt is necessary.

'No. No children. Felicity was the least maternal woman I ever met. No, she just carried on, as

68

one does because there's nothing else to do when someone you love dies.' Kate hesitates again. 'Well, you know that, don't you?'

Jess nods, remains silent.

'Well then, David came down to visit his daughter, who lives near Moretonhampstead, and decided to have a bit of a painting holiday. Remember, I didn't know him then. Anyway, he began a painting of Felicity's cottage, which is a beautiful old long-house, and she saw him sitting out there in the lane, found out who he was, and invited him in for a cup of coffee. They became lovers.'

Another pause.

'And?' asks Jess, fascinated by this little history.

'And David spent a wonderful few weeks discovering a different direction in his work whilst having an affair with Felicity. They were both widowed, but she'd had a lover for some years— an extra-marital diversion, you might say—so her reputation led David to believe that she would be quite happy when it was time for him to return to London.'

'What happened?'

'A tragedy happened. David genuinely believed that it had been one of those perfect little gifts that life sometimes gives us but he never imagined it as a long-term commitment. Felicity saw it differently. She'd unexpectedly fallen in love with him. After he'd gone back to London she tried to contact him, unsuccessfully, and then one evening she had too much to drink combined with too many of the tablets that she took for her migraines.'

'Oh, my God . . .'

'Yes. He couldn't ever forgive himself.'

'How terrible.' Jess remembers the words: *Bless you for everything. It's been perfect.* 'How could you get over something like that?'

'He didn't. Even though it was an accident—which everybody accepted that it was—he said that she wouldn't have been drinking so much if she hadn't been so unhappy. I met him a year after it happened and he told me all about it. I was able to fill in some facts about Felicity, which made it slightly more bearable for him, I think, but he never really got over it.'

'But you said it was Felicity who left you the painting.'

'She did. She left me everything she owned. I'd been divorced and I was struggling to make ends meet. Since I was the one to end the marriage I refused to take anything from Mark, except for Guy and Giles, and I think for some reason she felt sorry for me. I'd had an affair too, after my divorce, so I understood what she was feeling. I stopped my affair because I thought it might become a difficult relationship for the boys: they were still very young. I was in love with him so it was very painful. Felicity thought I was crazy. One day the boys would leave me, she said, and I'd be alone and, by the time she met David, that was true. Loving David changed Felicity. It softened her, made her vulnerable, and she poured it all out to me; how she loved him and how she felt so different. When I met him afterwards it was all such a shock. He came to my house looking for someone else and the first thing he saw was the painting, and so it all came out.'

'And you got married.'

'After a while. It took me a bit of time to leave the safety of not feeling anything. Loving hurts but

70

at least you know you are alive. David was a good man. He wanted to give; to share. He persuaded me that it's better to cut your feet on the glass than never to feel the sand between your toes. So I took my shoes off again and married him.'

Jess shakes her head. 'It's all so weird,' she says.

Kate looks at her sympathetically. 'Oldies emoting about their pasts? It's a bit gross, isn't it?'

'No,' cries Jess. 'No, I don't mean that. It's just that, coming here, it's like walking into a story. You and Cass and Tom knowing my grandparents and all being young together. And hearing all this about David. David Porteous! I mean, he's like an icon to me and now you're telling me all this stuff and that little painting is a part of all of that. Those words he wrote on it.'

'Poor Jess. Rather overwhelming as stories go, I'd say.'

'No,' says Jess vehemently. 'It's good. I've been kind of shut in since Daddy was killed and Mum took off to Brussels. Being an artist—' she looks faintly self-conscious, as if she might not deserve the title—'it keeps you on your own a bit. It's something that makes you need to be alone for most of the time. Well, it does for me, anyway. And then not wanting to keep having to explain about Daddy, and Mum getting married again, all those things kind of keep you a bit apart. And suddenly I've wandered into like a tapestry or something, with all these figures, and they're all coming to life round me. Hearing Tom talking about Granny was really, really bizarre. And the way he couldn't get over how much I was like her. Even after all these years he remembered her.'

'Tom never forgets a beautiful woman,' says Kate

drily. 'However many years it might be. I'm just glad you're not overwhelmed.'

'No. It's amazing. I feel a part of something again. I belong in the story.'

'Good,' Kate says. 'Well, let's hope the Trehearnes add something good to the story. We've been invited to lunch next week.'

*   *   *

Next morning Oliver telephones just after Kate's waved Jess off in her little car on a solo expedition. She's supplied Jess with an Ordnance Survey map and a flask of coffee, and explained that mobile phone signals are unreliable out on the moor.

'I'm sure she'll be fine,' she tells Oliver. 'She's very self-sufficient. So what's happening?' Oliver is using his mobile so she suspects that this is a private call.

'Gemma and the boys arrived yesterday,' he says, 'and Ma is wondering whether you'd like to come over to see them. I think she's going to phone in a minute, so this is just to prepare you.'

Kate is silent. She wrestles with the strong urge to say something rude. She's shocked at how much she does *not* want to see Gemma. Gemma has played around and messed up her marriage with Guy, and she, Kate, is going to find it difficult to stroll in and greet her daughter-in-law with the usual affection. Of course, there are the twins . . .

'Kate,' Oliver is saying, 'if you need time, just don't answer the phone. I thought you might find it hard to refuse if you were taken by surprise. They got an early flight and I went up to fetch them yesterday morning.'

72

'Then they'll all be exhausted,' says Kate quickly. 'I'll wait a few days, Oliver. Thanks, though.'

'Ma thought you'd want to see the twins.'

'And I do. Of course I do. But . . .'

'But it's rather tricky seeing them all here happily in the bosom of their family? And poor old Guy left in Canada?'

Kate gives a bitter little snort of laughter. 'Absolutely right. Can you imagine how hard that will be? Does Cass? How am I supposed to react? I don't know how to handle it and I don't see why it should be at the Rectory. I shall be outnumbered.'

'I think it will be embarrassing all round,' he says. 'I don't think Ma has quite taken it on board. Pa is angry but trying not to show it because of the boys. I really do believe it will be sensible to stay cool and prevent this from turning into some great drama.'

'I know you do. And I think you have a point— when I'm not feeling very angry. None of this is Guy's fault, after all. What am I supposed to say to Gemma? "How lovely to see you, darling. Welcome home. Shame the marriage didn't work out because of your flirtations and infidelity." What about my loyalty to Guy?'

'I do understand, Kate. That's why I'm phoning. I think everyone needs a bit of space.'

'Sorry, Ollie,' she says. 'Honestly, it's nothing to do with you. Sorry.'

'It's OK. Just don't answer the phone.'

'I shall go and do some shopping,' says Kate. 'Take Flossie for a walk. Thanks, Ollie.'

'See you soon,' he says.

*   *   *

Driving slowly in her little car, Jess gazes out at the unfamiliar landscape. The tors, piled like untidily squashed granite pillows, rear up out of fold upon fold of close-nibbled turf where small, hardy ponies graze, and whitish, bundly-looking sheep wander at the grey road's edge. She carefully manoeuvres the car around them, afraid that they might suddenly dash beneath the wheels, and then pulls up on the verge so as to be able to take in the unexpected glory that presents itself. She has no idea where she is but this doesn't worry her; there is a kind of magic in being lost in these untamed surroundings. She notes crimson berries clustering on a silver-lichened thorn; the herringbone pattern of the trampled bracken. It is the minutiae, the tiny details, that fascinate, though the strange power of this bleak wilderness beneath its infinite sky-scape continues to assault her senses.

She drives further off the road, into a small ancient quarry, switches off the engine and reaches for the flask of coffee. It is sheltered here, out of the sharp north-easterly wind, and Jess steps out of the car. She pours the coffee, wanders away, pauses to sip. The sun is hot and she turns towards it, closing her eyes, listening to the sore-throated rasp of a raven somewhere nearby. A rowan tree clings to the edge of the quarry's lip and, between its exposed bony, tenacious roots, she sees the faded foxglove.

Jess sets down her cup upon a ledge of rock and feels in her jacket pocket for her camera. The foxglove immediately brings David to her thoughts and she photographs it along with a patch of stunted yellow tormentil. She climbs a little way up the worn path out of the quarry but the wind

74

is cold up here and she turns back to drink her coffee perched in the car with the door open to the sunshine.

'Some people are frightened on the moor on their own,' Kate told her. 'I've never felt that. The moors and the sea have always been important to me. That sense of infinity makes me feel very peaceful. My problems are reduced by the sheer size of them and that calms me and heals me. Rather like God. Anyway, stick to the big roads and you'll be fine.'

'I'm not frightened of being on my own,' Jess answered. 'I'm used to it. Daddy encouraged me to be self-sufficient. He must have been fairly tough when you think about it. To come all the way from Australia at eighteen to join the army. Of course, he'd been born here so he had a British passport, and he had a few relatives here, but even so, it was a brave thing to do. He used to say that we shouldn't allow our lives to be controlled by fear and desire but I was too young, back then, to understand what he was really trying to tell me. I think it was important to him, though.'

She felt a bit foolish then, wondering if she sounded rather like a silly pretentious kid, but Kate didn't say toe-curling things like: 'He'd be so proud of you,' or anything like that. She simply held out an Ordnance Survey map and the flask. 'Enjoy,' she said.

Sitting in the sunshine Jess finishes the coffee, thinking about Kate and Oliver, Tom and Cass and David; she feels that she belongs amongst them, that she is a small part of their story. She is completely happy.

'I can't get hold of Kate,' Cass is saying. 'She's probably shopping.'

'Just as well,' says Tom grumpily. 'For goodness' sake, Cass, give us all a breathing space.'

Cass stares at him. 'What is the *matter* with you? Anyone would think you aren't pleased to see your daughter and your grandchildren.'

'I don't particularly want to see them like this,' he hisses, an eye on the door. 'Not without Guy. Not talking about divorce. I don't want this for them. You know that.'

'Neither do I,' she protests. 'Of course I don't. But things had come to a head and Gemma needs somewhere to go.'

'Well, just don't expect Kate to come rushing round with cries of joy,' he snaps. 'How d'you think she's feeling about it, for God's sake?'

'I'm sure Kate will understand,' says Cass rather uncertainly. 'She can see that Gemma had to make a stand . . .'

'She can see that Gemma was unfaithful, that she got herself into a mess and that Guy decided that the move to Canada was a nice clean break. Gemma very gratefully agreed. She didn't want to leave Guy then, remember? She said it very loud and clear.'

'I know all that,' whispers Cass crossly. 'But things haven't worked out. Mark was supposed to be retiring and leaving the running of the boatyard to Guy. But he hasn't. He's stayed around and Guy's just doing what he's told and getting very frustrated. Gemma says she can't stand it any more. I don't blame her. I remember Mark of old, and

76

how he was with Kate. I should think she'd have every sympathy with Gemma.'

'I don't agree,' says Tom stubbornly. 'Guy gave her a chance, a really big chance, and she should be giving him one now. Not running home to us with the twins. If they want to sort it out they should be doing it on neutral ground where nobody else is involved. It's difficult for us and impossible for Kate—'

'And embarrassing for everyone if Gemma or the twins hear you,' says Oliver, stepping through the slightly open door and closing it behind him. 'Amazing how whispering carries, isn't it? And just because it is whispering it makes one want to listen even more. They're all still asleep, actually.'

Tom glares at him and Cass laughs. 'God, you frightened me. Look, can't we have a kind of what-d'you-call-it? A moratorium, is it? Just a space of time where everyone comes off the boil and nobody asks questions.'

'It's interesting, isn't it,' says Oliver quietly, 'that Gemma doesn't want to discuss the divorce now she's here? I think she's bluffing.'

Cass and Tom stare at him and he nods at them.

'I think she's given Guy an ultimatum. It's not working as they'd hoped in Canada and she wants out, for all of them. Guy is dithering. He's busy, frustrated, confused and he won't talk. So she's decided to make the move. She's hoping that the shock will make Guy see sense. OK, it hasn't worked, she's told us all that. Guy and Mark quarrel, Guy can't really do what he wants to do. He's into the internet side of the business and Mark doesn't want to know. So let Guy come home and do it here and Mark can retire just like

77

he planned. That's what Gemma wants, but they're at an impasse and Gemma has decided to break it. It's a big chance but I think she's quite right. She's threatened divorce and it hasn't worked so she's simply walked out on him. But I don't think it's a divorce that she wants. She's hoping he'll follow them home before very long.'

'And what would you know about it?' Tom is still cross but he's listening; he would like Oliver to have a point, though he'll never admit it.

'Oh, I know I've never been married and all that, but I know Guy and my sister very well indeed and I think it's worth giving it time. Why not look on it as an extended holiday? If you start questioning Gemma about the future she'll begin to panic and think about making other plans and then other complications might arise.'

'I'm sure he's right,' Cass says quickly to Tom. 'I agree it's worth giving it time, anyway. We've got nothing to lose.'

Tom snorts. 'Except the cost of supporting three extra people indefinitely.' He glances at Oliver. He'd like to say 'four extra people' but Oliver contributes very generously to the household when he's staying and Tom can't, in all fairness, make such an accusation. Oliver grins at him.

'And on a fixed income,' he adds, using one of Tom's favourites phrases. 'I'll sub Gemma and you look after Ben and Julian. That's fair, isn't it?'

Cass bursts out laughing. 'I'm sure we'll manage between us. So that's settled then. No questions, no decisions.'

'And what about Kate?' asks Tom, reluctant to quit the field without a last small victory. 'I still think it's a bit much to expect her to come here knowing that Gemma has walked out on Guy.'

'I agree,' says Oliver. 'I think, to begin with, Gemma should take the twins to see Kate in Chapel Street. Once the first meeting is over it'll be easier.'

*   *   *

Two days later Gemma is driving back from Tavistock. Her meeting with Kate is over and she feels equal measures of guilt and relief. She's glad now that she decided to leave the twins at the Rectory. She and Kate couldn't possibly have had a heart-to-heart with Ben and Julian within earshot. Each time she thinks about her boys Gemma's gut twists with fear at the huge risk she's taking. It's impossible to imagine her life without Guy, and however could she explain to the nine-year-old twins that Daddy wasn't coming back to live with them? At the same time it was also impossible to remain in such a damaging situation.

Gemma wants to weep at the thought of Guy, back in Canada, furious that she's simply taken the boys and left; returning from two days away, delivering a boat, and coming home to find her letter. But he'll know why she's done it. She's talked, explained, pleaded, threatened divorce, but he simply won't respond. Even now he is still in complete denial. Although she has texted him he hasn't replied. He's clearly very angry. She's desperate to know how he is but some instinct warns her to remain silent now and wait. Guy has never been a demonstrative man but lately it's been getting much worse. It's like he's morphing into his father and becoming detached and cynical and sarcastic. Gemma shakes her head, gives a little shiver. Soon this might begin to affect the twins more seriously and she simply can't stand for it. And, just as importantly, it's not good for Guy to be like this. It's not just about her and the boys; it's about Guy too. She's simply got to get him home and she's chanced everything on this desperate course of action: the sudden departure and the threat of divorce if he doesn't follow. She clutches the steering wheel tightly as she imagines how Guy has reacted to her going. But the situation demanded a desperate remedy. Guy needs to come back and be in charge of his own life again. To be at the beck and call of his father is crushing him, sapping his confidence.

As she drives out of the town through Whitchurch she has to fight down her own guilt lest it disables her and makes her weak. If she hadn't played around, had a silly affair while Guy was away, the drastic move to Canada would never have happened; the offer to run the boatyard, to take over so that Mark could retire, would have simply remained a possibility at the back of Guy's mind. She knew very well that getting them out there had been a feather in Mark's cap, a kind of two-finger gesture to Kate, and very quickly she'd seen that Mark had no intention of allowing Guy any kind of real power.

She'd been fascinated—not in a good way—to see how Mark maintained control over his son with a mixture of biting sarcasm thinly veiled with humour—'Can't you take a joke?'—irritation barely concealed, and detachment. It was rather frightening: Guy has that same detachment, the short fuse, but he is capable of great affection and loyalty—and his sense of humour is genuine and not cruel.

Watching him with his father she'd felt the first stirrings of genuine fear for them all—and it was her fault. This was the price she must pay for foolishness, disloyalty, a quick physical fix, all masquerading as a harmless bit of fun. Guy, continually humiliated and frustrated, began to withdraw from her; Mark simply ignored her or treated her as if she were mentally deficient. She'd grown angry, had a few rows with him, but he was quick to point out to her how dependent she was, so far from home and at the mercy of his goodwill. Guy, trying to keep a balance between them, ashamed at his own inadequacy in defending her, grew more morose. And now there is the new wife, who is very anxious to assert her rights. Mark always seemed cool with living in the flat above the boatyard and renting the manager's house to Guy, but now his new wife doesn't see why she should be in the flat when there's a nice house going.

Gemma stops the car on the open moorland between Horrabridge and Walkhampton and gets out. Now that she has left, and Guy is on his own, what if Mark is able to influence him even more strongly; what if he persuades Guy that he is in the right, that he must not allow himself to be blackmailed? The conversation with Kate has made her a bit shaky, though Kate was understanding.

'I'm really sorry, Kate,' she said. 'I really, really tried. I promise. But I still love him and I want him back. I have to take this huge risk. Have I got it wrong?'

'Probably not,' answered Kate. 'If your instinct is telling you to do this then it's probably right.'

'It's head and heart, isn't it?' Gemma said

81

anxiously. 'It seems absolutely right one minute and then I have the mother and father of a panic attack the next.'

'It's a bit late for that,' said Kate drily. 'So let's hope you have very good instincts, darling.'

Gemma's having one of those panic attacks right now. The cool little breeze fans her hot cheeks and she takes slow breaths. The deep rural silence washes over her, calming her, and she can see the square tower of Walkhampton church amongst the trees. It looks solid and reassuring; like a rock. Gemma feels she might burst into tears. She's between a rock and a hard place: the slow disintegration of her family or divorce.

She gets back into the car and heads for the Rectory with dread in her heart. Everyone's being so tactful and discreet, it's humiliating. Even Pa is restraining himself. She can actually see the effort he's making and she just can't quite bring herself to explain about the ultimatum. Not just yet. Ma's OK, but Gemma feels a bit like a bone between the two of them. Pa wants everything cut and dried, and then she says things she doesn't mean and commits to things she's not ready for simply to shut him up. Ma comes to her defence, which generally leads to a row. She doesn't want it to be a big thing with the boys, and she's praying her gamble comes off before any damage is done. They're too young to know anything's really wrong and they believe that they've come back to live here and Daddy will follow as soon as he can.

She tries not to imagine a conversation in which she has to tell them that Daddy isn't coming back, and she thinks again about Kate and how she must be feeling; after all, Guy is her son. It was clear while they were talking that she was remembering her own relationship with Mark and trying hard to be fair about it all—but Guy is not Mark. Suddenly Gemma's longing for Guy is intense; tears sting her eyes, but she braces herself. The twins will be waiting for her and she must be strong and cheerful.

*   *   *

From the landing window Cass watches Gemma drive in and park the car on the gravel. She stands for a moment, head bent as if she has forgotten something, but Cass knows that she is bracing herself and she wonders how the meeting with Kate has gone. Gemma turns, swinging her bag over her shoulder, hurries towards the house and is lost to sight below the window.

Cass stands still, listening to the voices of the twins greeting Gemma in the kitchen and Gemma's cheerful reply. She wonders, not for the first time, why Gemma fell in love with Guy; why such a light-hearted, flirtatious girl should be attracted to a man who is so contained, so unknowable.

'There's much more to Guy than what *you* get to see,' Gemma had said once. 'That's why I love him. He's got something really special and it's all for me.'

Well, that's probably true; there is an integrity about Guy, a single-mindedness, which makes it all the more praiseworthy that he was prepared to forgive Gemma her faithlessness and give the marriage another go. Even so . . . Cass folds her arms, leans forward to rest her forehead against the cool glass. What Gemma has told her makes

83

her afraid: afraid that as he grows older Guy might harden into his father's mould.

She is glad that Gemma and the twins are home, away from Mark's influence, and she will do everything in her power to keep them here. Those little boys are so precious to her, so dear, that she cannot bear to think of them exposed to Mark's acid tongue and contemptuous glances. Guy, on the other hand, clearly adores his sons, and they him, so perhaps she is foolish to be so fearful.

All will be well now: they are home, safe, and if Guy returns then that will be good, and if not . . . Cass thinks of Kate and her heart aches. Kate is too honest to condemn Gemma for feeling about Guy as she once felt about Mark, but the truth is plain: if Gemma had not played around they'd all still be living happily in South Brent.

Cass straightens up, turns from the window as if escaping from something she no longer wishes to see, but the old familiar anguish grips her heart. Had she not been faithless all those years ago Charlotte, her first-born and Tom's favourite, would still be alive. Even now Cass cringes away from a vision of Charlotte watching, listening, gradually piecing together the unpalatable truth. And the terrible irony was that when at last Charlotte made her move, the affair was over. Charlotte's accusations involved other people and precipitated a terrible tragedy—even now Cass can hear the recriminatory words she screamed at her daughter—and then Charlotte, still in shock, saddled up and rode out on her pony, riding to her death. She was fifteen . . .

The twins come racing out of the kitchen. 'Granny,' they shout. 'Granny, where are you?' and

Cass switches her mind away from these thoughts and hurries thankfully down to join them.

*　　　*　　　*

'But the fact remains,' says Kate to Jess later as they sit in front of the fire, 'that part of me still feels very slightly resentful. Cass has always been able to disarm me, and Gemma is exactly the same.'

Kate was struck, during that conversation, by Gemma's resemblance to Cass and to Oliver, with her long blonde hair swept up into a knot, her blue eyes anxious. Once again the ghosts edged closer: Kate remembered the delightful baby Gemma in her pram, the pretty schoolgirl, the beautiful young bride and, last, the extremely attractive woman who was watching her over the rim of her coffee cup.

'Honestly, Kate,' Gemma had said, 'I had to do something. Mark is impossible and Guy just grows more silent and more unapproachable. *You* know!'

And Kate agreed; yes, she knows about that invisible barrier, which blocks any attempt at communication, the chill atmosphere and the numbing lack of physical affection.

'Oh, I know what Guy can be like,' Kate says now to Jess. 'And I know it's not always easy for someone like Gemma to cope with that unemotional, rather austere kind of character, but they've known each other all their lives so it's no good complaining about it at this late date.'

'How weird that must be,' says Jess, curled up at the other end of the sofa. She's fascinated by this new angle of the story. 'Were you pleased when they got married?'

'Yes,' says Kate, trying to remember. 'Yes, I was,

85

because they seemed to be so much in love, but I was a bit anxious because they are so completely different.' She hesitates, wondering how much she ought to tell Jess; how far she can go without being disloyal.

'You might as well tell her,' Gemma had said. 'She's going to be around for a while so it's easier for everyone, isn't it?'

'It's odd to think,' says Jess, 'that if Juliet and Mike hadn't gone to Australia I might have been part of all this. Daddy might have gone to school with Oliver and Guy.'

'Your father must have married very young,' says Kate.

Jess nods. 'He was twenty-two. I think it was because he was on his own over here and he wanted to have his own special person. Mum's parents had died in a car crash when she was quite young and they were a bit "babes in the wood" together, if you know what I mean. They looked after each other, though they were both quite strong people, and we had army friends, of course. But when Daddy was killed and Mum went off to Brussels all that fell apart. I think this is why it's so fascinating hearing all this stuff. It's like I'm being given a family again.'

'We haven't talked much about Juliet and Mike, though we probably will when we go to lunch with the Trehearnes. Johnnie knew Mike very well. Didn't Tom say that Juliet and Mike met at one of the Trehearnes' parties? You'll love the house. It's on the River Tamar, and the views are spectacular. In the summer they used to hold the parties outside in the sea garden.'

'The sea garden? What's a sea garden?'

'It used to be an old quay built up above the

86

saltings. Now it's grassed over, with a wonderful curving stone balustrade around the edge of the lawn, and the most amazing old ship's figurehead, Circe. She looks downriver towards Plymouth and the sea. The Trehearnes' ancestors were traders and in the old days the ships used to come right upriver. Circe was taken from one of them and she's simply magnificent. The legend has it that the sea garden was built by one old chap when he could no longer go to sea so that he could go out and stare down the river and listen to the gulls and watch the tide come sweeping up over the mudflats.'

Jess tries to imagine it. 'And is that where Juliet and Mike met?' She has a sudden vision of pretty girls in long dresses and handsome men in uniform moving in the sea garden; lights are strung above the balustrade and gleam on the dark water in the gathering dusk. She blinks, surprised at such a vivid mental picture.

'That's what Tom says.' Kate notices that Jess says 'Juliet and Mike' not 'Granny and Grandfather', as if she is seeing them now as the young couple they were then; as if she is in the story with them. 'Tom served with Mike, so he must have got to know him pretty well, though Mike was a couple of years older than Tom.'

'I wonder why they went to Australia,' says Jess rather wistfully.

'Exchanges happened quite often back then,' Kate says. 'Between us and Australia and Canada. Mark, my ex-husband, transferred to the Canadian Navy and then bought into a boatyard business when he retired from the service. Guy was doing yacht brokerage and delivery work over here, which is why he thought it might all work out when they moved to be with him.'

'You must be pleased that they're back.'

'I shall be happier when Guy's back, too. I can see why Gemma's given him the ultimatum but I hope she knows what she's doing.'

'You're cross with her for taking the risk?'

'I suppose I am, a bit,' admits Kate. 'That's what I meant about feeling resentful. Gemma had been playing about, you see, and Guy found out and it all got rather unpleasant. He decided that he would join his father in Canada so as to make a clean break from the mess here and she must choose whether to go or end the marriage. Gemma agreed that it was a fair deal. It worked for a little while but Mark is showing no sign of passing the business over to Guy, which was the plan, but has been playing a rather heavy hand and allowing Guy no scope. Meanwhile, Guy has been growing disenchanted and grumpy and Gemma is missing her friends and family. She's tried to persuade Guy to come back and now she's given him this ultimatum. I can well imagine that between Mark and Guy she's had a tough time, especially now Mark has married again, but it wouldn't have happened if she hadn't played around in the first place.'

'But did she play around because she was . . . well, bored with Guy?'

Kate sighs. 'Gemma simply can't resist a flirtation. Cass used to be the same. They have a kind of blindness. They don't see it as cheating: simply as harmless fun. Unfortunately it doesn't work like that, though when Guy found out that she'd actually had an affair he was very understanding about it. He could see that Gemma had been left alone too much whilst he was at sea, and he was prepared to give the marriage another try. She certainly wanted to. That's why she was prepared to go to Canada. We were all gutted that they'd be so far away, of course, but that was Guy's condition at the time. Now it's Gemma calling the shots.'

'Poor Kate. It's a bit tough on you, isn't it?'

'It'll be tough on all of us if Gemma's misjudged Guy. This is a very flawed and damaged family you're taking on, Jess.'

'That's why it feels so real,' says Jess contentedly.

*   *   *

'Stop looking so hunted,' Oliver says. He pushes his sister's glass of wine a little closer to her. 'There's nobody here we know. No one's going to pop up and question you.'

'I know.' Gemma relaxes a little, picking up the glass, glancing round the bar of the little moorland pub. 'But it's getting me down a tad. I just wish Pa would stop giving me little lectures about playing fair and about how it was all my fault in the first place. It makes me want to pack up and go somewhere else. I know he's right but I still think that this is the way I'm going to save our marriage.'

'Then stay with it.' He drinks some water. 'You know, they both played the field a bit, our dear parents, and I think Pa's frightened that you might lose something you love because you're not taking it seriously enough.'

She stares at him; gives a disbelieving little laugh. 'What? Sorry, Ol. Have I missed a point or something? You sound like "Thought for the Day". Anyway, what d'you mean "played the field"? After they were married? Come on.'

He hesitates. 'OK then, but this is in absolute confidence.'

She pulls a face. 'Good grief, Charlie Brown. OK. Cross my heart and hope to die.'

He smiles a little at the phrase from their childhood but quickly looks serious again; his gaze is inward, remembering.

'I expect you don't remember much about Charlotte. She was about fifteen when she died and you were about six. Do you remember her?'

Gemma thinks about their older sister. She frowns, trying to separate true memory from stories and photographs. She shakes her head slowly.

'It was such a long time ago,' she says. 'I just have this feeling of a kind person.'

'Yes, she was a gentle, quiet girl. Well, Ma and Pa had been having a slight relationship problem and they'd both been finding comfort elsewhere. On the day Charlotte went out on that fateful pony ride she'd found out something a bit unsavoury about Ma and they'd had a row. She was very upset and, as you know, the pony slipped at the edge of the quarry and they both went over. Ma can never forgive herself. She told me about it when you went out to Canada. She said that it had brought back terrible memories and she and Pa were just so relieved that you and Guy had sorted things out and the twins were happy.'

Gemma gazes at her brother with horror and fear. 'Charlotte found out something?'

'Ma didn't give me any details. Perhaps Charlotte overheard something—perhaps a telephone call—

90

and confronted Ma. Apparently there was a very bad scene and Charlotte just dashed out and got on her pony and rode off without putting on her hard hat. Ma said that the bitter truth was that her affair had been over for a while but Charlotte still suspected her of infidelity.'

'I can't believe that Ma would have messed around.'

'Can't you? I should have thought that it would be quite easy for you to understand the quirk of character that leads you to have flirtations and play the field.'

'Thanks,' she says grimly. 'I asked for that. But even so . . .'

'One doesn't like to imagine one's parents in that situation? True. Look, I'm saying this because they're both anxious that nothing like this should happen to you. Or the twins.'

'Shut up. Just shut up. You've made your point.' There are tears in her eyes. 'I can't take it in. Charlotte . . . Oh my God. Why are you telling me now?'

'For two reasons. First, so that you can understand a bit better why Pa is going on like he is. He doesn't want history to repeat itself. Second, I think you'll get another chance with Guy and you should think very carefully about it.'

'It's awful.'

'Yes, it's awful. But it explains things a bit, doesn't it?'

She nods. 'It's just such a shock. I mean, I know Charlotte was killed falling off her horse, but putting it into this kind of context makes it . . . Oh, I don't know. Oh God, however did they live with it?'

'With a great deal of heartbreak and difficulty.

But they had to carry on. Shit happens. Deal with it.'

She stares at him, shocked. 'There's no need to be so brutal about it.'

'I don't feel brutal. I've had more chance to get used to the truth and, like you said, it happened a long time ago. It's just that I don't want everyone going off half-cock. OK, Pa's being tiresome but now you know why, you'll be less likely to do something silly and rush off in a fit of temper. We have to think of Ben and Julian. They need stability right now.'

'I know they do,' she says defensively. 'I know that. This is for them just as much as me. More, if anything. They weren't particularly happy out there lately, you know.'

'OK. OK.' Oliver raises his hands pacifically, palms up. 'But it's going to be better now. They'll go to Mount House next week for the assessment and with luck they'll go straight in. It's amazingly lucky that the school has got space for them.'

Gemma subsides into the corner of the seat. 'I know. And I'm truly grateful that you're prepared to sub us the fees if they do get in, Ol.'

He grins sardonically. 'I hope Guy will feel the same. He and I were never great buddies and I suspect he'll find it just a shade difficult to cope with.'

'I know he will.' She makes a little face. 'That's tough. I am utterly thrilled at the chance to have Ben and Julian at Mount House. I think it helped with Mr Massie to know that they had a father and a few uncles there before them. That's going to be another shock for Pa. That you'll be shelling out for two sets of school fees.'

He shrugs. 'I can afford it and I'm their godfather as well as their uncle. He should be pleased to know they'll be settled.'

'He is, but he still feels it. It must be a bit tough for him knowing how wealthy you are.'

'I cry all the way to the bank. Are we going to have some lunch?'

She sits up straighter. 'Did you bring me here just to tell me that? About Charlotte.'

'It had to be said. I don't see how you ever get over losing a child, for whatever reason, but they've struggled on and tried to come to terms with it. It's easy to make harsh judgements about people when you don't know the truth about them. You're a big girl now and I reckon you can take it.'

'Would Mum mind you telling me?'

He shrugs. 'Probably not now. She didn't absolutely say it was a secret but I'd rather you didn't mention it to her. And certainly not to anybody else.'

'Good grief, no.' She shudders; frowns suddenly. 'D'you think Kate knows?'

He hesitates and then nods. 'Almost certainly. They've always been so close, haven't they? Come on, let's order.'

She watches him as he goes to the bar and she sees a reflection of herself: tall, elegant, blond, attractive. She wonders why he's never nailed a relationship, never committed; after all, there have been plenty of contenders.

'I get bored too quickly,' he said once. 'It wouldn't be fair.'

Selfishly she's rather glad; he's such a mate, always there when something crops up. More importantly, he's always on her side. A wife or partner might be a bit of a nuisance. The point about Oliver is that he doesn't make judgements, which is why, when he does get serious, she listens. Like just now . . .

Gemma drinks some more wine and tries to remember Charlotte. She reflects on the big age gap between six and fifteen, and the fact that Charlotte had been away at school for so much of the time. Oh, but how ghastly for Ma: what a price to pay for some foolish flirtation. How terrible it must be to have an argument with your child and then never see her alive again; to live with the aching thought that if she hadn't been so upset she'd have taken more care. She thinks about her twins, out with Kate for the day, and her heart is squeezed painfully with love and fear and a longing to protect. It occurs to her that Pa isn't simply being bloody-minded and cross with her; he, too, is trying to protect her—and the boys—from her actions.

Oliver glances across from the crowd around the bar, gives her a little wink. She grins at him and her whole body suddenly relaxes: thank God for Ollie.

'I shall be coming home sometime in the next fortnight,' she said to him on the telephone. 'Is there any chance you could be there? Can you make some reason for visiting? It'll be so much easier if you're around.'

And there he was, acting as a buffer state, making her laugh, taking charge of the twins, who adore him. Oh, he can afford to do as he pleases, she thought, he's made a packet, but not everyone in his position would be as kind as her big brother.

'So tell me about Jess,' she says as he sits down again. 'I still haven't met her yet. Is she as gorgeous as Pa says?'

'She's certainly a looker but not in an obvious way. She's got very long, very dark reddish-brown hair and her eyes are almost exactly the same colour. A very sweet, neat face, but not in any way vacuous. She looks keen, alert, very alive.'

Gemma's eyebrows shoot up. 'Well. That's a very detailed description. I can almost see her.'

'Kate's taking her down to meet the Trehearnes. You remember them? Mad Lady T and dear old Johnnie. Apparently they knew Jess's grandparents back in the day. I felt quite sorry for the poor kid to begin with, but she's absolutely loving it all. I like her a lot. Pity about the age gap but there it is. Clearly I've taken on Unk's mantle and I'm destined to be everybody's uncle.'

'Oh, I don't know. If I were just out of uni with my way to make in the world I'd think you were a jolly good catch.'

'I'll introduce you,' he says, 'and you can put in a word for me. Do you want another drink?'

*   *   *

Tom puts the newspaper aside and glances at his watch; a bit too early for the one o'clock news. Cass is off playing bridge, Oliver and Gemma have gone out to lunch, and he ought to be feeling a sense of freedom and relaxation. Instead he feels scratchy and cross. He doesn't want to have to think too much just at the moment. Gemma's return and the arrival of Jess have brought all sorts of memories rushing back, some of them good. He likes to remember those days when he was a young cadet, before he met Cass, hanging out with Johnnie Trehearne and Freddy Grenvile. The Trehearnes

95

were very generous with their hospitality and he went home with Johnnie and Fred from Dartmouth on many occasions for a weekend. The three of them became good friends though he was never quite so keen on sailing as the others. He never let on, of course; it did him no harm at all to be a close oppo of Dickie Trehearne's son and he took advantage of it.

Seeing Jess has brought it all back. He was knocked sideways by Juliet but she was more taken up with the older ones: Al and Mike and Stephen Mortlake. Now he tries not to admit the fact that he's slightly jealous of Oliver's growing friendship with Jess and the way that his elder son attracts women. Anyway, Oliver's too old for the girl, nearly twice her age. And he's got far too much money. It's always been a mystery to him that old Uncle Eustace was so impressed with Oliver; taking him into the business, leaving him his shares. He had a very high opinion of Oliver. And Oliver was very fond of Unk.

'It's not the same,' he said after Unk died. 'There's just no fun in the business any more. And it's grown far too big. I've had a very good offer for it and I shall take it.'

And so he had. He didn't ask advice from his father, talk it through with him, nothing like that. No. Just, 'I've had a very good offer and I shall take it.'

'For goodness' sake!' Cass cried when Tom said this to her. 'So what? Leave him alone. Why can't you be proud of him for doing what he does so successfully?'

Tom refolds the paper irritably, glances again at his watch. He was glad when Cass went off to her bridge morning, giving them both a breathing space. There have been quite a few rows lately about Gemma's predicament and—indirectly—Oliver's involvement.

'We've lost one daughter,' Cass shouted, 'and I don't intend to lose another. Gemma and the twins stay here until she's ready to move on.'

She actually said that: 'We've lost one daughter.'

He sees her clearly: Charlotte. She'd never have behaved as Gemma has; she was so sweet and gentle and loving. How he misses her and what a comfort she would have been to him now. He stands up and walks away from the table as if he can walk away from his pain; away from the fear that Gemma might precipitate just such another tragedy.

'That's simply nonsense,' Cass says, exasperated by his anxiety. 'This is all completely different. The twins aren't adolescent girls with feverish imaginations, and Gemma isn't playing the field any more. For God's sake, get a grip.'

He knows her anger is an outward expression of her own remorse and grief but that doesn't help. What will happen if Guy takes a firm stand and Gemma has to face the future alone with the twins? He asks Cass this question and she simply shrugs.

'Other women have managed,' she says.

And they both know that Oliver would take care of his sister and his nephews. Tom tries to decide why this knowledge irritates him so much; after all, he doesn't *want* to see Gemma and the boys suffer. He gropes towards an answer but can't find it. All he can see is Charlotte on one side, the scapegoat for his and Cass's misbehaviour, and Gemma, nonchalantly and uncaringly recreating just such another disaster, on the other. It's as if Charlotte has suffered for them all and his own sense of guilt seeks to assuage her spirit by punishing Gemma.

He needs a drink and it's time for the news. Tom makes himself a gin and tonic, switches on the television and sits down at the table.

TAMAR

The tide is making; slipping and sliding across the mudflats, advancing on the birds—seagull, shelduck, curlew—that scoop and probe at the edges of the deep-water channel. Downriver the two great bridges, Brunel's railway and the road bridge, one elegant structure superimposed against the other, are hardly visible in the early-morning mist; they look delicate, ethereal, strong as a cobweb. Along the littoral, the high-tide line is a litter of twigs and broken branches, seaweed and bladderwrack. As the salt water floods into the river's bed the boats begin to swing on their moorings and a white egret sails across their mast-tops, its reflection clear and dazzling on the mirror-like surface of the rising tide.

Standing at her bedroom window, Rowena peers short-sightedly at the magical scene. Her memory sketches in the things she can no longer see without her spectacles, and fills her deaf ears with once-familiar sounds: the plock of the seagulls' feet in the mud, the creak of the swinging hulls, the curlew's evocative cry.

Soon there will be the usual knock at the door and Johnnie, still in his dressing gown, will bring her early-morning tea. She will be brusque with him because it is her way; she has never learned to be tender. Only with Alistair, her first-born, her beloved; only with darling Alistair has she ever been able to be truly loving. They were alike, she and Al; tough, greedy, demanding, passionate. She understood him, gave way to him, shielded him from his detractors and, when he died, part of her died with him. It had been more than forty years since Al died but the past is still fresh; and now the child has come, looking just like her grandmother, and the ghosts with her.

And here is the knock at the door and she shouts 'Come!' irritably because she is still living in that moment of meeting Jess, seeing the girl's bright face and eager ways.

'Wait,' she snaps at Johnnie as he puts down the tray on the table by the window. 'Only a quarter of my head is working.'

Together they hunt for her hearing aids, for her spectacles, and she puts her teeth in, glaring at him as if it is his fault that she's ninety-two and furious because she no longer functions properly. Johnnie merely smiles at her; just like his father he is sweet-tempered, amiable, patient. And, just like his father, he drives her mad.

He pours her tea for her because he knows that her hands shake, and this irritates her too, and he knows it but can't help himself.

'Jess will be here later,' he says, quite unnecessarily because she has been counting the hours. 'Isn't it fun that she's going to stay? She really loves the old place, doesn't she?'

Just like his father, platitude after platitude— 'Five minutes on the bleeding obvious,' as Al had once put it, making her laugh—but, because

Johnnie is pleased at the prospect of Jess's arrival, she feels a sudden warmth towards him and she smiles as she reaches for her teacup and nods a little thank-you.

He goes out, leaving her to the silence, the river and her tea. She picks up the cup with care, prepared for the trembling of her hand, advances it cautiously to her withered lips, sips the hot reviving liquid. There is a clatter as she puts it into its saucer but her thoughts are back with the child; coming into the house, exclaiming at the great jar of spindleberries on the hall table, delighting at the view, struck silent in the sea garden as she stares up at Circe and out across the balustrade to the great bridges and the sea.

'Kate tried to explain it to me,' she said, 'and then I had a kind of vision of it . . .'

'Vision?' Rowena asked quickly, too quickly. Jess looked at her, partly surprised, partly embarrassed.

'Tom told me about the wonderful parties you had here when he was young,' she said, 'and, just for a moment, I could see it with little lights strung around and the girls in pretty dresses and the men in uniform.'

Now Rowena nods, remembering: yes, that's how it was. Warm summer evenings, with the moon just rising, and the pale, moth-like fluttering of the girls' dresses against the dark silhouettes of their companions, smart in evening clothes. And Alistair moving amongst their guests, debonair and amusing; the girls excited by his presence, their men flattered by his attention. He was too bright, too sharp, to be loved in the way Johnnie—and his father before him—was loved. No, Al's magnetism was like an electric current that could bring light, heat, power. It could sear and burn too, but it was irresistible.

He and Mike Penhaligon were a wicked pair.

'We're going hunting, Mother,' he'd say, leaning casually to kiss her. 'Don't wait up.' And she'd laugh, egging him on, glorying in his strength and beauty, and Mike, behind him, would laugh too. Once they'd gone, the room would seem a little duller, smaller, and Dickie would irritate her by making some remark about Al being too clever by half; too big for his boots. He was jealous of his elder son, of course; quiet, gentle Johnnie was much more to his liking.

Rowena pours more tea. The china spout of the teapot cracks sharply against the eggshell-thin cup so that tea spills in the saucer. She makes a face, reaches for a tissue and mops up. No harm done. She's back in the past, remembering Mike introducing Juliet; he was proud, besotted, his gaze hardly leaving the face of the delightful girl, who smiled with proper deference at the wife of an important senior officer. Juliet had smiled with the same sweetness that Jess smiled at her last Sunday, so that she'd gripped the girl's hand too tightly, trying to hide her shock.

As she finishes her tea she remembers how, more than forty years before, Alistair stood to one side, watching the introduction. For once his guard was down and she was taken aback by his expression; he looked angry, thwarted. Just so had he looked as a child when he'd been crossed, and she experienced a tiny thrill of fear. More than that, she was indignant that Mike had appropriated something that Al clearly wanted for himself. Generally it was the other way: Al was always first, best. Now, it seemed that Mike had won the prize and Al was furious. Next moment she wondered if she'd imagined it. Al was laughing, teasing Juliet, mocking Mike, but Rowena was watchful now. She saw how Al's eyes lingered on the girl and how the old easiness between him and Mike was gone. It seemed that Mike was the conqueror this time— until that evening of the Midsummer's Eve party in the sea garden.

Rowena replaces the delicate cup in its saucer and stands up. The small long-haired terrier, nestling amongst the flung-back bedclothes, raises her head and Rowena bends to stroke her with stiff, arthritic hands. 'Good girl, Popps,' she murmurs. 'Good girl.' She must crack on; get moving. Washing and dressing are arduous tasks that take time, and soon Jess will be here and she must be ready; watchful as she was forty years ago.

*   *   *

Downstairs, Johnnie drinks his coffee with Sophie in the kitchen.

'Odd of Mother to take such a fancy to Jess,' he says. 'I thought she might like to meet her but I was very surprised when she asked her to stay. I hope it won't make a lot of extra work for you.'

Sophie shrugs. 'Much less work than when the girls come home with the children. She looks the sort who will muck in.'

'I liked her,' he says, 'didn't you? Rather engaging. Must be odd for her to be here where it all began. To be honest with you I never liked Mike Penhaligon all that much. He was a bit of a bully.' He snorts with amusement. 'Ditto my dear elder brother, actually.'

Sophie grins at him. 'I think I'd already guessed that. When people die young it's too easy to sanctify them, isn't it? Especially if they die in a terrible accident. The living haven't got a hope.'

He looks at her affectionately. 'To be honest, I'd given up long before Al died. Mother was infatuated with him. There's no other word. Never mind. It's all over now.'

'I hope so.' She puts the list to one side. 'I shall dash into Bere Alston after breakfast, but if Jess arrives early the sail loft is all ready for her. I've made up the bed and given the whole place a good airing.'

'I still feel badly that you had to abandon your independence in the sail loft and move into the house when Mother had that attack,' he says.

'Don't be silly. It's much more sensible to be on hand when Rowena has her bad moments, as well as with Will here most weekends during term-time since Louisa went out to Geneva. Anyway, it's a while now since I felt the urge to bring home some lusty young man from the sailing club. Go and get dressed, Johnnie. Rowena will be down for her breakfast and she'll want you to take Popps for a run.'

*   *   *

Jess drives carefully along the lanes, paying attention, watching for signposts. She feels excited, nervous and guilty all at once.

'I don't know what came over me,' she said remorsefully to Kate after the lunch with the Trehearnes. 'When Lady T asked me to stay it just seemed right, somehow.'

'But that's what it's all about.' Kate was quite calm and laid-back about it. 'That's what this trip was for, wasn't it? Exploring, finding out about the past and Juliet and Mike. Lady T and Johnnie will have lots of stories to tell. I'm delighted she responded so positively. You really made a hit.

Jess nodded eagerly, relieved by Kate's reaction. 'She was amazed how much like Juliet I am. Just like Tom said. It's really weird, isn't it, that people remember her so clearly? No, but it's just that you've been so kind and I do really love it here in Chapel Street . . .'

'I know you do. And you can come back whenever you want to. Actually, it's worked out really well, Jess. Ben and Julian can come over and stay with me for a few days before they start school, and Oliver will probably enjoy a break from full-on family life too, so it's perfect timing. Go and enjoy yourself.'

'Thanks,' she said gratefully. 'It's another piece of the story, isn't it? Mike being such a close friend of the Trehearne family. Everything kind of interlocks and connects so that there are no beginnings and endings. The story just rolls on.'

'And you are a part of it,' said Kate.

So here she is, driving down to the Tamar, trying to remember Kate's directions—and, suddenly, she sees a glimpse of the shining river below her. With a quick glance in the rear-view mirror she swerves into the lane's edge and brakes, heart beating fast. Why should these little steep muddy lanes, that sinuous curve of water, the sheltering, gently rising hills, cause such a mix of emotions?

Suddenly, unexpectedly, she feels fearful: she

104

remembers that strange sense of *déjà vu* she experienced in the sea garden and again, oddly, in the sail loft.

'What a strange-looking place,' she said to Johnnie, staring at the long stone building with its low roof. 'What is it?'

'It's the old sail loft,' he told her. 'My great-grandfather was a keen sailing man. Very competitive. He had his own sails specially made. My girls used it as playroom and then Sophie had it as her own private quarters when she first came to live with us. Come and have a look. The boathouse is underneath.'

And he took her into the great light-filled space with windows along each wall and a huge glass door at the far end, set within a balcony. The room seemed to shake around her, the river light quivering and dazzling her, and Johnnie held her arm as if fearing that she might stumble on one of the rugs cast down upon the pale shining wooden floor. A short stairway, at the opposite end to the balcony, leads upwards to the bedrooms on a curving mezzanine floor rather like a minstrels' gallery. The kitchen and bathroom are tucked away beneath it at the back.

She tried to make light of her reaction. 'It's utterly amazing,' she said, rather breathlessly, laughing a little. 'Wow! What a place to work.'

And that's when Lady T, following behind them, made her offer.

'Well, why don't you come and stay with us for a few days, my dear? You could be here in the sail loft since you like it so much, and come over to the house for your meals and whenever you want company. We can get to know you better and you can explore the Tamar and perhaps find some inspiration for your work at the same time. We'd like that, wouldn't we, Johnnie?'

And he smiled at her, still holding her arm protectively. 'It would be splendid,' he said.

Now, Jess lets out the clutch, and drives on. She knows that it is time to step right into the story and take her place among the players.

*   *   *

Johnnie, with Popps at his heels, lets himself out through the back door, walks along the path between the big walled kitchen garden and the outbuildings to the higher ground where the lawn is surrounded by shrubberies of azalea and hydrangea. The tide is still making and a light north-easterly breeze rustles in the reed-beds; perfect conditions for a sail. Scrubbed down and ready for the winter, *Alice* lies at her moorings out on the deep-water channel. Inherited from his grandfather, she is Johnnie's passion. He's spent years restoring her, working on her, and his greatest joy is taking friends sailing in her.

As he strolls across the sloping land, watching the sun glinting on the cottage windows across the river in Cargreen, he reflects that had Al lived he would have inherited the house when their father died. It would have been Al's boat out on the river, his children running along the corridors and sitting around the dining-room table; his dogs following that rabbit's trail over the hard dry earth beneath the tree-tall hydrangeas.

Instead, Al's bones lie fathoms deep somewhere off the Gribben Head. Johnnie wanders slowly,

106

glancing back at the plain Georgian façade of the house, remembering the games he and Al once played here and down on the river: smugglers, pirates—the games were always water-based. The boathouse and the disused sail loft were perfect for these activities, along with the small sailing dinghy that Al was given on his ninth birthday. Johnnie learned quickly to follow where Al led, to be a good lieutenant: no sneaking or tattling. Al could do no wrong with their mother and he soon saw the wisdom of staying in his big brother's shadow.

Standing by the balustrade at the edge of the sea garden, his hand on the sun-warmed wood carving of the old ship's figurehead, Circe, he recalls the night of Al's death. The four of them crewed regularly for each other: Al and Mike; Johnnie and Fred. They'd been sailing out in the Western Approaches and, as night fell, were heading home, running before a strong south-westerly, which was gusting to gale force. Al and Mike had the midnight watch: he and Fred were in their bunks below. It was Mike who gave the alarm; Mike's voice echoing down the hatchway: 'Man overboard!'

Johnnie remembers being woken by raised voices, the boat's sudden gybe, being nearly thrown from his bunk. He and Fred scrambled out together, confused and frightened, jostling up the companionway where Mike was struggling to release the life buoy.

'Take the helm!' The words were snatched and flung away by the wind but they hurried to obey him. Mike had the life buoy in both hands then, and was lifting it, hefting it over the side, grabbing for the cockpit searchlight. 'Put her about!' he yelled. As black choppy water slopped into the cockpit,

Fred seized the helm and put it down, ducking as the boom swung over his head. Together they brought the boat under control while Mike swung the searchlight to and fro. They'd patrolled the area until dawn, waiting and watching, shouting in turn, but there was no sign of Al.

Later, Mike said that he'd just been going below to make coffee in the galley when the sudden squall hit the boat. It must have caught Al by surprise, he said, for he'd lost control, been struck on the head by the boom and knocked overboard as the boat gybed. His body has never been recovered.

Johnnie's hand automatically smoothes the carved, painted wood of Circe's gown, hearing again the raised voices followed by the boat's sudden lurch. The figurehead stands above him, staring downriver towards the sea, chin lifted, as if she is waiting for the tide to lift her upon its bosom and give her life again.

There is the sound of a car's engine in the lane behind the house and, calling to Popps, he hurries back to welcome Jess.

*   *   *

Rowena is before him, waiting impatiently. She has always been impatient: anything that is drawn out, slow, drives her almost insane. Long anecdotes or explanations, watching somebody doing something that she can accomplish in half the time, guarantee a tension inside her that makes her feel she might explode. So she hurries out to the car, bringing Jess into the sunny morning-room and ignoring the kitchen where Sophie will have put the coffee things ready. Rowena cannot understand the modern passion for entertaining in the kitchen; much nicer in this pretty little panelled room where she writes her letters and reads than in the rather dark, north-west facing kitchen.

Popps comes bundling in behind them, barking excitedly, and Rowena says, 'Quiet, Popps. You remember Jess,' and Jess bends to stroke the little dog, gently rubs the small velvety ears between her fingers.

'It's a funny name,' she says, suddenly overcome with shyness. 'Is it short for Poppy?'

'Johnnie's to blame,' says Rowena. 'When she was a puppy she'd howl when she was left alone and Johnnie said she sounded like Lucia Popp warming up for a concert. "Popp's off again," he'd say, and the name just stuck.'

Jess laughs, glad of the distraction with the little terrier, beginning to feel less nervous.

'We always had black Labradors at home,' she says. 'Mum wasn't really a dog person but Daddy hated to be without a dog.'

'Did he?' Rowena sits down at the big round rosewood table where newspapers and magazines are scattered. There are letters half out of their envelopes, and a yellow painted china pot with pencils and pens standing in it. Her hands stray amongst the letters, tidying them. 'What was he like, your father?'

Before she can reply, Johnnie speaks from behind her.

'Good morning, Jess. So you found your way to us. Well done.'

Jess turns to him, almost with relief. There is an intensity about the older woman that is very slightly unnerving.

'Kate gave me very good directions,' she answers, 'but I certainly had to concentrate.'

'Then you deserve some coffee,' he says. 'Sophie hoped she'd be back before you arrived but I'm sure she'll have left something ready.'

'Can I help?' she asks, smiling at Rowena and following him out with Popps close behind them.

Rowena listens to their voices, and to the patter and click of Popps' claws, as they cross the hall. She sits quite still, folding and smoothing the pages of a letter from an old friend and pushing them back into the envelope, hardly aware of what she is doing.

In the kitchen Jess helps Johnnie to put the coffee things onto the tray. She feels completely at ease with him, he is so kind and amusing and relaxed, and she likes it here in the warm, muddly kitchen with the percolator popping.

'We simply couldn't manage without Sophes,' he's saying. 'Thank God she never wanted to leave us. When the girls and all the children come in the holidays I'd be utterly out of my depth without her. And she's wonderful with Will.'

'I'm looking forward to meeting Will,' says Jess, arranging biscuits on a hand-painted blue and yellow plate.

'Will's ten going on forty.' Johnnie puts the coffee pot onto the tray. 'He has three little sisters who drive him right round the bend, poor chap, and it's made him old before his time.'

Jess laughs. Suddenly she's happy again, all her nerves and fears put to rest by this delightful man. In an odd way he reminds her of her father; perhaps it's the military influence.

'He's lucky to have you here,' she tells him. 'I

110

used to go to friends for exeats and Sundays out once Daddy died. Brussels was just too far. Will's lucky to come back to his own home.'

'It's lucky for us, too. We love having him out, teaching him to sail. Can you manage the plate if I take the tray? Mother prefers to have coffee in the morning-room.'

Jess hesitates. 'The thing is,' she says confidentially, 'I don't quite know what to call your mother. She said not to keep calling her Lady Trehearne last Sunday but I simply can't call her Rowena. Can I?'

'What did she say about it?'

'She said that I could call her Rowena . . .' she hesitates, 'but that it might be fun if I could call her Great-granny like all the other young ones do.'

His blue eyes narrow as he smiles. 'Between you and me, they call her the granny-monster, but never mind.'

'But even so.'

He sees her discomfiture and puts the tray back on the table.

'The thing is,' he tells her, 'that, to my mother, you're one of a group of people who have been a part of the family for ever. Mike and Juliet were around so much, you see. Mike was my brother's closest friend from childhood onwards. Then there are my daughters and their husbands and innumerable sprogs. She simply sees you as one of this extended family. It would probably give her a great deal of pleasure if you could manage it, but you must feel comfortable, too. It's awful when people want you to call them things you feel unhappy with.'

Jess nods, and he picks up the tray again, and

they go back to the morning-room.

*   *   *

Later, on her own in the sail loft, Jess has time to collect her ideas and thoughts, and try to make sense of them. The great room swims in sunlight and river light; it is as if she is enclosed in a shining bubble. She goes out onto the balcony to get her bearings.

Across the river a small village of huddled cottages lies in the shelter of the hill. As she watches she sees a small rowing boat move out of the shadows along the waterfront, heading towards one of the bigger boats at anchor. Once again she has the oddest feeling that this has happened before; that the scene is familiar. Perhaps Juliet once stood here, her hands on the sun-warmed balustrade, and watched the boats on the Tamar and the birds wheeling low over the water. This thought doesn't upset her; she simply has a great longing to understand this strange sense of connection.

Both Johnnie and Lady T—after so much time with Kate she simply can't help thinking of her as Lady T—were both pleased when she told them that she loved sailing. 'Daddy taught me,' she said, and Lady T gave a little cry of triumph, quickly suppressed, as though an important point had been made.

'We'll go out tomorrow,' Johnnie said, 'just to give you a feel of the river. If you'd like to.'

Jess looks back into the room, wondering how she can make her own impression on it; give it a personal touch. Her belongings are too few to make

112

any impact on such a space, but she puts her laptop and notebooks on a round mahogany table under one of the windows and carefully unpacks the little painting Kate has given her.

'But I want you to have it,' she said, when Jess protested. 'It belongs to you now. David would have been so pleased. It's the next stage in its own story.'

'A sign,' Jess said. 'Or a portent. Thank you so much. I can't believe I have my own David Porteous painting.'

She looks around for a place to stand its little lectern: on the low table, which has books and magazines on it? Or on the shelf between two of the windows? Nowhere seems quite worthy of it. So she puts it carefully beside her laptop and notebooks, hoping that it might inspire her. Despite the fact that she wants to upload some photographs from her camera to the laptop and study them, she is drawn back again to the balcony. Perhaps, after all, this will be too much of a distraction; she will get no work done.

The little rowing boat is now empty, rocking gently, attached by its painter to one of the bigger boats; a figure, silhouetted against the sun, moves about on its deck then disappears below. A cormorant flaps slowly upriver and lands on one of the buoys; it balances, stretching its wings, its crucifix-shape perfectly mirrored in the glass-like surface of the water.

Jess takes a deep, contented breath: she will take her camera and walk along the river bank.

*   *   *

From the kitchen's side window, Sophie sees her go

113

through the little wicket gate.

'Good,' she says with satisfaction. 'I'm so glad she doesn't feel she has to stick around being polite. Rowena seems a bit on edge. Is there something you're not telling me?'

Johnnie is kicking off his shoes at the end of the short passage by the back door, to put on his gumboots, and she comes away from the window to look at him from the kitchen door.

'What d'you mean?' His voice is slightly muffled as he bends down to tuck his jeans into his boots.

'She's edgy,' Sophie insists. 'All bright and alert as if she's expecting something to happen. Something to do with Jess.'

'Oh, surely not. She's just enjoying having a young person around. Mother's always enjoyed the company of the young.'

He's got his boots on now and he turns to look at her. His expression is blandly cheerful, open, and she looks back at him thoughtfully. 'Come off it,' she wants to say to him but, just for a moment, she feels she is being warned off. His eyes narrow with amusement, as if he recognizes her dilemma.

'I'm off to mow,' he says. 'Last cut of the year, I'd say. Everything's fine, Sophes. It's just having Jess here brings back memories for all of us. Times past and all that stuff. It's that Proustian moment.'

'Good,' she says brightly. 'That's OK then. But I'm not making madeleines for tea so don't think it.'

He laughs and goes out, and she turns back into the kitchen, thinking about Rowena: that little edginess when Jess is there, and the look of inward concentration when she isn't. It's as if Rowena is doing a complicated mental jigsaw puzzle, fitting in

114

the pieces, trying them for size. And it is clear that Jess is an important piece of the puzzle. Even in her nineties the older woman's mental acuity is still formidable but Sophie feels anxious. She is not by nature fanciful but she is worried by the intensity of Rowena's reaction to Jess and how it might affect her health.

Sophie glances from the window again and sees that there is no sign of Jess. It's good that the girl is already feeling the freedom of making herself at home—yet the little niggling anxiety remains.

*   *   *

Jess steps out cautiously along the high-tide line, picking her way across the saltings. Here and there the narrow lane is separated from the river bank by stands of spindleberries and thorn and the yellow buddleia *weyeriana* and, when the way before her looks too muddy, she squeezes between their branches to get back into the lane.

The tide is on the turn: in the deep-water channel the current is running fast, the surface is choppy and rough, yet across the mudflats the water lies smooth and calm. She stops to watch a small motorboat speeding downriver with the tide, its bow wave rippling from shore to shore. The man on the yacht has come back on deck and stands to watch the noisy little boat. He remains standing, looking towards her now, and instinctively she waves to him—she knows that water-borne people are usually friendly—and after a moment he raises a hand in response.

For some reason this pleases her, makes her feel at home, and she walks on, listening to the

115

dry rustling of the reeds and the plaintive bubbling call of the curlew. It is hot here in the sunshine, orange and white butterflies flit above the sedges, and she snuffs up the rich vegetative smell of mud and seaweed and rotting wood. She takes some photographs of the spindleberries and the *weyeriana* and wanders on again, enchanted by the magical beauty and the peace.

*   *   *

'It's still so hot, isn't it?' says Sophie. 'It's amazing for October. Shall we picnic in the summerhouse? It seems a shame to waste such a glorious day being indoors. Pity the tides aren't right; we could have all gone sailing after lunch.'

'I'm hoping we can get out for an hour or two tomorrow morning just to see how Jess makes out,' answers Johnnie. 'Get down to the Hamoaze if the wind's right. Shall I help you carry?'

'Yes, please. I'll get some things together and put them on a tray.'

'Is Jess back?' asks Rowena, coming into the kitchen. 'It must be nearly lunchtime.'

'We were just saying that a picnic in the summerhouse might be good,' says Sophie. 'Nice for Jess, too. Informal and fun.'

'The young enjoy picnics,' adds Johnnie.

'She's not a child,' says Rowena, irritated by this banal remark. 'I'm sure Jess is quite able to manage a knife and fork at the dining-room table. However . . .'

The 'however' hangs in the air as she turns away and goes out: it is her unspoken if reluctant permission, and Johnnie and Sophie exchange

116

quick glances of amusement. They hear voices outside; Jess sounds as if she's apologizing and Rowena is reassuring her.

'You're not at all late. And we're having a picnic in the summerhouse. I thought you'd like that. You'll be able to imagine what it was like when we had our parties. Juliet loved parties and picnics . . .'

The voices fade away in the direction of the sea garden.

'She is impossible,' says Sophie. 'And I still think that something's going on. I know Mike was Al's best friend but I've never seen Rowena quite like this before. She's not even like it with her own grandchildren.'

Johnnie picks up the tray, which is loaded with knives and forks and plates, and sets it down again.

'I think it's all come as a bit of a shock,' he says. 'Jess looks exactly like Juliet did, and I have to admit it's quite uncanny. Al had a thing about Juliet, you know, and Mother believed that Al should have been the one to marry her. She always believed that Al should have whatever he wanted, even his best friend's wife. But it all happened a long time ago and I think that Mother's managed to convince herself that, because they were all such close friends, Juliet belonged to Al as well as Mike. And so Jess belongs, too. Perhaps it's her way of reliving the past and remembering them all, and especially Al, in a happy way. After all, she's ninety-two and we can't blame her if she gets confused.'

'Her brain is as sharp as a razor,' says Sophie, 'but I can see that she might want to rewrite history a bit in an attempt to remember happy times as she would have liked them to be. I suppose even

117

Rowena might be capable of the odd attack of romantic nostalgia, though it seems rather out of character.'

'They *were* happy times.' Johnnie sounds as if he is trying to convince himself. 'Al and Mike were great oppos but they were competitors too, and Mike got Juliet. Al was certainly very taken with her. Anyway, I think Mother wants to think of them when they were all very young together. Like you said, she's airbrushing out what she doesn't want to remember.'

'Odd, though, in a way. If Juliet came between Al and Mike you'd think that Rowena might resent her and not want to meet her granddaughter, let alone be so friendly. It would be a fairly normal reaction, wouldn't it?'

Johnnie frowns, as if he is trying to see it from his mother's point of view.

'I told you, I think it's just a question of Mother seizing a chance to talk to anyone who has any kind of relationship to Al, however distant. It gives her a chance to live things through again, to talk about the parties and the dancing and the fun. She's going to show Jess the old photographs and do all that stuff. It's doing her good, I'm sure of it. Look, we'd better crack on or they'll wonder where we are.'

He takes the tray and goes out. Sophie begins to stack the second tray: a loaf of new bread, cheese and butter, pâté. As she washes some cherry tomatoes she thinks how typical it is of Johnnie not to be resentful of this streak to the past that doesn't seem to include him. His and Freddy's exploits are not referred to when Rowena talks of the past: there is only one Golden Age in Rowena's memory.

'What you have to bear in mind,' he said once,

118

way back, when she was exasperated on his account, 'is that Mother and Al were so alike. They were cut from the same cloth. I think she found him easy because she couldn't hurt him. He was tough and confident, and whatever happened he'd simply bounce straight back. Just like she does. Sensitive, needy people irritate her. She can't bear to look on the wounds she inflicts upon them and she simply hasn't got the patience to be kindly and thoughtful. She's always said that the worst trait anyone can have is a need to be loved.'

Sophie knew that he was touched by her partisanship but slightly amused by it, and she soon realized that, in his own way, Johnnie was just as tough as his mother. He managed it without putting backs up or alienating people but he was no pushover. Nevertheless, Johnnie, and his father before him, had a deep-down kindness, a generosity of spirit, that was missing in Rowena.

'And after all,' Freddy said, when she talked to him about it, 'Johnnie's still here, isn't he? And his children and their children. All able to enjoy this glorious place. Poor old Al didn't win in the end, did he?'

Thinking about Freddy, Sophie reminds herself that she must phone and invite him over to supper when Tom and Cass Wivenhoe and the Mortlakes and Kate Porteous come for the great reunion that Rowena is planning. She'll need two extra men, and Freddy'll want to meet Jess, too. Anyway, it'll be good to have him here; he's always such fun to have around.

She picks up the tray and carries it out to the sea garden.

*   *   *

The summerhouse doors are open to the sunshine, and Johnnie has already unloaded the contents of his tray onto the table. He's set a canvas chair for his mother outside in the sunshine and Jess is putting out another.

Rowena leans on her stick, watching them. She doesn't sit down just yet simply because she knows that Johnnie is anxious that she should do so.

As if, she thinks irritably, I'm too old to remain upright for more than five minutes.

She stares away across the river, towards Cargreen, but superimposed upon the granite walls of the cottages and the pub she sees Jess's face. Truly, it is as if Juliet has come back to them and Rowena's heart aches for Al—to see him just once more, strolling towards them with his sexy slouching walk and his wicked grin. Her longing is so great that, when Johnnie gently touches her elbow and says, 'Why don't you sit down, Mother?' she snaps at him, 'Don't fuss!' shrugging her arm away and nearly toppling over.

She turns quickly, hoping that Jess hasn't seen her flash of temper, but the girl is in the summerhouse with Sophie, sorting out the food.

'Are you hungry, Rowena?' Sophie calls, and this gives her the opportunity to go across to them. She's not hungry but she'll make a pretence of eating something. Jess smiles at her so sweetly that she longs to touch the girl's hand, to stroke that long dark red-brown hair. How attractive she is; no wonder all the boys fall in love with her. For a moment Rowena is confused; looking around for the boys, for Al and Mike and Stephen. And then

120

she remembers that this is Jess, not Juliet, and she feels rather weak, and her heart beats unevenly in her side.

Johnnie is beside her again. 'I'll carry your plate,' he says.

He helps her to her chair and gives her the plate and, as usual, his kindness irritates her and she longs for Al to be there, to make some witty, acerbic comment in her ear that only she can hear.

At last they are all gathered around, eating, talking. Johnnie is telling Jess the family history, about the book he is writing, and Sophie is planning for this weekend when Will comes out for his exeat.

'If the weather stays like this we'll get some sailing in,' she says. 'Will always loves to get out on the river. Lucky the tides are right.'

Rowena makes some reply but all the while she is planning for that moment when she and Jess will be alone so that together they can look at the photographs and reassemble the jigsaw of the past.

*   *   *

Jess refuses when Sophie suggests that she goes with her to fetch Will.

'He might be a bit shy,' Jess says. 'And three-handed conversations are always tricky. Anyway, it'll give you a chance to warn him I'm here and he can ask questions about me without feeling embarrassed.'

She remembers her own journeys to and from school and how it was so much nicer if she had one of her parents to herself; sitting in the passenger seat, feeling grown up. She doesn't want to take that away from Will although, as soon as he makes his way to the sail loft to find her, she realizes that she probably needn't have worried. He is a poised, confident little boy with the occasional faraway expression of someone who lives in other worlds; he is thin, with fragile wrists and bony knees, a mop of blond hair and a serene look in his blue-green eyes: Johnnie's eyes. Jess falls in love with him at once.

'I wish *I* could sleep in the sail loft,' he tells her enviously, 'but I'm not allowed. We do in the hols when my sisters come over from Geneva and my cousins come to stay, but I'm not allowed on my own. Mummy says I can when I'm twelve.'

He gazes at her with his amazing eyes and Jess stares back at him; she feels an odd desire to fulfil his every wish.

'Perhaps,' she begins tentatively, 'since I'm here, you could stay tonight in the sail loft with me?'

The small thin face lights up. 'Could I?'

'Well, I don't see why not.' Jess glances round for Sophie or Johnnie, anxious lest she is breaking some kind of rule. 'Shall we ask Johnnie? Your grandfather. What d'you call him?'

'Grando,' says Will at once. 'Grando's cool. He'll be OK with it but Sophie might not.'

'Well, we must go with what Sophie says,' Jess tells him firmly.

'OK,' he says cheerfully. 'It's good out on the balcony, isn't it? I took some really cool photos this summer from the balcony.'

'I take photos, too,' says Jess. 'I like to draw from them.'

'D'you upload them onto your computer?'

She nods. 'You can blow them up to a good size so that you can really study them.'

He gazes at her, impressed. 'Sophie says you've

122

won a really cool award. Have you got any of your work with you?'

'No. I've left it all with a friend in Bristol. I'm hoping to start something fresh but really I'm having a holiday.'

'D'you like sailing?'

She nods, and he looks away, slightly shy for the first time.

'I could take you out if you like,' he says casually. 'I've got a Heron dinghy in the boathouse. It's my own.'

'Wow? Your very own?' It's her turn to be impressed. 'I'd love it.'

His gaze swivels back to her, bright, almost mischievous. 'Would you? The tides are good this weekend.'

'You've got a date,' she tells him. 'But had we better check with . . .' She hesitates, can't quite bring herself to call Johnnie 'Grando', '. . . with Sophie? I'm a guest, you know. I have to play by the house rules.'

'OK,' he says cheerfully. 'Shall we go and ask if I can stay here tonight? I can bring my stuff over.'

He pauses at her table to look at her camera. 'I'd like one like this,' he says wistfully. He peers at the little painting. 'Did you do this?'

'No. It was done by the artist whose Award I won. David Porteous. Do you like it?'

He bends nearer, studying it. 'Mmm. It looks real, doesn't it? Like you could pick the flower, and the water actually looks wet. What does the writing say?'

Jess hesitates. It is odd to be in a position to explain the words to this little boy whose gaze is fixed so intently on the painting. She almost feels as if she is betraying a confidence.

'It says, "Thanks for everything. It's been perfect." David Porteous gave the painting to a very close friend who died not long afterwards.'

The sea-green stare is turned upon her and she feels faintly unnerved by its focus. 'And did the friend give it to you?'

She shakes her head. 'No, she—it was a woman—left it when she died with lots of other things to a friend of hers called Kate, who later married David. Kate gave it to me because I won his Award, in the hope that it would inspire me.'

His eyes widen, drift, as if he is imagining the story she has told him, seeing the characters in his mind's eye.

'That was nice of her,' he says. 'And it must be very valuable too, so it was generous as well. You'll have to get it insured.'

'Yes,' says Jess, slightly thrown by the practical turn to the conversation. 'Yes. I must. Let's go and find Sophie and see if you're allowed to spend the night here.'

*   *   *

Rowena decides to wait a few days before she makes her little test with the photographs. Though she finds it almost impossible to contain her impatience, some instinct warns her that it will be wise to let the girl settle in. She knows that her own excitement has communicated itself to Jess and made her slightly wary. There must be no tension when Jess sees the photographs; no suggestion of a hidden agenda; simply a happy moment looking at old snapshots in order to put some meat on the

124

bare bones of the past.

Carefully she plans it. Sitting there in the sunny morning-room, she shuffles the photographs, opens albums, peers into big brown envelopes bursting with snapshots. Ever since that day in the Bedford, when Kate told them that Jess was coming to stay, Rowena has been planning. She hasn't much evidence to support her long-held suspicion but such that she has she marshals; pieces of the jigsaw. She can see these pieces clearly before her as if they were laid on the table with the photographs: each piece represents a small scene that plays and replays itself in her mind's eye.

Once again she sees Al dancing with Juliet at the Christmas Ball on HMS *Drake*, holding her too tightly, his eyes closed, whilst Mike watches from the bar. She hears Juliet's voice, strained and desperate, whispering just outside these morning-room windows: 'I should never have married him, I know that now. I thought I was in love with him. I really did. How was I to know? What shall we do?' and the low, murmuring response: 'We must be very careful.'

She remembers Juliet as a house guest, staying for a week whilst Mike is at sea. Juliet, slipping away to the sail loft, along the river bank, and, after a while, the shadowy figure of Al following her.

Last and most important: the Midsummer's Eve party. The sea garden is a magical place: reflections jitter and dance on the smooth black surface of the water; shadowy figures dance or lean against the balustrade beneath Circe's imposing figure. The tall lavender hedges are pale, cloudy shapes, their scent still lingering on the warm air.

And the voices, whispering: the first is urgent,

demanding; the other is frightened. Juliet's dress is in disarray, her hair loosened. Al's face is buried against her throat but her face is twisted away from his, her hands on his shoulders.

'Listen,' she is saying, still in that desperate whisper. 'Please just listen to me. I'm pregnant, Al. Just for God's sake, listen . . .'

And now, as the weekend passes, Rowena waits. She watches Jess and Will: sailing in his little dinghy, joking together at lunch, in the sea garden. Now, as she glances from her bedroom window, Will perches on the balustrade with his back to Circe, explaining something to Jess, his arms gesticulating wildly; Jess leans beside him, listening. Popps is with them, playing with an old tennis ball. Its yellow coat is torn, ragged and discoloured, and she seizes it in her teeth and tosses it into the air as if it were a rat. Suddenly Will leaps from the balustrade, catches the ball and goes racing over the grass with Popps behind him. Jess turns to watch them, resting her elbows on the balustrade, laughing as the boy and the dog wheel round and round the sea garden.

Jess's likeness to Juliet is so strong that Rowena half expects to see Al and Mike coming across the lawn to join her. Her heart hammers too fast for comfort and she sits back in her chair, taking deep breaths, willing herself to be calm. Now is not the moment for one of her tiresome little attacks. She must be ready, strong. After tea Sophie or Johnnie will take Will back to school and then she must decide whether or not to show Jess the photographs. Part of her longs with such intensity to do it that she feels quite ill; part of her hesitates, draws back from it, fearing terrible disappointment.

Yet she feels the significance of Jess's readiness to feel at home here; her easiness with Johnnie and now with Will. Already she is part of the family. The girl's vitality makes her, Rowena, feel young again; the spirits of the past press in around her: officers with their girls, Juliet and Mike—and Al. If she closes her eyes she can see him: dark brown eyes, black hair, strong, athletic. Dickie, Johnnie and Will are all cut from the same genetic cloth: blond, blue-green eyes, not much above average height. Al and she were alike. They'd chuckle together at the same jokes, he encouraged her to be outrageous, whispering in her ear and egging her on.

She smiles, eyes still closed, feeling him near.

'Mother,' he says. 'Mother . . .' and she feels his breath on her cheek as he touches her arm.

She gasps, eyes flying wide open, her knuckles against her mouth, as Johnnie bends anxiously over her.

'Mother,' he says again anxiously. 'You were asleep. Sorry to wake you, only tea's ready and we have to get Will back. Are you all right?'

'Of course I am,' she says crossly, her heart still crashing in her side, furious at his foolishly concerned expression, resentful that he isn't Al. 'And I wasn't asleep. Why are you creeping about? What? Oh, wait, I haven't got my ears in.'

She fumbles impatiently on her table for her hearing aids and snaps at him again when he attempts to help her. Feeling ill, but refusing to show it, she goes downstairs with him to have tea with her great-grandson before he returns to school.

'Jess is coming with us,' Will tells her gleefully.

'I'm going to show her my dormitory.'

She smiles at him, and at Jess, and her heart aches with hope—and disappointment. The photograph session must be postponed after all.

'That's very nice,' she says to him; she's very fond of the little fellow. 'Boiled eggs,' she says to Jess. 'It's a tradition. The boys always had boiled eggs and soldiers for tea at the end of an exeat and now we do the same for Will.'

'So did I,' says Jess. 'So it must have been a tradition in my family, too.'

'And,' says Will, leading the way into the kitchen, 'Jess is coming to watch me play rugby.'

'Is she?' Rowena smiles at Jess. 'So it sounds as if you won't be leaving us just yet?'

'Not quite yet, if it's all right with you.' Jess looks slightly embarrassed. 'I'd love to stay for a few more days.'

'Well, you've certainly got to be here for the reunion supper,' says Sophie firmly. 'Johnnie says Freddy must come over for it, and he's trying to think of anyone else apart from Kate and Tom and Cass and the Mortlakes who will remember Mike and Juliet.'

Rowena sips her tea and watches Will eating his egg: she wonders, for the first time, how Jess might react to the bombshell that could be waiting to explode.

*   *   *

'You could invite Oliver,' Jess says when Sophie says that she needs an extra man for the reunion supper party. 'Cass and Tom's son. Do you know him?

128

'Oliver?' Sophie frowns, shakes her head. 'Rings a bell but I don't remember him.'

'I think he'd be great at a party,' Jess says. She feels that it would be good to have Oliver there; he is *her* friend, someone apart from all these people who know each other and share a history. She really likes Tom and Cass, and Kate, of course, but she's beginning to feel very slightly overwhelmed by the thought of being the focal point at the reunion supper. She is certain that Oliver will take the pressure off somehow.

Sophie is watching her curiously. 'Oliver,' she repeats. 'Good. We'll invite him too. Anyway, it'll be rather nice for you to have somebody of your own age around.'

'Oh, but he isn't,' Jess says quickly, anxious lest Sophie should leap to the wrong conclusions. 'He's not that young, he's more your age,' and flushes furiously. 'Not old,' she adds quickly, whilst Sophie bursts out laughing. 'I didn't mean that. Oh hell.'

'Forget it,' says Sophie, amused. 'I shall look forward to meeting him.'

Presently she seeks Johnnie out in the Growlery: his little den, which is lined with his Patrick O'Brian and C. S. Forester books, and an astonishingly vast collection of sailing manuals. He sits on a small folding chair, frowning at the computer screen.

'Is this a bad moment?' she asks, head round the door.

'Mmm? No,' he mutters. 'What is it?'

'Oliver Wivenhoe. Have I ever met him?'

He turns on his chair to look at her. 'Oliver? He's the older son, isn't he? A rather clever sort of fellow, if I remember. Went to Cambridge and got a First. You might have met him when you first arrived but I've only seen him once or twice since he went to university. He lives upcountry. Why?'

'It seems that Jess has met him and is rather taken with him. She'd like to invite him to the reunion thrash. Is that OK?'

'Why not? Sounds a good idea.' He turns back to the screen, stares at it grumpily.

'Writer's block?' she asks sympathetically.

'Ridiculous idea, this book,' he says. 'Writing the family history. I mean, what's the point?'

'It's fascinating,' she tells him. 'Your merchant forebears and those wonderful ships and the Tamar when it was a real working river. There must be hundreds of photographs you can use. Rowena's got stacks of them. She's having a session with Jess in the morning-room, actually. Come and have some coffee in the kitchen.'

He saves the document and turns round in relief. 'I think I will,' he says.

*   *   *

When Jess woke that morning she had the strangest sensation that there were other people with her in the sail loft. She pulled on a long woollen cardigan and thick socks over her pyjamas, and went out onto the gallery-landing and down into the big room, staring about her in amazement. Thick clouds of white mist curled and lapped at the windows; the light was eerie and cold. The sail loft felt isolated, cut off, and she shivered and hurried into the small kitchen to fill the kettle and switch it on.

Even as she did so she was aware again of a presence; the echo of a light footstep on the shining wooden boards, muffled laughter suddenly quenched. She turned her head, listening, but she wasn't frightened; she was filled with an odd kind of joyfulness as she made her tea and carried it to the balcony window. She didn't slide it open but stood, sipping her tea, watching the mist drifting above the river.

As the sun rose higher so the cloud was diffused with golden light, thinning and shredding, and she could see shadowy black shapes: the boats riding ghostlike at their moorings. The mist became patchy, tangled in the trees across the valley, blowing like smoke above the chimneys of Cargreen. The sun grew stronger and Jess slid open the window and stepped onto the balcony, drawing her cardigan more closely around her. She could hear the faint splash of oars and saw a rowing boat slipping across the river, approaching a boat at anchor in the deep-water channel. The dinghy disappeared behind the hull of the bigger yacht and then she saw the figure of a man aboard, busy, clambering over the deck. She heard the puttering of an engine and the boat began to move away from its mooring, the man at the helm. As he drew level with the sail loft he raised a hand to her and she waved back, watching the boat disappearing downriver with the tide, leaving the dinghy bobbing in its wake at the buoy.

*   *   *

By the time Jess joins Rowena in the morning-room, the mist has vanished and the room is full of sunshine. Photographs, carefully sorted, lie on the polished surface of the mahogany table, and Jess leans forward to look at them. As she reaches to

131

pick one up Rowena moves quickly, forestalling her.

'This one first,' she says. 'I've put them into a kind of order,' and Jess sits back obediently and waits to be shown.

After the first few photographs she begins to realize that the older woman is deliberately leading up to something. These are snapshots taken of parties, dances, gatherings, where no particular person is the subject of the photo. All are black and white, slightly grainy, but the mood is clear: these are happy times. There are several shots of the sea garden *en fête*, with Circe presiding; a benevolent and beautiful hostess.

The next selection is more personal: several young officers in uniform posing slightly self-consciously for the camera but still too small for identification, though Rowena names them, and Jess peers to look at the slightly blurred, youthful faces.

'But this one,' Rowena says, 'is clearer,' and she offers a large, more official photograph and sits back waiting for Jess's reaction.

The bride is beautiful, with flowers in her long shining hair. She wears a simple white dress with a high boned-lace collar and long lace sleeves. She gazes at the camera with a kind of pleased surprise. The groom, in full dress uniform, proud and confident, stands protectively beside her with his hand on the hilt of his sword.

'You haven't see this before?' asks Rowena.

Jess shakes her head, unable to speak: the likeness is almost shocking.

'Juliet sent it to me after the wedding. You can see now why you've had such a reaction from us all.

132

It's as if Juliet has come back to us.'

Still Jess stares at the photograph, at Juliet and Mike.

'It's such a pity that it's black and white,' Rowena is saying, 'but colour was almost unheard of back then in the sixties. And then there's this one that might interest you.'

She places a large photograph on the table and Jess takes it up, still preoccupied by the picture of Juliet. She stares at the small group in a close-up photograph taken on an official occasion by a professional but in an unguarded moment. The six young men are relaxed, simply smiling into the camera. And this time the shock is even greater. She recognizes Mike at once from the wedding photograph, but another face—one she knows most intimately—transfixes her. Some sixth sense warns her that this is what Rowena is waiting for; it is towards this moment she has been leading. Jess glances up at her and sees the older woman's tension, her eagerness, but still she can't control her shock.

'Who is this?' she asks faintly, putting the photograph on the table, pointing at one of the young faces.

Rowena takes a deep, deep breath. Her whole body relaxes and she cannot disguise her joy.

'That's Al,' she says. 'My son.'

Her heart hammers so fast that she can barely breathe. She leans back in her chair gasping for breath, and Jess leaps up and races to the door, calling for Sophie, for Johnnie.

They come running and bend over Rowena, looking for her medication, and under cover of all the activity, Jess takes the two photographs and

133

slips them beneath the silver tray on the sideboard. Quickly she sweeps the other photographs together, muddling them, stacking them into large brown envelopes and folders, leaving others in piles, and then she stands back, waiting, biting her lips.

'Is she OK?' she asks anxiously.

Rowena lies in the chair, waiting for the medication to take effect. Even in her exhaustion, she looks triumphant, as if a great point has been gained.

'We need to get her to bed,' Sophie is saying to Johnnie.

'Give her a minute,' he answers.

At last, between them, they half carry Rowena to the little lift, which has been installed in what was once a pantry, and, with Sophie crouching beside her, she is carried to the next floor. Johnnie runs up the stairs to meet them on the landing.

Jess waits at the morning-room door and, as soon as he is out of sight, she takes the photographs from beneath the silver tray. Quickly she darts out through the back hall and across the lawn, skirting the shrubbery, to the sail loft. In her bedroom she hauls her rucksack from beneath the bed and only then does she pause to look again at one of the photographs. She scrutinizes it carefully: the likeness to her father is there in the lift of the chin, the set of the eyes—and the smile, especially the smile. There are tears in her eyes as she looks at the young happy face. It is such a strong likeness to the man she remembers, yet it was taken more than twenty years before he was born. She tucks the photograph quickly into her rucksack and hurries back to the house before she is missed.

'The reunion thrash has been postponed,' says Tom, tracking Cass down to the small laundry room where she is ironing. 'That was Johnnie on the phone. Lady T's had another bad angina attack and she's been ordered bedrest.'

'Poor old thing.' Cass sets down the iron and carefully folds one of Oliver's shirts. 'Not to be taken lightly at her age. Is Jess still with them?'

Tom nods, trying to quell an uprush of irritation: why should Cass iron Oliver's shirts? Why can't he iron his own shirts?

'I'm perfectly happy to do some ironing for Ollie,' says Cass, correctly interpreting Tom's frown. 'He's driving Gemma to South Brent so that she can spend a few days with Debbie Plummer. You remember Debbie? They worked together at the dental practice. Gemma phoned her earlier for a chat and Debbie invited her over. Lovely for Gemma to see darling Debbie, and good for all of us to have a breathing space now that the twins have started at Mount House. So is the party postponed indefinitely or have we got another date?'

'Not yet. They're waiting to see how Lady T gets on. So, still no news from Guy then?'

Cass selects another shirt: Tom's shirt. 'If there is, Gemma isn't telling me. I think that's why she was so glad to get away. Now the twins are at school I think she's finding it much more stressful, just sitting here waiting.'

'It's madness,' Tom says angrily. 'I've always said

135

so. Simply walking out with the children. He'll call her bluff, I know he will.'

'And would that be so bad?'

He stares at her, shocked. The iron glides to and fro over the crisp striped cotton; the familiar, comforting smell of hot damp cloth fills the little room.

'Are you serious?' he demands. 'Don't you care if their marriage breaks up?'

Cass sighs inwardly. 'I'd care very much indeed if I could believe that they still love each other. I'm just not sure that they do. In which case I'd rather Gemma and the twins were here.'

'You never liked Guy, did you?' Tom perches on the end of the little deal table where the laundry basket sits.

'Not much,' answers Cass. 'No. He's too much like Mark, and I saw how it was with Kate and Mark. I didn't want that for Gemma. If it had been Giles I'd have been much happier. Giles is much more . . . human. Gemma needs love like plants need the sun, and Guy is such a cold fish.'

'But Gemma loves him,' Tom insists. 'She wouldn't have gone to Canada otherwise. It was a perfect moment to leave him if she'd wanted to but she didn't.'

Cass folds the shirt and selects a long cord skirt. She turns it inside out and draws it over the ironing board. 'I know she didn't, but I wonder how much of that was to do with guilt. She'd had an affair and had been caught out, risked everything for a foolish moment of passion. We've been there, haven't we? We can't condemn her for it. I certainly can't.'

Tom heaves a huge, rather self-pitying sigh: he hates these kinds of discussions. They force him to confront his own weaknesses and failures; to remember his own infidelities and, much worse than all these, the death of Charlotte, who adored him. The reminder that, just briefly, he was prepared to put her at risk for the sake of a lustful moment of physical madness still has the power to reduce him to tears. He turns away, sticks his hands in his pockets and stares out of the window.

'We were both equally to blame,' Cass says, knowing what he is thinking. 'I remember Kate saying back then, that kind of passion is like a terrible illness that destroys all sense of past or future. Only the present matters, burning you up so that you're prepared to consign duties and responsibilities and even your loved ones to the flames. And when the fever passes it's too late. The damage has been done.'

And Charlotte was our scapegoat, bearing the weight of our confusion and passion; riding her pony out, too overwhelmed by her own fear and vulnerability to take sensible judgements. He doesn't say the words aloud, fearing another shouting match; instead he says, 'Have you told Kate how you feel? That you don't mind if Gemma and Guy divorce?'

'Of course I haven't,' Cass says irritably. 'Kate and I hardly know what to say to each other at the moment. It's a wretched situation. She blames Gemma and I blame Guy, but deep down we know it's much more complex than that.'

She pushes the iron along the skirt's seam, steam hissing, remembering Kate's love and support through those dreadful months after Charlotte's death. She hates the Tom Tiddler's ground that stretches between them since Gemma

137

came home; each publicly defending her own child whilst privately acknowledging the other's dilemma. It seems impossible that they should be unable to have a normal conversation without resentment creeping in or sharp words being spoken: impossible that she and Kate, after all these years, should be in such a position. While Gemma remained in Canada it was possible to skirt the issue; small skirmishes but quick retreats back into the warmth and constancy of their long relationship. Now, with Gemma and the twins here, it is as if the lines of battle need to be more clearly defined.

Cass shakes out the skirt. She knows that it is unfair to put all the blame on Guy. She and Gemma are too alike for her to ignore that trait that leads Gemma to flirt, to regard the occasional sexual encounter as unimportant as a session at the gym or a game of tennis. She does blame him, however, for taking Gemma and the twins to Canada—to Mark.

'I never liked Mark,' she says, 'and he never liked me. Gemma doesn't like him either. I can't imagine why Kate ever married him. I know Guy isn't such a cold fish but I'm afraid that, as he gets older, he might turn into Mark—if you see what I mean. I hate going out there and having him there in the background looking so smug and vindictive. It must be hell for Kate when she goes out to visit them. Even worse now that he's married again, not that Kate cares about that. I think she's relieved, actually. She feels a bit less guilty for walking out on him.'

Tom whistles a little tune just under his breath. 'What you really hate is Mark having the satisfaction of thinking that he's won. That's why you want them back, isn't it?'

'Partly.' Cass lays the skirt beside the shirts. 'Mostly because I miss them so much and I know that Gemma isn't happy there. Nor, by the sound of it, is Guy. Anyway, she's made up her mind and it wasn't anything to do with us. We didn't influence her and I'm not going to beat myself up if Guy doesn't come back.' She switches off the iron. 'Shall we have some lunch? Oliver said he'd grab something on the way back from South Brent.'

She goes out, passing him without a glance, and after a moment he follows her downstairs.

*   *   *

Kate packs a few things into an overnight bag. She doesn't need much; after all, she's going home, isn't she? A different home in a very different setting, but home just the same. She straightens up and looks around her bedroom, at the familiar belongings. It's odd and unsettling to have two homes but this one at least belongs to her. The cottage at the end of the row in St Meriadoc is Bruno's, though it feels—and looks—like home. She's confused by the concept of having two homes; it's already beginning to feel divisive. She misses the sound of the sea, the tall, bleak cliffs—but it's good to wander out into the town or to drive up onto the moor, to know that the twins are only a few miles away at school.

So why not simply keep both cottages and go between the two of them? After all, she managed to move and live happily between the house in Whitchurch and David's house and studio in London. But that was different: the truth is that the house in London was never truly home to her.

Perhaps David felt the same about the house in Whitchurch but the marriage worked nevertheless. Married late, each with grown-up children, they'd both been glad of the space they'd given each other. She'd retained responsibility for her house and David for his so that their children had been almost unaffected by their parents' marriage. Nobody had been required to make choices or give anything up. David was an artist; his workplace was sacrosanct but beyond that he was very flexible. Bruno is like him in that respect.

Kate takes the bag and goes downstairs, checks that the kitchen is tidy, plugs switched off, and wanders through to the sitting-room. She's thinking of Gemma and Guy and the twins now, of Cass and Tom, of Bruno; oh, the different kinds of love: love for one's children, for friends, for a lover. Her heart is divided amongst them all and she longs for a solution that answers their needs and her own.

The danger is, she thinks, that when we love we demand too much, we grow possessive because our hearts are searching for perfect love. Perhaps no human person is capable of it; perhaps only God can offer it, but still we long for it . . . and the words of St Augustine's prayer come into her mind: 'O Lord, You have made us for Yourself and our hearts are restless till they rest in You.'

True intimacy, she decides, requires both closeness and distance . . . like dancing. But how difficult it is to know when to move closer and when to draw back. Sometimes we invade the other person's space, become too needy, and sometimes we hold ourselves apart, fearing to make demands, but giving the impression that we are unwilling to commit.

We double-guess each other, thinks Kate, Bruno and I. How dangerous that is. Privately, secretly, I set him little tests but, since he doesn't know the questions, how can he hope to pass? Perhaps he's doing the same to me.

She is glad that she's made this decision to go to St Meriadoc; to be proactive rather than waiting, always waiting, to see if Jess needs her, or Gemma or Cass. She telephoned Bruno to tell him—she didn't have to but decided she would—and to ask outright if she could come to supper.

'Then,' she said, 'I shan't have to worry about serious shopping. I've got some basic stuff . . .'

And he was so pleased.

'I've got a cassoulet on the go,' he said. 'Great. Will you go to the cottage first? OK then. Just come over when you're ready.'

Oh, the foolish relief; the ridiculous happiness at his reaction.

I wonder, thinks Kate, if I shall ever grow up.

She has one last thing to do: she will make a call to Oliver and then she will be free to go.

*　　　*　　　*

Oliver has a pint and a sandwich at the pub in Cornwood and then heads up onto the moor. He drives quite slowly, listening to his Norma Winstone CD, stopping for a string of horses who come clattering out of Tinpark Riding School, clip smartly along the lane and then disappear onto Ridding Down, the rider at the rear raising her hand to him as he idles along patiently behind them. At Cadover Bridge a woman is throwing a ball for two Labradors who plunge into the river, leaping and splashing, their wet sleek black coats glistening in the sunshine. When he reaches Lynch Common he pulls the car off the road to check his mobile. There is a voice message from Kate.

'I'm going down to St Meriadoc for a few days,' she says. 'I feel edgy, and anyway I want to collect a few things. I wonder if you'd like to use the cottage while I'm away? I think it might do us all good to have a break from one another and you might like a bolt hole yourself. Let me know. Cass has got the spare key for emergencies.'

He sits in the warm November sunshine, looking across Burrator reservoir towards Sheepstor, thinking about it. His instincts tell him that something crucial is about to happen between Guy and Gemma, and he needs to be at hand for it. At the same time the prospect of a break from his parents is tempting. He presses buttons and Kate answers at once.

'I'm on my way back,' he says. 'Just picked up your message. I think it's a very good idea. Thanks.'

'Oh good. I've been dithering about whether to stay or go but I think we're all getting on each other's nerves and this seems an ideal opportunity. Cass and Tom won't mind you coming here, will they?'

He laughs. 'I think they'll be delighted. The timing is perfect. Thanks, Kate.'

'The bedroom Jess used is all made up. I'll leave you some rations—milk and stuff—but you'll want to get some food in.'

'Don't worry about that. Have you heard from Jess?'

'Yes. She sounded a bit odd when we spoke but Lady T has had an angina attack so Jess is probably

142

upset. They want her to stay on, though, and she seems keen. But look, Ollie, I've given her your mobile number. Do you mind? It's just that I feel I'm rather abandoning her, though it's no great distance from St Meriadoc if there's a problem.'

'Of course I don't mind. And I'm sure she's quite safe with the Trehearnes.'

'I know. But I was the one who invited her down and she doesn't know any of us particularly well. If she has a wobble I'd like her to feel she can come back to Chapel Street, and she sounded pleased to have your number. Apparently she's asked if you can be invited to the reunion supper or whatever it is. I said you'd probably be delighted to go.'

'OK. Tell her I'll be around if she needs me. I'll collect some things from the Rectory and be over.'

'Great. Thanks, Ollie. Look, I'm just leaving now so I shan't see you. Could you tell Cass? It's all a bit sudden but I really need a breathing space.'

'We all do. Send over Jess's mobile number, would you? Thanks. Stay in touch.'

He puts his mobile back in his pocket. Cloud shadows drift across the bleached grassy slopes where sheep graze, moving slowly; the calm waters of the reservoir glitter below him. A buzzard rises, circling out of the trees, borne upwards on invisible currents, each flap of its wings taking it higher. Two crows come out of nowhere to hassle it, dive-bombing it; a pair of aerial fighters driving it out of the valley towards the stony summit of the tor.

Oliver turns the car and drives down the lane to the Rectory.

*   *   *

143

Tom and Cass are still sitting at the kitchen table with the remains of lunch between them.

'It's just not the same without a dog,' Oliver says as he comes in. 'It feels weird.'

'We don't need a dog,' Tom says at once, just as Oliver knows he will. 'If you need a dog, get one yourself.'

'I don't need a dog,' protests Oliver. 'I'm too peripatetic. It's the Rectory that needs one. It's too big without one. You'd like one, wouldn't you, Ma?'

Cass cannot quite hide her relief at his return. It seems, just now, that whenever she and Tom are alone they argue about Gemma, so Oliver's teasing is a welcome distraction.

'Listen,' Oliver says, sitting down, reaching for the cheese and cutting a slice. 'We've had this idea. Kate and I. She's shooting down to St Meriadoc for a few days so I'm going over to Chapel Street.'

'Why?' asks Tom immediately, irritably. 'Why do you need to go to Chapel Street simply because Kate's going to Cornwall?'

Oliver beams at him kindly. 'Don't you want me to go? Will you miss me?'

Cass, who has also helped herself to a sliver of cheese, nearly chokes.

'The thing is,' Oliver is saying, since Tom remains furiously silent, 'Kate thinks Jess should have somewhere to go if things get difficult down on the Tamar. I expect you've heard that Lady T isn't well?'

'Yes,' snaps Tom, not wishing Oliver to think that he's ahead in the information stakes. 'They've cancelled the reunion thrash. But I still don't see

144

why you need to be at Chapel Street. If Jess has a problem, though I can't imagine why she should, she can come here. Her grandparents were our friends, not yours.'

'Well, that's true, but the point is that Jess and I are friends, you see. That's what matters. It's the age thing, isn't it?'

Tom thinks of the beautiful, desirable Juliet and of Jess as if they are one woman and feels a stab of jealousy.

'Good grief, you must be nearly twenty years older than she is!' he cries.

Oliver shakes his head sympathetically. 'But at least not old enough to be her grandfather,' he points out gently.

Cass gets up from the table, stifling laughter, hoping Tom isn't going lose his temper.

'Well, it sounds like a good plan to me,' she says briskly. 'It could well be that Sophie will have her hands full with Lady T, and Jess might feel she's in the way. After all, she hardly knows them. And to be honest, sweet girl though she is, I wouldn't want to cope with her just now. Kate's key is in the dresser drawer, Oliver. Do you need to take any food or will you shop on the way into Tavistock?'

Tom pushes his chair back with an expressive snort, which indicates that Oliver is old enough to attend to his own catering. Oliver hesitates, scenting a new tease, but Cass looks at him, eyes narrowed warningly, and he grins at her.

'Kate's leaving the essentials and I expect I'll pop round to the pub for supper. I'll go and pack.'

She smiles back at him. With Oliver she is really at ease: he understands but never judges. He teases but is never cruel; he makes her laugh and reminds

145

her of her dear old dad, that old soldier for whom he was named.

Cass turns to look at Tom, who is packing the dishwasher; he is still frowning. She would like to alleviate his anxieties about Gemma, to explain that she understands how he is grieving afresh for Charlotte, but it's never quite that simple. She's learned that, though they both suffer equally, they are not necessarily best placed to help each other. They both share the blame and, when the pain of loss is very bad and they are over-emotional, then it is a quick and slippery slope that descends from the comforting of each other to the tempting, self-easing apportioning of the responsibility.

'If only you hadn't . . .'

'It's a pity that you . . .'

The least breath of criticism can turn a moment of loving comfort into a blazing quarrel.

Meanwhile, Oliver has defused the recent argument over Gemma and this is an opportunity for reconciliation.

'Rather nice,' Cass says cheerfully, 'to have some time on our own, don't you think? Wasn't that what you were saying yesterday?'

'I suppose so,' Tom says grumpily—and she smothers a sudden desire to laugh and instead makes a little face at his back.

'Good, then,' she says lightly. 'So everyone's happy.'

*   *   *

The cottage is warm and welcoming. Oliver closes the front door behind him, drops his overnight bag in the hall and goes into the living-room. He looks around, aware of a sense of familiarity. There is none of the homely clutter that comes with years of living, but neither is there the impersonality of the holiday cottage.

'It's tricky,' Kate told him. 'Most of my really precious stuff went to St Meriadoc when I moved down but the cottage is so much smaller that I couldn't fit everything in. I had to get rid of all the really big pieces when I sold the house in Whitchurch but there were a few things I hung on to and put into store. Luckily most of it fits in here, which is really good. After all, I may not spend much time here but it needs to look like home, too.'

Well, it does look like home; the sort of home Kate has made through forty years of naval quarters, hirings and cottages, and one that Oliver recognizes. The table probably started life in a French farmhouse, and none of the wooden chairs or cushions quite match. He couldn't begin to recount all the occasions that he and his siblings, and Guy and Giles, have sat around that table on those faded cushions; gingham and flowered and chintz. Flossie's spare basket is under the window, and he can remember the bentwood rocking chair from his earliest childhood. The paintings on the wall are of the Newlyn School of Art, and a couple of Paddy Langworthy's, and a mix of paperback novels, autobiographies and children's books jostle together on the bookshelves with a pile of CDs.

At the end of the table, against the wall, two or three rolls of unframed photographs are piled together. Curiously he takes one and rolls it flat across the table. Mount House School 1976.

Before my time, thinks Oliver—but the scene is a familiar one. Mr Wortham, with his golden

147

retriever, Winston, beside him, sits in the middle of the front row of little boys. Oliver recognizes Matron, and here are the twins, Guy and Giles, standing together. It is almost impossible to tell them apart, dark-haired and serious in their navy-blue, high-necked jerseys and grey corduroy shorts, staring rather self-consciously at the camera.

Oliver lets the photograph roll up, takes another one and spreads it flat. Blundell's School 1981. It is Petergate House's photograph, and here is Mr Denner sitting in the front row and he, Oliver, is sitting beside him, beaming happily.

He bends closer, looking at that much younger Oliver in his new tweed jacket and long grey flannel trousers. How grown-up he'd felt. Giles and Guy stand at each end of the middle row, and now he can see the difference between them: Giles smiles, easy and relaxed with the boy next to him, as if they are sharing a joke. Guy stands slightly apart, staring uncompromisingly at the photographer as if he is weighing him up.

Oliver remembers Mr Denner, how he'd say: 'Good! Good! Good!' all in one breath and how they used to mimic him behind his back, but affectionately because Mr Denner was very popular. And, quite suddenly, here is another memory: a painful memory mixed with the smell of old books and leather. He is with the twins in their study whilst his mother explains that Charlotte has been thrown from her pony and killed because she wasn't wearing her hard hat. Hugging him tightly she tells him that it's best if he doesn't come to the funeral; that it will be better for him to remain at school and that the twins will be there if he needs them.

Now, staring at those young, unformed faces, Oliver remembers the shock, the disbelief, and how, afterwards, it was Giles who put his arms around him and held him when at last he began to cry.

The photograph springs back into its roll just as the doorbell peals. He puts the photograph with the others, giving himself a moment to recover, and then goes out into the hall and opens the door. On the doorstep, with that same uncompromising look, stands Guy Webster. They stare at each other disbelievingly and then speak together.

'What the hell are you doing here?'

* * *

Guy follows Oliver into the hall, closing the front door behind him. He drops his grip beside the overnight case, glances around.

'Where's my mother?' he asks.

Instead of answering, Oliver opens a door off the hall and politely waits for Guy to pass into the room. Guy hesitates for a moment. Irritation, never far from the surface, is mounting. It's as if Oliver is the host here; he has taken charge of the situation. Guy walks past him into the living room. He's never liked Oliver. Though he is several years younger, Oliver has always had an innate confidence, an ability to be in the right place at the right time and always with the right people: scads of A levels, the First from Cambridge, Unk taking him on as a partner and leaving him his very lucrative business. And now he's had the nerve to pay the school fees for his, Guy's, children. He looks at his brother-in-law with barely concealed dislike, thinks about the overnight case in the hall.

'Is my mother here?' he asks again.

'No, she isn't.' Oliver makes a gesture that could be interpreted as a mixture of sympathy and apology. 'She's gone down to St Meriadoc for a few days. Did anyone know you were coming home?'

'No,' answers Guy shortly. He looks around the room with a speculative expression; taking it in, summing it up. 'I spent last night with a friend in London and hired a car. So what are you doing here?'

Oliver is clearly amused at the direct question. Guy is expecting conflict, accusations, and is prepared, aggressive. Oliver hesitates, then rather than take a conventional approach to the prodigal son—or, in this case, brother-in-law—he decides simply to wrong-foot him.

'Dear old Guy,' he says lightly. 'How good to see you after all this time, completely unchanged. I was just looking at some photographs of you.'

'Photographs?' Just as Oliver hopes, Guy is thrown completely off his stride. 'What photographs?'

'These.' Oliver bends over the table and unrolls the Mount House photograph. 'See? You and Giles at the end of the row here.'

As Guy stares at the rows of little boys he is unexpectedly filled with a number of memories and sensations that confuse him: easy companionship, physical freedom, security. He was very happy at prep school.

'Could be your twins, couldn't it?' murmurs Oliver. 'A kind of continuum.'

Before Guy can answer, Oliver unrolls another photograph: Blundell's. He and Giles stand at opposite ends of the row and now the memories are

150

different. The responsibility of exams and the adult world were beginning to press in: life was real and life was earnest. He lets the photograph roll up and looks at Oliver.

'I was remembering Charlotte,' Oliver says, as if he is answering a question. 'That was the year she died. Ma told me in your study, d'you remember? How long ago it seems.'

Guy is silent. He is struggling with indignation. By showing him the photographs, recalling the tragic scene at Blundell's, Oliver has got under his guard and it is more difficult now to say the bitter words that have been running in his head ever since Gemma told him that Oliver has offered to pay the school fees for the twins. Once again he has the upper hand and Guy rages silently.

'Kate asked me to stay for a few days,' Oliver says. 'She's told you about Jess winning David's Award . . .? Yes, well, it seems Jess might need to come back, so Kate thought someone should be here in case. Why didn't you tell her you were coming? Does Gemma know?'

'Nobody knows. This whole thing has got completely out of hand.' Guy feels frustrated. That last row with his father, the silent house, empty and oddly lonely without the twins and Gemma, the sudden need to see them and to get everything sorted out, has driven him to this mad journey. It never occurred to him that his mother would be away—but then he wasn't thinking particularly clearly. He planned to confront Gemma, to take her by surprise . . .

Oliver is watching him with a compassionate look that makes him even more angry. He mutters some imprecations below his breath and Oliver

151

bursts out laughing.

'Look,' he says. 'I can go back to the Rectory if you'd rather be alone. It's not a problem. But why don't we walk down to the pub and have a pint first? Then you can come back and phone Kate and I'll disappear. It hasn't been a particularly happy scene at the Rectory, you know. My parents don't actually approve of Gemma walking out on you and tension is running high. Gemma's spending a few days with a friend and I grabbed the opportunity to get out too. I'm very glad to see you, to tell you the truth. You can tell us what's really going on.'

Guy snorts. 'What the hell makes you think I know?'

Oliver shrugs. 'OK. So let's have a pint anyway. Can't hurt, can it?'

*   *   *

'. . . And that's where it stands,' Guy says later; quite a bit later.

They've had a few pints and some supper at the pub, and now they are back in the cottage and Guy is holding a glass of rather good malt whisky that Oliver has provided.

Guy is no longer angry but, during the course of the evening, has mellowed, even been amusing, but now he's becoming morose. Oliver, filling his own glass, remembers this pattern from a few previous occasions when he and Guy have spent time together. His brother-in-law has always needed a little lubrication to enable him to relax. It's been a good move to take him to the pub, to watch him unwind and to discover how things really are between him and Gemma.

152

He's even been able to persuade Guy that putting the twins into school needn't be the end of the world. It's required all his persuasive powers to assuage Guy's pride about the school fees but very gradually Guy's animosity has become less apparent and he's been quite open about his own situation.

'I want them back,' he says now, sitting in the rocking chair, his long legs stretched out, crossed at the ankles. 'This isn't a subject for negotiation. We've got a home, I've got a job, and if Gemma doesn't like being away from her family and friends she should have damn well thought of that before she made it impossible for us to stay here.'

'I agree,' says Oliver. 'I can see that she isn't in a very strong position to start calling the shots but from the little she's told me it sounds as if you haven't been all that happy yourself.'

Watching the curl of Guy's lip, the drooping of his eyelids, he wonders if he's made a tactical error: Guy dislikes any show of disloyalty.

'Gemma hasn't said much at all, you know,' Oliver adds mildly. 'She admits she doesn't get on well with your father but that's hardly news, is it? Let's be honest, very few people get on well with your father, do they?'

He can see Guy fighting with that strong sense of loyalty, his dislike of gossip, and suddenly Oliver feels a real sense of sympathy for him.

'Gemma has told me, not my parents, that she feels that you're becoming like him. Less communicative and more touchy. It's worrying her.' Oliver nearly says 'frightens her' but knows that will be too emotive for Guy; he will respond less sympathetically if he believes that Gemma has been dramatic. 'She said that she doesn't think you're particularly happy either; she certainly isn't, and she believes that it's beginning to affect the twins.'

'So we throw it all up and just come back here and begin again? Where? How? With what? And why the hell should I? I've done all that once, remember.'

The anger is returning and Oliver remains silent, thinking.

'Is she wrong?' he asks at last. 'Are you happy, Guy?'

Guy nurses his whisky, staring into the glass. 'It's OK,' he mumbles at last. 'It's a beautiful country but I admit the work is a bit frustrating. Dad isn't retiring any time soon, as we thought he would, and he's not all that open to new ideas, though he's considering my plans for sailing cruises, like I told you. That would be really good. He was furious when Gemma buggered off, of course, and annoyed that I've taken time off to come over to see her. It really hasn't helped. I'd just got him into the right mood for agreeing that my idea is a good one and now there's all this damned fuss.'

'Gemma hasn't said anything about this.'

Guy looks very slightly embarrassed. 'I decided on a need-to-know basis,' he mutters. 'Didn't want anyone to get excited until Dad finally agreed to it.'

Oliver is silent. Guy looks a little discomfited at his own high-handedness.

'Shall you tell her when you see her?' asks Oliver.

Guy shrugs, drinks some more whisky. 'I don't know. This has probably set it back again. Dad's not keen on new projects and all this has made him angry. I think he suspects I might change my mind and move back here.'

Another, longer silence.

154

'And might you?' asks Oliver at last. 'After all, couldn't you start your sailing cruises or whatever over here?'

Guy gives a contemptuous snort. 'Can you see my father funding it over here? It's like pulling teeth to get him to agree to anything that might expand his own business.' He swallows the last of the whisky and stands up. 'I'm going to bed. Stay if you like. Anyway, you can't drive now.'

'Thanks.' Oliver remains where he is; an idea slowly forming. 'Any plans for tomorrow?'

Guy hesitates at the door, frowning. 'Not now. Not if Gemma is staying with Debbie. I need to think about it. Why?'

Oliver gives a little shrug. 'Jess is down on the Tamar with the Trehearnes. She's invited me over and I wondered if you and I might go together. Kate knows them very well. Do you remember the Trehearnes?'

Guy pulls his mouth down, considering, shakes his head. 'I don't think so.'

'Well, I'm sure Jess would love to meet you. She's very fond of Kate and there are all sorts of connections with the past, apart from her winning David's Award. We could take her out to lunch or something.'

Guy shrugs. 'Whatever. I haven't got any really smart clothes with me.'

Oliver smiles. 'Oh, I don't think that will matter. Well, we'll discuss it in the morning. Sleep well.'

'Thanks for the whisky.'

He goes out and Oliver is left alone.

*   *   *

155

Upstairs, in Kate's bedroom, Guy drops his grip onto a small chair and goes to draw the thick curtains across the darkness. The material is silky soft, warm, and he fingers it, bunching it, turning to look around the room. He recognizes the furniture from the house in Whitchurch. The brass bed with its patchwork quilt used to be in the spare room, the Lloyd Loom chair with its embroidered cushion has come from his own bedroom; once, many years ago, his toys used to sit in it. The elegant white dressing table and the little stool were in his mother's room, and he stoops to look at the photographs: David, with his eyes screwed up against the sunshine; Ben and Julian with Gemma, clowning; he and Giles, aged about eight, grinning cheerfully. Small, informal photographs in rather battered frames; evocative and unsettling.

The evening, beginning with those other photographs, has softened him, weakened him. Over the last few weeks he's worked himself up for battle, using those hours of the long-haul flight to feed his resentment and anger, preparing himself for the fight ahead. He'd planned how he'd arrive, taking everyone by surprise; his mother would be anxious, worried about Gemma and the twins, but on his side. He'd decided that he'd see Gemma here at the cottage, on his own territory, catching her off guard.

Instead he's been confronted by Oliver, by memories and sensations, persuaded to talk things through so that now he feels tired, his self-righteous rage dismantled, and suddenly he longs for Gemma, to fall onto that bed with her and forget everything in the familiar warmth of her embrace.

As he unpacks his grip his thoughts slip back

to those days before he was married, to his little cottage in Nethercombe Court in South Brent. Although he'd known Gemma all her life, the ten years between them prevented any really close relationship as children. Then they met up by chance just after he'd bought the cottage in the courtyard development and was running his brokerage from Dartmouth, and she was at Hungerford training to be a Norland nanny. Back then he was emotionally involved with his neighbour, the beautiful Nell, and Gemma was going out with a young naval officer, yet their friendship flourished, based on the familiarity of a shared past, ease of companionship and old childhood jokes. During her holidays she came driving over to see him in Cass's little car and he took her out sailing and they went for long walks with his golden retriever, Bertie. Yet, because of the beautiful, elusive, newly widowed Nell, he persisted in treating Gemma almost as a younger sister; it was when she finally believed that their relationship would never be anything more than friendship that Gemma made her move.

Now, Guy sits on the edge of the bed and allows himself to picture the courtyard of attractively converted barns and cottages at Nethercombe on one particular December evening twelve years ago.

It was a pleasant scene at dusk; lights twinkling from the windows and smoke rising gently into the frosty air. He was returning from a stroll along the beech walk with Bertie when he saw Gemma hurrying across the bottom of the drive. It looked as if she had been to his cottage and, finding it empty, was going away. His feeling of disappointment that he should miss her was unbelievably sharp and he let out a loud shout, which made Bertie jump. Gemma either didn't hear or ignored the call and hurried to where her car was parked. He raced down the last few yards, his feet slipping and sliding on the gravel, whilst Bertie skittered from side to side, ears flattened, trying to keep out of his way. As he came level with the entrance to the courtyard's arched entrance Gemma's little car was just backing out of the space allocated to his visitors and he ran towards her, waving his arms. Still she didn't seem to see him but pulled away and vanished down the drive and out into the lane.

He stood perfectly still, a prey to several different emotions. He was confused by his disappointment and the other quite unreasonable feeling of rejection and hurt, as if she had deliberately ignored him and had been trying to avoid him. Why on earth should she come into the courtyard if she didn't wish to see him? He wondered if she'd put a note through his door and dashed over to his cottage, feeling in his pocket for his key. There was a note lying on the mat; a folded piece of paper. He snatched it up.

Dear Guy,
Just to say that I shan't be over this holiday. I suspect that I'm a bit of a nuisance to you and you've been very sweet about it but I won't bother you any more. We'll still be friends, won't we? It's been fun.
Love, Gemma

He was back out of the door in a flash, stuffing the note into his pocket, encouraging Bertie into the back of the car, leaping in, turning and racing

158

down the drive with spurts of gravel flying from beneath the wheels. He knew just which way she would go and he turned the car onto the Ivybridge road and headed for Cornwood. As he drove across the moor, his brain reeled as it grappled with his thoughts. It was as though a curtain had been ripped away in his mind and he saw what an unutterable idiot he'd been. He realized that his determined adulation for Nell had blinded him to the glaringly obvious truth. He thought of the pleasure he felt when he saw Gemma, the comfort and confidence she gave him, the ease and happiness he experienced in her company. It was Gemma, the real flesh-and-blood girl with her teasing, loving ways, that he loved; not the dream that he'd built round the ethereal Nell and which he'd persisted in keeping fixed before his eyes. Oh, yes! Nell was beautiful, vulnerable, alone. And that had woken his chivalrous tendencies and made him believe that he was in love with her. He'd been like a sixteen-year-old, infatuated by a film star; there was no reality in it. He knew, now, why he'd been unable to imagine Nell in the role of mistress and wife. As he drove, he put Gemma into the role with no difficulty at all. His heart started to pound furiously and he hit the steering wheel several times with his clenched fist.

'Fool!' He cursed himself aloud, and Bertie cowered in the back, scrabbling to keep his balance as the car fled round corners and up hills.

He was out beyond Wotter before he saw her tail lights, and he drew close up behind the little hatchback and flashed his headlights at her. Still she drove on without slackening her speed, and finally, in desperation, he overtook her on the long stretch before Cadover Bridge. He glimpsed her startled face as he flashed past, his two offside wheels bumping over the rough moorland verge, and then he pulled in front of her car and gradually slowed down until she was obliged to stop. He was out of the car and opening her door before she had even grasped that it was him and she gave a cry of relief as he hauled her out of the car.

'Guy! I didn't realize it was you. I wondered whatever was going on!'

'Why did you go away?' he demanded, holding her shoulders and giving her a little shake. 'Didn't you hear me shouting to you?'

'I left you a note,' she said evasively, looking up at him rather shyly. She pushed the hair out of her eyes. 'I put it through the door.'

'I saw it,' said Guy contemptuously. 'Never saw such rubbish in my life.'

'Was it rubbish?' she asked, and he bent suddenly and kissed her. He felt dizzy and weak, and he clutched her to him, her face crushed into his shoulder.

'Absolute bloody rubbish,' he mumbled against her hair. 'But it was my fault. I've been a monumental fool.' He swallowed hard, pushed away his instinctive urge for self-preservation and caution, and spoke the simple truth. 'I love you.'

She strained away from him, peering at him in the fast-fading light.

'Oh, Guy. Really and truly? I love you, too. I have for ages. Years.'

He laughed and held her close.

'Since you were in your pram? I'm delighted to hear it.' And he bent and kissed her again.

Presently she realized that she was shivering.

160

'What shall we do?' she asked, her eyes enormous with love. 'We're halfway between the courtyard and the Rectory. D'you want to come back with me?'

'No,' said Guy at once. He had no desire to face the Wivenhoes *en masse* whilst he was feeling so unlike himself. He needed to get used to these feelings and to be alone with Gemma. 'Could you bear to come back with me now? I'll drive you home later and we'll pick up the car on the way.'

'Or,' said Gemma, with her familiar provocative smile, 'I could stay the night with you. I'm sure Ma and Pa would understand. Us all being such old friends.'

'You'll do nothing of the sort,' said Guy, his old puritanical instincts coming to the fore. 'It would be all over Nethercombe in minutes. We'll wait.'

'Heavens!' said Gemma in mock dismay. 'I'm not sure I can. How long do you suggest?'

'I've been thinking. I'm going down to pick up a boat from Fowey just after Christmas. Like to come along?'

'Love to,' she said. 'As long as you don't order me about too much!'

Now, remembering the happiness and the fun of those first weeks, and that wonderful journey from Fowey to Dartmouth, frustration and whisky curdle in Guy's gut and he rips open the zip of his grip, grabs his sponge bag and goes out to the bathroom.

Downstairs the light is still on and he can hear Oliver's voice, very faint; silence, then a burst of laughter. For one furious moment Guy wonders if he's talking to Gemma, warning her, and then remembers that Oliver promised he wouldn't tell her or Cass and Tom. Despite his dislike for his

161

brother-in-law, Guy knows he can trust him. He goes into the bathroom, shuts the door and turns the shower on.

*   *   *

Oliver switches off his mobile. What luck that Jess was still up and ready to have a chat. She sounded rather muted, slightly preoccupied, but that's fairly normal, given that her host has been taken ill.

'I'd love to meet Guy,' she said. 'Come and have coffee with me in the sail loft and we'll take it from there. But I know Johnnie and Sophie will want to see you, too. And Guy. He's the sailor-twin, isn't he? Johnnie can show him his boats. About eleven, then. Great.'

Oliver sits for a moment, debating whether this is a good plan. At least it will be a distraction for Guy; give him time to cool his temper and remember how much he loves the West Country. And at some point he'll visit his sons at school—another happy reminder of his own childhood—but, meanwhile, a visit to neutral territory, to acquaintances ready to be friends, with a shared passion for sailing, should assist the process.

Pleased with the evening's work, Oliver gets up and turns off the lamp. He doesn't admit to himself his own pleasure at the prospect of seeing Jess again.

She is waiting for them at the end of the drive, a small figure wearing denim dungarees over a high-necked jersey, her long red-brown hair tied back. She waves enthusiastically to Oliver, who waves back, then gives a sideways glance at Guy, who is summing her up with his usual uncompromising stare.

'No need to frighten her to death,' suggests Oliver. 'You could even try smiling.'

'Shut up,' mutters Guy, and gets out of the car. He has already decided that he is going to use his not inconsiderable charm and, before Oliver can introduce them, he's holding out his hand, saying, 'You must be Jess. I'm Guy Webster, David Porteous' stepson. Congratulations on winning his Award,' and Jess is looking very slightly shy and smiling back at him.

She says something about Kate and how kind she's been inviting her to Chapel Street, but Guy has caught sight of the sail loft and the river.

'Pretty good here, though,' he says. 'Better than the town, I should think.'

His gaze is taking in the boats at anchor out in the deep-water channel and he instinctively moves towards them, with Jess still at his side, talking to her as he strides across the grass. She turns to look back at Oliver, gives a little apologetic shrug as she hurries to keep up.

'That was quick work,' murmurs a voice from behind him, and Oliver swings round to see a fair-haired woman surveying him with amusement.

'It wasn't even much of a chat-up line, either. Does he always cut you out like that?'

Oliver is aware of a very odd sensation; as if everything—the world, time, sound—has briefly stopped and now jolts on again but in an entirely different way. Nothing will ever be quite the same again. He shrugs, pretending resignation.

'Story of my life,' he says. 'Are you Sophie?'

She nods. 'And you're Oliver. Jess has told me about you, and Johnnie thinks we must have met in the distant past. And that must be Guy. Where d'you think he's taking her?'

'It'll be the boats,' says Oliver. 'My brother-in-law is a single-minded fellow. I apologize for him. I don't think he can have seen you there. I didn't either.'

'That's OK. I can sympathize with that. I'm a sailor myself, and it's spectacular here, isn't it? Come in and have some coffee while he gets it out of his system.'

'Thanks. Jess said something about having coffee in the sail loft. I don't want to muscle in . . .'

'When Jess told us you were coming Johnnie said to be sure to bring you in,' Sophie says firmly. 'He's looking forward to meeting you again. He says it's years since he saw you.'

Oliver follows her into the house just as Johnnie appears from another room across the hall. He stretches out a hand in greeting.

'Oliver,' he says. 'It's been a long time since we've seen each other but I'd know you anywhere as Cass's son.'

As they all go into the kitchen a bad-tempered little terrier comes stiff-legged from its basket by the Aga, growling at Oliver, and Johnnie says, 'Oh, shut up, Popps,' and scoops the little dog into his arms. Sophie grins at Oliver and he grins back at her and suddenly he is happier than he has ever been in his life.

He watches her as she makes coffee, liking the line of her jaw and her muscular shapeliness; her skin is still faintly tanned by summer winds and the sun, and her mouth is wide and curling. She smiles now as Jess and Guy come into the kitchen and Popps starts barking. Oliver stands up to make introductions and Guy says, 'That's a beautiful classic yacht you've got out on the river, sir. Jess says you restored her yourself,' whilst Jess soothes Popps, and again Oliver's eyes meet Sophie's and it's as if they are magically set apart from the talking, laughing group.

He sits down at the table again and looks at Jess, trying to bring her into focus. Johnnie and Guy are deep in conversation about boats and sailing, Sophie is pouring coffee into white china mugs.

'How are you?' he asks Jess, and now that he is concentrating on her he sees that her eyes are shadowed, thoughtful.

'OK,' she says. 'I'm fine,' but she looks away from him, biting her lip, and her hands, partially hidden beneath the table, twist and turn as if she is washing them.

'Is something wrong?' He keeps his voice low.

She shakes her head but still looks uncertain. 'I'd like to show you something,' she says. 'Just you. When we go over to the sail loft.'

'OK,' he says. 'When we've had coffee?' and she nods, smiles quickly at Sophie, who is passing coffee to her, and turns to listen to Johnnie, who is now talking about sailing in the Fastnet.

165

'I'll just go and check on Rowena,' says Sophie.

When she's gone Oliver relaxes in his seat, taking deep breaths as if he has been running very fast. Slowly the room swings into focus: the terrier back in its basket; Guy's animated expression as he listens to Johnnie; the jar of spindleberries on the table. He is content to be held in this moment, this little space of time, before she returns and something quite new begins.

*   *   *

'What a place,' murmurs Guy. He stands in the sea garden, staring up at Circe, gazing downriver towards the two great bridges. 'It's crazy. I spent the first twenty years of my life around Tavistock and I never knew this was here. Well, the Tamar, of course. Pentillie Castle. Cotehele. Morwellam. But I've never sailed here. For some reason I did all my sailing out of Dartmouth.'

It is clear that Johnnie is flattered by Guy's reaction to his home and its surroundings.

'We could sail tomorrow, if you like,' he offers. 'Take *Alice* out and make a day of it. The tide's right but we'd need to get off by eight o'clock latest. How would that suit you?'

Oliver almost laughs at Guy's expression: he looks like a five-year-old on Christmas morning.

'I'd love it,' he says at once. 'It would be great.'

'That's settled then,' says Johnnie.

He begins to explain that the sea garden was once a quay, how the old sailing boats and barges used to come right upriver, and Guy listens, fascinated. They wander away towards the boathouse.

So much, thinks Oliver, for getting in touch with Gemma and trying to sort things out.

He wonders what is in Guy's mind: clearly he feels that one more day won't matter; after all, Gemma doesn't know that he's in the country.

'We email quite a lot,' Gemma said, 'but he's useless with a mobile. I insist that he has one but he never switches it on. He's a very bad communicator. Thank God Ma got on to Skype when we went out. At least I can sometimes get him on that, and the boys love it, of course.'

He strolls behind Guy and Johnnie, across the lawn, but when Jess and Sophie come out of the house he changes direction and goes to meet them.

'The boathouse is next on the agenda,' he tells them. 'Johnnie's invited Guy to go sailing tomorrow.'

'I wonder which boat he's taking out,' says Sophie, alert at once; keen. 'We could get hold of old Fred and make a day of it.' She raises her eyebrows at Oliver. 'I think you said that you're not a sailing man? You don't fancy a day's sailing in the Channel?'

He shakes his head, smiling. 'Not me, lady. But Guy will be in his element.'

She laughs. 'A landlubber,' she says.

Another look goes between them, acknowledging this thing that has happened to them, and with it an odd sense of acceptance. There is none of the anxiety or tension or fever that is often present at such moments; just this deep-down happiness. Sophie turns away to follow Guy and Johnnie; Oliver looks at Jess, sensing her relief.

'Is this a good moment to show me whatever it is you want me to see?'

He follows her up the steps and into the sail loft. Whilst he wanders through the large light room she disappears into her bedroom and presently reappears with a photograph.

'Lady T showed me this,' she says, holding it out to him. 'It's got Mike in it. I wondered if you'd recognize anyone else.'

He takes the big black-and-white photograph and studies the young men.

'Which is Mike?' he asks. 'Mike's your grandfather, right?'

He notices the faintest of hesitations before she answers.

'Yes,' she says. 'That's Mike.'

As she points at one of the young men Oliver gives a cry of recognition. 'There's Pa,' he says. 'Look, here. And that's Johnnie beside him, surely. You can see the likeness when you really look. So that's Mike, is it? But I don't recognize the other three. Do you know who they are?'

'That one,' she says, pointing, 'is Al.'

'Who's Al?'

'Johnnie's older brother. He died in a sailing accident.'

'Oh, yes, I remember now.' Oliver looks more closely, then shakes his head. 'Didn't Lady T tell you who they were?'

'She'd just told me about Al and then she had a really bad angina attack. Sophie thinks she's had a very slight stroke as well. It was really scary.'

'How awful for you. But look, Johnnie will know who they are. Why not ask him?'

Jess takes the photograph, shakes her head. 'I don't want to do that. Not just at the moment. It's to do with something she said, and there's another

168

thing as well.'

She stands, indecisive, as if she is wondering whether to confide in him, and then Guy and Johnnie pass by outside the window and there is a little knock at the door. Jess slips away with the photograph and Oliver opens the door.

'Would Jess mind if Guy has a look?' asks Johnnie. 'Bit of a cheek with Jess in residence . . .'

Oliver hesitates, glancing round for Jess.

'Of course it isn't,' she says from behind him. 'Come in. It's the most amazing place, Guy.'

Oliver watches as Guy walks the length of the sail loft, exclaiming in delight while Johnnie explains why his grandfather had his sails specially made, and they all go out on to the balcony. Jess glances back at Oliver, gives him a little smiling nod as if to say: 'All's well, don't worry.' He hesitates but she nods again, more firmly this time, and he turns and goes out; across the lawn to the house, to Sophie.

*   *   *

'I've taken Popps up to keep Rowena company while she has her lunch,' says Sophie.

Her fine fair hair swings forward as she leans to stir the soup and she tucks it behind her ears. She puts a tray of rolls into the oven and some bowls to warm. A bottle of claret stands warming by the Aga.

'Is Guy a wine or a beer man?' she asks. 'I've got some Jail Ale.'

'Definitely an ale man,' answers Oliver. He pulls out a chair and sits down at the table. 'I'm driving but I think a glass of wine wouldn't be out of order. This is very kind of you, taking us all in. First Jess

169

and now me and Guy. Especially when you've never met any of us before.'

'Oh, Johnnie loves having visitors. He's never happier than when the house is bulging at the seams. Rowena's the same, though she can't handle it like she used to.'

'And you?'

'Me? Oh, I love it too. And Jess is no trouble at all. It's such a shame that Rowena's been taken ill but she's very anxious that Jess should stay.'

She pours wine into two glasses and passes one to Oliver. He lifts his glass, looking at her, and she looks back at him. Her eyes are the colour of warm clear amber.

'It seems that Jess has something on her mind,' he says.

'Yes,' she agrees. 'I thought that it was you.'

'Me?' he says, startled.

Sophie's mouth quirks into a little smile. 'She talks about you rather a lot. And when we were planning the reunion supper she asked if you could be invited.'

He is silent, thinking quickly: it is crucial that there should be no misunderstandings here.

'She's Kate's protégée. You know, winning the David Porteous Award and so on. I think Jess was rather taken by the idea of coming down to the West Country to find her roots but a bit daunted by the age gap when she arrived. I'm quite a bit older than she is, but even so I think she was relieved to meet someone who was younger than her old granny. More like an uncle, wouldn't you say? I felt it was my duty to rescue her.'

Sophie laughs. 'How noble of you.'

'Oh, I'm all heart that isn't armpit.'

170

'And, of course, it doesn't hurt that she's extremely attractive.'

'That was a bonus,' he says blandly. 'Do we have to keep talking about Jess?'

'You started it,' she reminds him. 'What would you like to talk about?'

'Your mobile telephone number, for a start, before everyone comes back,' he says, 'and then about a good place to have dinner.'

*   *   *

'I'll drive myself over tomorrow morning,' says Guy. 'Johnnie's invited me to breakfast so that we can go down with the tide.'

Driving carefully in the narrow lanes, Oliver thinks about this. It's been discussed at lunch and finally decided that Jess will join Guy and Johnnie whilst Sophie stays to keep an eye on Lady T.

'I can go sailing any time,' Sophie said. 'You'd like to go, wouldn't you, Jess?' And Jess nodded and said that she'd like to go with Guy and Johnnie if Sophie really didn't mind.

Thinking about it, Oliver suspects that Jess doesn't want to be left alone with Lady T and that it has something to do with the photograph, but he can't think what it might be. He wasn't able to talk to her again except for a few words after lunch.

'You can come back to Chapel Street any time you like,' he told her quietly. 'Don't be put off because Guy's here for a few days.'

'I'm fine,' she said. 'Really. I want to be here for a bit longer.'

'If you're sure.'

She sensed his anxiety and smiled at him. 'Really,

171

I'm OK. And don't mention the photograph to anyone, will you? It's just a private thing.'

'If you say so.'

'Honestly. I promise I'll phone you if I have a problem or need to talk.'

'OK then,' he said.

Later, Sophie said, 'Why not come and have lunch with me since they'll be away all day? Come early,' and he agreed with deep secret pleasure.

Now, he glances sideways briefly at Guy. 'So are you planning to see Gemma at all?' he asks lightly.

'Of course I am,' answers Guy irritably. 'What d'you think I am? I'm picking her up from Debbie's tomorrow evening. They're off to the theatre tonight. Debbie's booked tickets and Gemma doesn't want to cancel.'

Oliver's eyebrows shoot up. 'You've spoken to her?'

He feels rather than sees Guy's withering look. 'Of course I've spoken to her. What did you expect?'

Oliver finds that he has no answer to this and remains silent.

'I was a bit worried when Johnnie said we'd have to come back in on the tide but he thinks we'll be in by about seven. Plenty of time to drive over to Brent.'

'And then . . .?' Oliver hesitates. 'Shall you both go back to the Rectory? Or will you bring her to Chapel Street?'

'For God's sake!' Guy gives an explosive snort of amused contempt. 'Are you kidding! Gemma's booking us into a little hotel we both like near Dartmouth.'

Oliver laughs. 'I think I've underestimated you.'

'Yes,' says Guy drily. 'I expect you have.'

'And don't tell me: you've also arranged to go to Mount House to see the twins.'

'Gemma was going to sort something out for the weekend. It's a Sunday out. But Jess was saying that there's a home rugby match on Saturday afternoon. Will—is his name, Will?—is playing so she and Sophie and Johnnie are going to support him. I thought we'd make up a little party. I'd like Gemma to meet them all.' He pauses. 'Perhaps you'd like to come, too,' he says offhandedly. 'Since you're the great benefactor, so to speak.'

'Thank you,' says Oliver humbly. 'I should love to.'

*   *   *

When Oliver arrives the next day he knocks on the back door, which is open, and goes in. He calls 'Hello' and finds Sophie in the kitchen with a very good-looking man. They are sharing a joke, very much at ease, and Oliver is surprised at his instinctively hostile reaction.

'Sorry,' he says. 'You didn't hear me knock.'

'Oh, hello, Oliver,' says Sophie, still laughing at the joke. 'Come on in. This is Freddy. Freddy Grenvile. He lives across the river in Cargreen. This is Oliver Wivenhoe, Fred.'

'I'm sure we must have met,' Freddy says, taking Oliver's outstretched hand. 'Tom and I are old oppos. How's your gorgeous mother?'

And now, shaking his hand, Oliver can see that indeed this fellow is much older than he first thought. His hostility vanishes though he remains aware of Freddy's vitality and charm.

173

'I came over to see why I'd been left out of the boating party,' he's saying. 'I just happened to see *Alice* going downriver while I was having breakfast and I wondered who her crew was.'

'What he means is,' says Sophie, 'he was peering through his binoculars as usual and he didn't recognize Guy. He's a terribly nosy man, I warn you.'

Freddy laughs. 'I admit I was curious.'

'I've been telling him about Jess,' says Sophie, pouring coffee for Oliver. 'One way and another he keeps missing meeting her so I've been satisfying his insatiable curiosity. And then I was explaining about Guy.'

'I remember Kate, of course,' says Freddy. 'But I'd rather lost the plot with the next generation. It's getting to be a real blast from the past, isn't it?'

'You could come to lunch tomorrow and meet Jess properly,' Sophie suggests.

'Didn't I tell you I'm off to the States?' he asks, finishing off his coffee, putting down his mug. 'I'm going to catch up with a very old friend. I thought you knew. I told Johnnie ages ago.'

'You didn't tell me. And Johnnie didn't say anything about it. Perhaps he's just been taken up a bit with Jess.'

She looks very slightly put out and Oliver sees that Freddy feels uncomfortable.

'Come with me,' he says dramatically. He puts his hand to his heart. 'Fly with me, Sophes.'

She begins to laugh. 'And wouldn't you be horrified if I said "Yes"? You'd better get going before the tide drops any more or you really will be up the creek without a paddle.'

Freddy grins at Oliver. 'She's such a prosaic

woman,' he says. 'No sense of romance. We shall meet again, Oliver. I gather there's going to be a reunion supper for young Jess. Tell Tom and Cass I'm looking forward to seeing them. It's been too long.'

They follow him into the passage and he goes out, raising a hand, closing the back door behind him, and Sophie and Oliver look at each other.

'You'd never want to leave this place, would you?' he asks softly. 'You are so much a part of it; of all these people.'

She looks startled; almost alarmed. 'They're my family,' she begins, uncertainly—and then, suddenly, a bell begins ringing insistently from somewhere in the house. Sophie gives a little exclamation that is partly exasperation, partly relief.

'Rowena,' she says, resigned. She pauses for a moment, and then says, 'Come and meet her.'

It is Oliver's turn to look startled and alarmed. 'Won't she be a bit surprised?' he asks. 'I mean, she doesn't know me.'

'She can recall Tom and she's heard that you're coming to the reunion supper. Come on. It'll cheer her up. But remember she's very weak and her brain wanders a bit at the moment. She's sharp for a while and then she completely loses it. She's on a lot of medication.'

They go together up the wide curving staircase and along the landing. The bell has stopped ringing now. Outside one of the doors, Sophie pauses.

'Wait,' she says quietly. 'I'll call you.'

Oliver stands at the landing window, looking across the river to the hills opposite, where a tractor is ploughing, followed by a cloud of seagulls who swoop and turn above the fresh-turned earth. A small dinghy glides out from Johnnie's slip, a figure at the oars pulling strongly across the river: Freddy rowing home.

'She'd like to see you,' says Sophie from behind him, and Oliver turns and follows her into the room. 'I'm afraid she's just a tad confused but never mind. Go with the flow.'

The old woman is propped about with pillows; her small face turned eagerly towards the door. Beside her, under the quilt, Popps stirs about and growls softly. Rowena shushes her, smoothing the rough head, and Popps subsides again.

'This is Oliver,' Sophie says. 'Tom's son. You remember Tom, Rowena? Johnnie's friend.'

Rowena's gaze is keen and fierce and she holds his hand tightly in her little claw; her rings dig into his fingers.

'Sit down,' she mutters. 'Do you know Al?'

He shakes his head and sits down on the chair pulled up close to the bed, still holding her hand. 'My father, Tom,' he says carefully, 'is Johnnie's friend.'

'Johnnie?' She frowns, closes her eyes, but she still holds tightly to his hand. 'Juliet has come back,' she says clearly. 'Juliet.' Her eyes are open again, watching him. 'Do you know Juliet?'

He hesitates and looks at Sophie, who makes a little face then shrugs and nods.

'Juliet,' he says, as if agreeing with Rowena. 'And Jess,' he adds, unwilling to lie outright. He remembers his conversation with Jess and feels uncomfortable. These are not just the woolly wanderings of a confused mind; there is something very important here though he cannot guess what it is.

176

'Freddy's just been to see us,' Sophie says cheerfully, coming closer, bending over the bed. 'He was sorry not to go out sailing with Johnnie and Jess.'

'Freddy and John,' says Rowena. Unexpectedly she laughs and Oliver has a glimpse of what an attractive woman she must have been. 'Johnnie and Fred. Freddy and John. They were inseparable, you see. But they weren't naughty. Not like Al and Mike.' She lets go of his hand suddenly and her head turns towards the door; she is listening intently, as if she is expecting someone. 'Juliet has come back,' she says softly; she puts a finger to her withered, shrunken lips. 'Is Al coming too?'

Oliver's eyes slide round to meet Sophie's and she bites her lip and very slightly shakes her head.

'Not yet,' she answers. 'Come now, Rowena. It's time for your medicine. Oliver has to go.'

He stands up thankfully, and the old woman stares up at him.

'Goodbye,' he says. He doesn't quite know how to leave her but Sophie gently pushes him away and he goes out onto the landing, standing at the window and taking a deep breath of relief. Rowena's confused intensity and her frailty and vulnerability have shaken him. He remembers how she laughed and how, suddenly, he saw a glimpse of a young, vitally attractive woman. How terrible for such a personality to be old; reliant and helpless.

Sophie comes out of the room, shuts the door and crosses the landing to stand beside him at the window. He draws her to him, puts his arms round her and kisses her. She responds readily, warmly, but when they draw apart she looks up at him questioningly, eyebrows quirked.

177

'Just because we're young, and we're strong, and we can,' he answers, and they go downstairs together with his arm still holding her close at his side.

*   *   *

They sit together at the kitchen table, the coffee pot between them.

'I hate seeing her like that,' says Sophie. 'It's just so not Rowena.'

'It's a bit weird, the Juliet thing, isn't it?'

'From what everyone says Jess is an absolute ringer for her grandmother and I think it's completely thrown Rowena.'

'It's thrown my old pa as well. What's this about Al?'

'Jess has revived all the old memories. I think that, in her confused state, Rowena thinks that if Juliet has come back then Al might come too.'

Oliver thinks about Jess and the photograph.

'So there was a little group of friends,' he says carefully. 'My father was Johnnie's friend and Mike was Al's. What was that about Freddy? Is that the Freddy I met earlier?'

Sophie nods, cradling her mug of coffee in both hands.

'Johnnie and Freddy were the younger ones. Al and Mike were the top dogs. There were a couple of others. They all trained at Dartmouth together. Your father was one of them, wasn't he?'

'Yes. Al and Mike were a couple of years senior but they all seemed to hang out together. I just wondered who the others were.'

She looks at him curiously. 'Why?'

He remembers his promise to Jess; shrugs. 'Oh, just trying to get the whole picture.'

Sophie puts down her mug. 'I feel there's something going on. It started when Rowena first knew that Jess was coming to visit. She began to get out all the photographs.'

'Photographs?'

'She's got hundreds of them. We'd begun to sort them out a while back when Johnnie started to write his history of the family, about his merchant forebears and the sailing ships that used to come right up the river. And then his grandfather was a very keen sailor and raced in the America's Cup. He had some amazing boats. The *Alice* was one of them, built specially for him in 1908. So there were all those photographs to be sorted for the book, and then Rowena began to make a collection of the family ones. When she knew that Jess was coming she got very excited and put them all out in the morning-room. She wanted to show Jess what it had been like in the sixties when her grandparents had been here as young people. There were parties in the sea garden, and the boys when young and in uniform, and girls in ball gowns and stuff like that.'

'And this worried you?'

Sophie frowns. 'Rowena was so intense about it all. I couldn't quite see why this girl was stirring up so much passion in her. Yes, of course it's fun to see an old friend's granddaughter, and all that, but Rowena hadn't seen Juliet or Mike for forty-odd years and, as far as I know, there hadn't been any contact. It puzzled me.'

'Was Johnnie surprised?'

'Oh, you know Johnnie. Everyone's welcome and it's all great fun. I mentioned it to him but he simply said that it was a chance for Rowena to talk about Al. He was her blue-eyed boy, the favourite, and she never got over his death. Apparently Al fancied Juliet and was furious that Mike got there first, so it seemed a bit odd that Rowena remembered her with such affection. I talked to Fred about it too, but he agreed with Johnnie. So that was fine—but then there was the angina attack.'

'And what do you think now?'

Sophie shrugs. 'I don't know what to think. Rowena was showing Jess the photographs when she had the attack. Jess was very upset, of course. She had no idea that her appearance would cause such consternation. She said that when she saw the photograph of Juliet at the same age she was completely taken aback but she could at least see why everyone was reacting the way they were.'

'So the impression is that this shock has swung Rowena off balance and back into the past.'

'I think so. I think that looking at the photographs with Jess, thinking about Al, caused the attack. The trouble is, each one she has weakens her. She's got several other health problems so it's a worry. Poor Jess feels in some way responsible, though it's not her fault.'

'Yet she wants to stay.'

'She loves it here. To be honest, I think she's a bit shell-shocked by it all, but she loves Johnnie and Will, and she's doing some work as well, she says. Are you worried about her?'

'Only that with Kate down in Cornwall I've been left a bit *in loco parentis*, but Jess is old enough to take care of herself. Anyway, I've got to go upcountry for a few days soon to some meetings so I'm glad she'll be here with you rather than in

Chapel Street on her own or with Guy. Who, along with my sister and their twin boys, is a completely different kind of complication.'

She looks at him sympathetically. 'You seem to take your uncle role very seriously. What's Guy's problem?'

Oliver groans. 'How long have you got?' he asks.

*   *   *

When Oliver has gone, Sophie goes out across the lawn to the sea garden and stands leaning against the balustrade. Circe towers above her, watching for the *Alice* to return.

Sophie feels almost as confused as poor old Rowena up in her bedroom. She hasn't expected to feel like this again; unreasonably happy, missing him already. The world is looking rather sparkly, new-rinsed specially for her, and little brightly coloured sails flash to and fro across the shining water beneath the two graceful bridges. At the edge of the sea garden the elegant acer trees gently shed their leaves, yellow and crimson, and orange spindleberries are vivid in the hedges.

Sophie's heart is filled with joy at this beauty, which seems to be totally at one with the warmth of the love she is experiencing. At the same time she can't quite see the future.

'You'd never want to leave this place,' Oliver said. 'You are so much a part of all these people.'

And it's true. How could she leave them—Rowena, Johnnie, little Will—to fend for themselves?

People are leaving their families all the time, she tells herself. And the families manage; find other people to help them. She puts out a hand to touch the wooden folds and pleats of Circe's dark red skirt. Johnnie had her repainted last year; shiny black coils of hair, scarlet smiling lips, blue and white bodice. Sophie looks up at her; she'd miss Circe, and sailing with Johnnie and Fred, and Christmases here on the Tamar with Louisa and all the family.

Suddenly, now that Oliver is not near her, she is filled with panic. She wonders if she's imagined the whole thing and if he's merely been chatting her up. She recalls each moment of their meeting: remembers that sense of familiarity and ease combined with a happy excitement that she's never experienced before. When he kissed her outside Rowena's room she'd known for certain then. Kisses are so important, so revealing.

Sophie smiles to herself; confidence returns at the memory of that kiss. She approves of Oliver's compassion. She likes it that he was moved by Rowena's helplessness; that he's worried about his sister and Guy, and about Jess. He will understand that she cannot simply turn her back on the Trehearnes and together they will sort something out.

She gives Circe a final pat and goes back across the lawn to make Rowena a cup of tea.

*　　　*　　　*

The sailors return, happy and tired. *Alice* is back on her mooring and Guy says hurried farewells, drives away in his hired car.

'He's nice,' Jess says at supper. 'He seems a bit formidable at first, not very forthcoming, but he's

182

so passionate about boats. It's rather sweet, really, like Will with his Heron.'

'Passion is so attractive, isn't it?' Johnnie glances at Sophie and is amused, and slightly surprised, to see a flush of colour wash over her cheeks. He's been aware of the attraction between her and Oliver but hadn't realized how serious it might be. 'It's like Jess here,' he goes on, not wanting to embarrass Sophie, 'with her painting and drawing. Because she is passionate about it she infects other people with that passion.'

'Gosh! Do I?' It's Jess who is embarrassed now. 'I hope I don't go on about it.'

'Of course you don't,' says Sophie quickly, cross with herself for blushing. 'No more than Guy does with his boats. I agree with Johnnie, he comes alive with it, doesn't he? I think he could have spent hours in the Growlery looking at those old photographs. He was fascinated by your book.'

'He's a first-rate sailor and he's got some very good ideas about classic boat sailing,' says Johnnie thoughtfully. 'Taking people to sea simply for the experience or on training courses. He's been trying to persuade his father to back it out in Canada.'

'I think,' says Sophie, standing up and piling plates together, 'that Guy's family is hoping that he'll move back.'

'Yes,' says Jess, getting up to help. 'His wife is back already and his boys are at Mount House. We're meeting up at the rugger match on Saturday.'

'Yes, he told me. I didn't quite get it,' says Johnnie. 'I assumed the boys had come back to go to school and that Gemma was returning to Canada once they were settled. Guy was at Mount House, wasn't he?'

183

'And Oliver,' murmurs Sophie. She has that foolish need to say his name aloud. 'And his brother,' she adds quickly.

Johnnie watches her speculatively: she's got it bad, poor old Sophes.

'Will is looking after them,' says Jess. 'Guy's boys, I mean. Ben and Julian.'

'So Guy's wife,' says Johnnie, who wants to get his facts straight, 'has moved back permanently?'

Sophie and Jess glance at each other, wondering which one of them has the most reliable information.

'Gemma is Oliver's sister,' says Sophie. 'You probably gathered that. Oliver says that Gemma's missing her family and friends and that Guy's father is a rather difficult man. He's not giving poor old Guy much leeway and Guy's very frustrated. They have lots of rows and Gemma doesn't like it. She's come back with the boys and is hoping that Guy will follow, though neither of them knows quite what Guy would do to earn a living.'

Jess puts some cheese on the table, glad that she hasn't been called upon to explain the situation. She isn't sure that she's qualified to explain to Johnnie the things that Kate has told her. Clearly Sophie doesn't think that Guy's private life is a secret.

'He told me he used to run a yacht brokerage,' Johnnie says. He cuts a piece of cheese, looking preoccupied.

'That's right,' says Sophie, putting biscuits and fruit beside him. 'But I think Guy's a bit more ambitious than that now.'

He looks up at her. 'Mmm,' he says vaguely. 'That wouldn't surprise me.'

'So you approve of Oliver?' asks Jess.

She and Sophie are clearing up together; Johnnie has gone into the Growlery to check emails and put in some work on the book. Sophie's reaction to Oliver has begun to penetrate Jess's preoccupation and she is surprised how pleased she is at the prospect of Sophie and Oliver getting together.

'I do, rather,' says Sophie, back turned as she stacks the dishwasher. 'You don't mind?'

Jess snorts with laughter. 'Of course I don't. I like him, too. To be honest, I rather fancy him. Why wouldn't I? He's really good-looking and such fun, and there's something . . . well, I don't quite know how to put it. Reliable isn't right. It makes him sound a bit boring, doesn't it?'

'I know what you mean, though,' says Sophie. She turns round, quite composed now, enjoying the opportunity to talk about him. 'He'd get you out of a fix. He might not be able to actually deal with it himself but he'd always know a man who could.'

'Yes,' says Jess. 'That's absolutely it. He's really with it.'

She longs to probe and question but she restrains the desire to know more.

'It's a bit tricky, though,' says Sophie. It's rather a luxury to have another woman to chat things over with; a change from Johnnie and Fred. 'I mean, I can't quite see how we'd go forward.'

'But you want to,' says Jess quickly. She has an absolute longing for this to be a proper romance. 'Don't you?'

'Yes,' says Sophie, after a moment. 'I think I do.

Weird, isn't it?'

'It's wonderful,' says Jess contentedly. 'Love at first sight.'

'I was a bit afraid that I was poaching,' admits Sophie. 'You seemed keen for him to come to the reunion supper and you talked about him quite a lot. And you've been a bit quiet lately, since Rowena showed you the photographs.'

It is Jess's turn to be discomfited. 'It's only because Oliver is much younger than all the others,' she explains quickly. 'And I suppose I was a bit bowled over by him to begin with. I mean, he's something, isn't he? But it was never a serious crush. Honestly. I'm utterly thrilled that it's happened to you and him. It's another part of the story.'

'Story?'

'Well, like me winning the Award and meeting Kate, and Tom and Cass, and coming here to see where Mike and Juliet met. And then me looking so much like Juliet.' She hesitates and gives an odd little sigh. 'It's been a terrific shock.'

'And you're part of the story?'

Jess nods. 'I feel connected. I like it.'

But she looks rather forlorn and Sophie feels a little stab of anxiety; even fear.

'It'll be fun, won't it?' Jess is saying. 'All of us going to the rugby match on Saturday. Like a big family.'

'Yes,' agrees Sophie.

She sees the connection between Jess and herself. The Trehearnes and their friends have become her family in a way her own relations never have. It seems as if it will be the same for Jess. They mustn't allow her to drift away; she must continue

186

to be part of the story.

TAVISTOCK

'This is so weird,' says Gemma as Guy unlocks the door with Oliver's key and lets her into the cottage in Chapel Street. 'Are you sure your mum doesn't mind?'

'She suggested it.' Guy puts their bags inside the door. 'She's coming up on Monday.'

'It's a nice little house, isn't it? I really like it. With all Kate's things here it feels like I've known it all my life.' Gemma takes a carrier bag of food and milk into the kitchen. 'I'll make some tea and cheese on toast.'

Suddenly she feels terribly tired. It's been exhausting trying to keep calm, knowing how Guy hates any form of histrionics, yet determined to win him back to her. As she fills the kettle and switches it on, takes the milk and a loaf and eggs and cheese out of the bag, she thinks back over the past few days.

To begin with it was such a joyful shock, hearing his unemotional voice telling her that he was in the country just for a week; that he'd hired a car and driven down the previous afternoon and was staying with Oliver in Chapel Street. For a moment she couldn't comprehend it. Why should he be in Chapel Street, and with Ollie of all people? Why hadn't he let her know he was coming? Frustration, disappointment and anger threatened to overwhelm her joy and relief in knowing that he'd come at last.

'So what am I supposed to do?' she cried. 'I'm in South Brent with Debbie and she's got theatre seats booked for tonight. Honestly, Guy. I can't believe you could do this without warning me that you were coming. I could have met you somewhere . . .'

Her disappointment deprived her of words but Guy remained quite calm. He was going to lunch with these friends of Oliver's on the Tamar, he told her. No, he couldn't remember what they were called but the girl had won David's Award. There was no need to cancel her arrangements with Debbie. He'd come over and fetch her the next day. Gemma wanted to scream at him. He made it sound as if it were perfectly normal to travel all this way to see her and then postpone their meeting for twenty-four hours while he spent the time with complete strangers.

She willed down her anger; it was crucial the meeting between them should work. If she raged at him he might easily catch the next plane out.

'But what then?' she asked. 'Does Ma know you're here?'

'Nobody knows. It was a spur-of-the-moment thing,' he answered. 'I ran into Oliver by mistake. Just as well he was staying here, actually. It hadn't occurred to me that Mum might be down in Cornwall.'

He sounded surprised, even aggrieved, and she closed her eyes, took a deep breath. Don't say it, she told herself silently. Just don't.

'So where shall we go when you pick me up?' she asked instead. 'Shall I tell Ma . . .?'

'Not likely!' he said. 'We need to be on our own for a couple of days. Let's go to that hotel just outside Dartmouth where we went on honeymoon.'

The suggestion surprised her, got under her guard. Suddenly her resentment fell away and she simply wanted to be with him.

'What a brilliant idea,' she said. 'Oh, Guy. I'm so glad you've come over. I'm missing you so much.'

'Mmm,' he said. 'Will you book it or shall I?'

'I'll do it,' she said. 'And what about the boys, Guy? You'll want to see them?'

'Of course I shall,' he said irritably.

He was always irritable if his affection for Ben and Julian was called into question, and she hastened to allay his irritation.

'As long as you haven't got to rush back before the weekend, that's all. It's a Sunday out so we can collect them after church. They'll be over the moon to see you.'

'OK then. Book two nights. Look, Oliver's wanting to get on. I'll phone again later.'

For the next twenty-four hours she swung between joy and anger; anger winning, especially when he phoned again that evening to say that he'd been invited to go sailing the next day and would be over rather later than he'd first planned.

'And can you get a taxi to the hotel?' he added. 'I don't want a public reunion scene in Brent.'

She suppressed an urge to scream loudly and throw her phone at the wall, but then he began to tell her about the boats and how he'd met Jess and someone called Johnnie whose grandson was at Mount House with Ben and Julian.

'There's a rugby match on Saturday afternoon,' he said, 'and he's suggested we might all meet up and watch Will play. What d'you think? Ben and Jules might like that, mightn't they?'

And once again she swallowed down her wrath

189

and agreed that they would. His voice sounded much more relaxed, almost ebullient, and she wanted to encourage the mood. Afterwards, though, resentment surged in her gut: why should she tiptoe round him, reading the storm signals and reacting to them so as to keep him happy? Why shouldn't she have the luxury of speaking her mind and getting it out of her system?

At this point Oliver phoned.

'Are you spitting nails?' he asked brightly—and all her spleen and fury erupted and she raged at him.

'Sorry,' she said wearily at last. 'Sorry, Ol. You just walked straight into that. But honestly! Can you get inside his head? I mean, what does he *think*, for Christ's sake?'

'I know, old love,' he said, 'but the point is: he's here. That's what you wanted. That's what you were counting on. And he hasn't come to say, "That's it. Finis." Listen, he's cross. Oh, yes, he's very cross. He'd worked himself into a good old self-righteous state by the time he got here but he can't keep it up, dear old Guy. I took him to the pub last night and today we've been down on the Tamar with the Trehearnes and he's relaxing nicely, coming off the boil, and, what's more, he's really connecting with his roots again. Waxing lyrical about the Tamar. He's fallen in with the plan to meet up at the rugby match—I expect he's told you—and a day's sailing tomorrow will just be the final thing to put him right back on course. If you can't work the old magic after that, well, I'll be very surprised. I'll clear out and you can stay here when you get back. I'll give Guy the key.'

And when at last she saw him she knew that

Oliver was right and it was a good thing that Guy had had the space and time to unwind before they met.

As he came into the hotel bedroom where she was waiting she recognized his relaxed, contented look that generally followed stringent physical exercise taken in a boat out at sea. She got up and walked into his outstretched arms and, as she hugged him tightly, her own tensions and resentment flowed out of her. Desire flared in her and she wanted to drag him down on the bed behind them. Instead she let him go just a fraction before he would have released her and smiled up at him.

'Good day, by the look of it.'

She was instantly rewarded for her restraint.

'Brilliant,' he said. 'Sorry I'm late, but honestly, Gemma,' he shook his head in a kind of bewilderment, 'you should just see that place. God, I'd kill for something like that on the river. I'd forgotten how beautiful it is down there on the Tamar.'

She let him talk on, watching him, feeling a huge affection for him.

'I'm looking forward to meeting them all on Saturday,' she said at last. 'It was a great idea that we should go to the rugby match. The twins are so excited at the thought of seeing you.'

'Are they? Well, I'm looking forward to seeing them too.' He looked around, stretched, suddenly seized by embarrassment.

But she was ready for that, too.

'Shall we go down and have a drink?' she suggested. 'You look very respectable, given that you've been sailing all day.'

'I stopped off for a quick shower at Chapel Street,' he said. He was clearly relieved at the prospect of a drink; at the postponement of anything more intimate. 'A beer would go down well. Or a very large gin and tonic.'

'Come on then,' she said lightly, slipping her hand into the crook of his arm. 'You must be starving.'

Later, as they sat at their table with coffee, she decided that she must talk to him seriously. The dining-room was half empty and they'd been given a table in the bay window with no near neighbours. The chintzy curtains were drawn and there was a sense of intimacy. Guy's face was calm but she could tell that he might withdraw into his more usual detachment at any moment. They would make love later, no doubt about that, but she didn't want this crucial issue muddled with any emotion aroused by physical passion. She could use it to her advantage but it would be cheating.

'This was a good idea of yours, coming here,' she said, pouring some more coffee. 'Can you imagine us at the Rectory with Ma dashing about trying to be tactful and Pa glaring at us?'

'No,' he said, his face lighting with his rare smile. 'That's why I went to Chapel Street.'

'You must have been really pissed off with me,' she said lightly, 'not to tell me you were coming.'

He looked at her, an intent look, as if he was measuring the gravity of her statement. 'I was,' he said at last. 'Just blinding off into the blue with the boys, saying you weren't coming back.'

'I'm not going back, Guy,' she said softly. 'I meant it. And I did give you a few warning shots across the bows, you know. It can't have been that much of a shock.'

He drank some coffee. 'I felt as if I'd lost control,' he said honestly. 'That's what really made me angry, I suppose. That you could just go like that and there was nothing I could do about it.'

She leaned towards him. 'It was the only way, in the end, to make you hear me. I couldn't take any more of it. You were always so silent and preoccupied. Short with the boys, arguing with your father. I felt utterly and absolutely alone.'

She noted the jut of his jaw, the way his eyelids drooped over his grey eyes, and knew that anger was not very far away. Still, she waited for him to speak; she would not think of placatory words that might help him to some face-saving way out, nor would she hasten to agree that she'd been to blame in the first place.

'So what d'you suggest?' he asked at last.

His long brown fingers turned his coffee cup round and round in its saucer, and he watched it, refusing to look at her.

'Why did you come?' she asked in return.

'Oh, to have a good rant,' he said. His eyes narrowed, as if he were laughing at himself. 'To bawl you out and insist on your return.'

'So what's changed your mind?'

He looked at her then. 'What makes you think I've changed my mind?'

She shrugged, holding his stare. 'Something has, hasn't it?'

He looked past her, his eyes widened as if he were seeing visions, and she held her breath.

'I'd forgotten,' he said at last, 'how beautiful it is here in the West Country. And how much I feel a part of it. Oh, Canada is beautiful too, in a different way, but this is . . . home. I hadn't realized how much I missed it.' He shook his head, suddenly embarrassed. 'It sounds crazy.'

'Does it? Not to me,' she said. 'It's why I came back. This is where I belong and I want it for Ben and Jules. If we'd been wonderfully happy out there perhaps things would have been different, but we weren't. And it's not just me, Guy, it's you too. You're not happy. I love you and I want to be with you but not like that. Oh, I know it's not fair on you and that it's my fault we went in the first place. Do you think I ever forget that? So I wanted to give it a try to make up for everything. And you wanted to go too, didn't you? It had been in your mind for a while so it was an obvious solution at that time. And we've both given it a try but it hasn't worked.'

'So what now? What about my father?'

She sighed. 'If I really thought Mark would care it might make a difference. But he won't. He doesn't like me—he makes that very clear—and he's not particularly interested in the boys. And as far as you're concerned I think it's more a question of him needing to be in control. He will be angry, just as you were when I walked out, but there won't be a great deal more than that behind it. I'm sorry to be so brutal but that's how I see it. And his cold approach seems to rub off on you so that our relationship suffers too. I really can't cope with any more of it, Guy. If it sounds like an ultimatum that's because it is.'

There was a little silence, and then she said, 'What were you seeing just now, Guy?'

'Boats,' he answered. 'Boats out on the River Tamar and an old grey house and a sail loft.'

She pushed back her chair and stood up, and he

looked up at her quickly, and just for a moment he looked anxious and frightened. She held out her hand to him.

'Come on,' she said. 'Let's go to bed.'

*　　　*　　　*

Now, as she makes tea and takes the slices of toasted cheese from under the grill, remembering how she and Guy made love, she can hardly keep herself from smiling. Yesterday they had the whole day to themselves, exploring old haunts, and this morning, after breakfast at the hotel, the drive across the moor was magical. Now she must prepare for the rugby match, for Guy's reunion with his sons, and for the meeting with these new friends. Oliver has sent a text saying that he'll see them at the school.

Guy appears behind her. 'How are we doing? The match starts in less than an hour.'

'It's ready,' she says, piling plates and mugs onto a tray. 'We'll have this in the living-room. By the way, I never asked you how Oliver was with Jess.'

He follows her down the hall, watches her put the tray on the table.

'With Jess?'

She glances up at him. 'He's rather taken with her. Trust you not to notice. He's afraid that he's too old for her.'

Guy frowns. 'I should have said that it was Sophie he was rather taken with, not Jess.'

'Sophie? But he's only just met her, hasn't he?'

Guy shrugs, takes a bite of toasted cheese. 'How long does it take?'

Gemma grins at him. 'It took you quite a while,'

she says. Then, suddenly serious: 'What are we going to do, Guy?'

He finishes his toast and drinks some tea. 'I don't know yet. I need something to come back to and we need somewhere to live. Dad won't set me up here. Why should he?'

'But you'll come back?'

He takes a deep breath. 'Yes, I'll come back.'

'Oh, darling.' She wraps her arms round him quickly, wanting to forestall any remark—'What choice do I have?' or 'You've twisted my arm'— that might lead to a downturn of self-pity. To a different kind of man she might have said 'Let's go to bed,' but Guy isn't that sort of man. He'd suspect the suggestion as a feminine attempt to strengthen her position by exploiting his physical need and she rejects it. Her position is a tricky one: she can't openly exult because it will look as if it's been a game that she's won. If she expresses gratitude he will be uncomfortable.

Guy solves the dilemma in his own prosaic way. He hugs her, releases her, and says: 'If you don't get a move on we'll be late for the match.'

Gemma wants to weep with relief but she doesn't. She plays it by his rules. She can afford to: she's won.

*   *   *

While he waits for her to get ready to go, Guy remembers again those early, happy days and he smiles reminiscently. She made a chink in his carefully constructed, self-protecting armour and through it injected her warmth, her easy light-heartedness and love of life. With her, he was more able to relate to other people, to take life more lightly. Without her, his future looked bleak. Her ultimatum, back then in the form of the note through his door, was just as effective as her flight from Canada is now.

'What are you thinking about?'

Gemma stands at the door, ready to go, watching him.

'I was remembering chasing you up over the moor twelve years ago, and that boat trip from Fowey a few weeks afterwards,' he answers.

She knows at once what he means.

'I was remembering it earlier. I always think of it when we drive along that way like we did today. Through Cornwood and Wotter, across to Cadover Bridge. I remember your lights flashing in my mirror and my hoping it was you but afraid to stop in case it wasn't.'

'And you remember us bringing the boat back from Fowey?'

She laughs. 'Of course I do. You were quite romantic in those days.'

'It was fun, though, wasn't it?' he persists. 'We enjoyed those trips collecting and delivering boats, when we used to go to sea together, before we had the boys.'

She looks at him, slightly puzzled. 'Yes, it was good. Why?'

He looks thoughtful, shakes his head. 'Nothing. Just a little idea.'

'We should be going,' she says. 'Have you got the door key? Come on, we'll be late.'

*   *   *

'I think it's outrageous,' Tom says. 'He's been back in the country for five days and hasn't had the courtesy even to come and see us. We've been looking after his wife and children for a month . . .'

He's been working outside all day, sweeping leaves; his ancient navy jersey is unravelling at the cuffs and the knees of his old cords are worn bare. He stands in his thick white submariners' socks, with his back to the sink, arms folded across his chest. Cass is making tea and he knows he is in the way but he isn't going to move. He stands sturdily, stockily, chin jutting.

'Oh, for goodness' sake,' cries Cass, deliberately jerking his elbow as she reaches for the sugar. 'She's our daughter. They're our grandsons. Stop talking like some Victorian spinster aunt. Guy and Gemma need to get things sorted. How are they going to do that here with us around? Use your sense.'

'They've been in Chapel Street.'

'But Kate isn't there, is she?'

'Guy didn't know that, did he?'

Cass rolls her eyes, pours the tea. 'Kate is his mother. Naturally he went there first. Just as Gemma came to us. How would you have felt if Gemma had gone to Kate first when she and the boys came home? It was just lucky that Oliver was there. And, anyway, what does it matter as long as things get put right between them? That's what you wanted, wasn't it?'

Tom is silent, trying to overcome a huge attack of self-righteous rage. He feels that Gemma has cheated and lied to them: allowing them to think she was still with Debbie when she was with Guy and then staying at Chapel Street instead of coming back to the Rectory.

'She's not twelve any more,' says Cass. 'She's a married woman with children. Do you want this tea or not?'

'That's what I said when she wanted to run back home in the first place,' he cries indignantly, ignoring the tea. 'That she should take responsibility for herself and her marriage, and not come back to us when she falls at the first hurdle.'

'Is this a private war?' asks Oliver from the doorway, 'or can anyone join in? Just to say I'm off to this rugby match. See you later.'

He disappears before Tom can answer. Cass dashes to the door.

'Tell Guy we'd love to see him if it can be fitted in before he goes back,' she calls after him. 'Perhaps lunch tomorrow with the twins?' Oliver raises a hand in acknowledgement and Cass comes back into the kitchen.

'Fitted in,' snorts Tom. 'I notice *we* aren't invited to this match with our grandsons and the Trehearnes.'

'The boys aren't playing.' Cass sits down at the table. 'Will is playing. Jess and Sophie are going and it's a chance for all the young people to be together.'

'What about Johnnie?' demands Tom at once. 'I bet he's going.'

'Probably he is,' answers Cass wearily. 'Tom, what is your problem? From the few texts that Gemma has sent Oliver it looks as if this whole thing might work out. Guy has come over, as Gemma hoped he would, and it seems as if he might be prepared to move back. This is what we're all hoping for. What is the matter with you?'

Tom fumes silently. He cannot say that the

199

matter is all bound up in his jealousy of his elder son who, like some latter-day Machiavelli, seems to be organizing everyone as usual.

'I'm fed up with being used,' he says. 'We stand about waiting to be told what's happening, grateful for a crumb of information, whilst Oliver goes in and out as if we're a bloody hotel. I mean, what's he doing here? He's been hanging around for weeks. Why isn't he doing whatever it is he does in London or wherever, and making himself even more money?'

'Oh, come on,' says Cass impatiently. 'Do you understand nothing about your children? It's my guess that Gemma told Oliver that she was planning to make the dash back home and she wanted him around as a buffer. She's always relied on Oliver to help her through difficulties since she was a little girl. He came down so that he could be at hand if she needed him. And she did. He's got the boys into Mount House, kept her spirits up and effected an introduction to the Trehearnes.'

Tom stares at her indignantly: why should Gemma need to rely on her brother when she has a father to support her? And what's this about an introduction?

'How d'you mean?' he asks. 'We've known the Trehearnes for ever. Why should we need Oliver to introduce any of us to them?'

'I didn't say we did. But he's introduced Guy to them, and now Gemma will meet them.'

'And?'

Cass is silent for a moment. 'I don't know,' she says at last. 'I just think that somehow it will be important.'

'I'm dreading going back to the Rectory,' Gemma confides to Oliver at half-time. They stand a little apart from the others at the edge of the pitch. 'I just know there's going to be a huge scene with Pa.'

'He deserves his chance to blow off some steam,' says Oliver tolerantly. 'Ma was getting an earful when I came out. He'll get over it.'

'D'you think we should all go over to lunch tomorrow? We could pick the twins up after church and take them up to the Rectory.'

'Definitely not,' says Oliver at once. 'Dear old Guy seems in an unusually mellow mood just now but I think that that would be a step too far. Pa simply won't be able to help himself saying something provocative and all our good work might be undone.'

Gemma's eyes stray to the tall, lean figure of her husband, deep in conversation with Johnnie.

'I'm sure you're right,' she says unhappily, 'but I just feel a bit bad about the Aged Ps. They've been very patient.'

'That's what parents do,' says Oliver robustly. 'They put their children first. Your duty is to your boys and that means getting it right with Guy. And talking of parents, has he spoken to Kate?'

'He talked to her last night. She's coming up from St Meriadoc on Monday morning and I shall push off into the town to give them some time on their own.'

He looks at her, eyebrows raised. 'That's very . . . tactful of you.'

Gemma shrugs. 'Kate's been very good to me. I'm not sure I'd want me as a daughter-in-law.

Anyway, after lunch on Monday I shall drive back to London with Guy, see him off on Tuesday morning and then catch the train down. Will you pick me up from Plymouth?'

'Of course.' Oliver is watching Guy and Johnnie. 'Well, it seems that your tactics have worked. I have to say Guy's looking very positive. Even jolly.'

'He is, isn't he?' Gemma bites her lips. 'Oh God, Ol, I couldn't bear it if anything went wrong now.'

*   *   *

'They are terribly alike, aren't they?' says Jess from her place beside the picnic hamper where Sophie is pouring coffee from a Thermos into an assortment of small mugs.

'Yes, they are.' Sophie resists looking across to where Gemma and Oliver are standing together.

'Really attractive,' says Jess with a sigh. 'They're lucky to be so tall and elegant.'

Sophie hands her a mug. 'Sure you're not in love with him?'

'Oh, no,' says Jess at once, taking the coffee. 'No, that's all over. It was infatuation. I'm utterly in love with Will. When he scored that try I thought I might die of pride.'

'He's a sweetie,' admits Sophie. 'Listen, I've had an idea. Why don't we invite them all to lunch tomorrow? What d'you think?'

'Oh!' Jess sips her coffee, her eyes bright. 'What a great idea. What else would they be doing, I wonder?'

'Well, Gemma says the boys want to spend time with Guy, of course, though she doesn't particularly want to go to her parents' place . . .'

'The trouble with Sundays out,' says Jess, 'is that it's difficult to know what to do all day if it's too far to get home. Will doesn't know how lucky he is just to be able to come out to you. We used to have to spend the day in a hotel or at a cinema, or going for a walk if the weather wasn't too awful. I suppose they'll take the twins to Chapel Street after church and then probably yomp out over the moor or something.'

'I was thinking that they could have the morning just being together and then come down a bit later for lunch. Sort of kill two birds with one stone. Time together as a family and then some entertainment with us.'

'I think it's a brilliant idea,' says Jess. 'Ask Gemma and see what she thinks. Will would be thrilled. He can show off his boat and the sail loft, and then they can all come back together after tea.'

'I suppose,' says Sophie, allowing her eyes to drift to where Oliver stands, 'it might be nice to invite Oliver as well.'

She is still not used to this odd sensation of joyousness when he is near—or how colourless life is when he is absent. These are unfamiliar sensations, they operate at the extremes of her emotions, and privately she is revelling in them.

'Of course he must come,' says Jess firmly, and then blushes. 'Sorry,' she says. 'That sounded a bit pushy. After all, I'm only a guest myself.'

'Rubbish,' says Sophie happily. 'You're definitely one of the family now. You belong here. Don't you feel it?'

A little pause.

'Yes,' says Jess. 'Actually, I think I do.'

TAMAR

Rowena dozes, slipping in and out of sleep. Sometimes, when she wakens, her thoughts are sharp and clear. Now is such a time. Her room is full of light; watery reflections slide and slip over the cream-washed walls and she can hear the harsh cries of the gulls out on the river. She thinks of Jess, of her shocked expression when she saw the photograph, the sharp intake of breath and her question: 'Who's that?' as she pointed to Al. Rowena feels deep satisfaction: her suspicions—her hopes—have all been founded on the truth. Those carefully hoarded memories, those pieces of the puzzle, have been pieced together to make a whole picture at last.

Once again she sees Al dancing with Juliet at the Christmas Ball on HMS *Drake*, a slow smooch in the shadows at the edge of the floor. He's holding her much too tightly; the silky chiffon skirt of Juliet's long, pale ball gown floating and clinging to his dark uniform. Mike at the bar, getting the drinks in, turning to watch them and his rather foolish, half-drunken expression hardening into watchfulness.

She hears Juliet's voice, strained and desperate, whispering just outside the morning-room windows one warm spring evening. 'I should never have married him, I know that now. I thought I was in love with him. I really did. How was I to know? What shall we do?' and the low, murmuring response: 'We must be very careful.'

She remembers Juliet as a house guest, staying

204

for a week whilst Mike was at sea, slipping away to the sail loft, along the river bank and, after a while, the shadowy figure of Al following her.

And, most important, the Midsummer's Eve party in the sea garden; reflections jittering and dancing on the smooth black surface of the water; shadowy figures dancing or leaning against the balustrade beneath Circe's imposing figure. The tall lavender hedges, pale, cloudy shapes; their scent still lingering on the warm air.

The whispering behind the summerhouse: the first voice urgent, demanding; the other frightened. Juliet's dress in disarray, her hair loosened. Al's face buried against her throat but her face twisted away from his, her hands on his shoulders.

'Listen,' she is saying, still in that desperate whisper. 'Please just listen to me. I'm pregnant, Al. Just for God's sake, listen . . .'

Then, the last small link in the long chain that links Rowena to the past, to Al. The letter from her friend in Australia.

'. . . no more children. It seems that Mike's been firing blanks . . .'

It must have been hard for Mike, watching Juliet's son growing to look more and more like Al. No wonder they quarrelled and the boy left Australia as soon as he was old enough and came to England to join the army.

Rowena stirs restlessly, chafing against her physical weakness. She is allowed up for short periods to sit in her chair by the window, and soon she'll insist on going downstairs. Johnnie fusses, of course—he's always been a fusspot, like his father—but before very much longer she will be strong enough to bend his will to hers.

Jess has been up to see her, of course, but usually Sophie or Johnnie has been hovering about somewhere and Rowena has been unable to speak openly with the girl. She must see Jess alone and this time there must be no more confusion or half-truths. She could tell at once that Jess had recognized Al; that she'd seen the likeness between him and her own father. Rowena feels the sharp familiar claw of pain rake at her heart. How tragic that they should have both died so young; how cruel that she should never have seen Al's son.

Al's son. With a deep sigh of satisfaction she relaxes again into her pillows. He'd had a son—and now there is his granddaughter, Jess, who, in her turn, might have more sons. A feather of anxiety brushes Rowena's drowsiness, lightly ruffling her sense of wellbeing, and she frowns. Some kind of allowance must be made for Jess. If Al's son had lived then this house and everything in it would be his, not Johnnie's.

Rowena struggles to grapple with this thought but suddenly she is too tired, too weak to pursue it. Later she will think of it again and decide how restitution might be made.

*   *   *

When she wakens it is late afternoon and the room is full of shadows. From the sea garden she can hear the shouts and laughter of the boys and her mouth curves into a smile at the thought of them playing there. She must get up, go down and join them. She raises her head, which feels weighty, too heavy for her neck to support, and she lies back again with a little gasp. Frowning now, she strives to recall

206

something she was thinking of earlier; something that must be put right before it is too late.

Slowly, slowly, she struggles up, willing herself into a sitting position, swinging her legs over the side of the bed. How tired she is. She sits for a while on the edge of the bed, marshalling her strength. She's been ill; she remembers now. Memories flit about her head like bats in the shadows, and all the while she can hear the children laughing.

Painfully, she stands upright and shuffles across the room to the tall sash window. She stands clutching at the curtain, staring down. The boys are there, she can see them playing whilst Circe stands guard above the three of them: Al, Johnnie and young Fred. She can see Johnnie's blond head but the other two are in the shadows. She lifts a hand and taps on the window. The effort is so feeble that they cannot hear her—and, anyway, they are too far away.

As she subsides into her chair she decides that she must have been very ill. Yet still she strains forward, hoping to see the boys playing, climbing the balustrade to look up at Circe, but the sea garden is empty. She sinks back again and closes her eyes.

When the bedroom door opens she turns to see Dickie coming towards her. Someone is behind him and he is saying, 'We were wondering how you are, Mother. The boys are having their tea before they go back to school and Jess has brought you yours.'

Rowena frowns; she feels frightened, confused. Why does Dickie call her 'Mother' and who is Jess? The girl is looking at her anxiously, putting down the tray, coming closer. And now, suddenly, Rowena's mind is clear again and she sees that it is Juliet and she recalls that Juliet has had a child, Al's child.

Her whole body is shaken with joy—but there is anxiety, too. She remembers that this has to be made clear; that there must be no mistake. Urgently she reaches out and seizes Juliet's wrist, pulling her down so that the girl has to kneel beside her.

'It is Al's child, isn't it? His son,' Rowena says, and she is so happy that her heart seems to explode in her breast and her eyes are full of tears because the girl is nodding, and she too is crying. She puts her forehead down on their joined hands so that Rowena can feel the wetness of her tears.

And Dickie is there, bending over them anxiously, and Rowena wants to tell him about Al's son but suddenly she cannot speak, cannot breathe, but still she clasps the girl's wrist until her strength fails and darkness comes.

*   *   *

It is Gemma and Guy who take Will back to school with the twins after tea.

'Great-granny is ill again,' Sophie tells Will. 'We must call Dr Alan. Can you be a good boy and go with Julian and Ben? Grando and I ought to be here. Do you mind just this once?'

And, of course, Will agrees at once, wanting to look grown up in front of these new friends. He is perfectly happy to go back to school with them but sorry not to see Jess, who seems to have vanished.

'You'll see her next time,' Sophie assures him. 'I expect she's with Great-granny. Now, what do you need to take? Did you bring anything home with you?'

And there is the usual flurry of collecting belongings, and farewells, and the car goes off up the drive and the house is quiet again.

Sophie and Oliver sit together, with Popps in her basket, while Johnnie is talking to their doctor on the telephone. Oliver holds her hands whilst she weeps, and then Johnnie comes in and says: 'Alan's on his way, thank God. It's too late, I'm afraid, but he wants to come and see her. I would have hated just to call out an ambulance.'

Sophie wipes her cheeks. 'I'm so sorry,' she says. 'Poor little Jess. What a wretched thing to happen.'

Johnnie is visibly shaken. 'It was very quick,' he says. 'We must be grateful for that. It was that thing about mistaking Jess for Juliet again. Mother suddenly seemed quite worked up about it and grabbed Jess's wrist and started talking about Al. Poor Jess is in shock.'

'Where did she go?' Sophie stands up. 'I was getting Will off before he realized anything was really wrong and she said she wanted to be on her own for a moment. Could she have gone back to the sail loft? I don't think she should be alone.'

'I'll go and find her,' says Oliver. 'You need to be around for the doctor. I'll see to Jess.'

'And we were all having such a wonderful time,' says Sophie woefully. 'Oh, poor Rowena, up there all on her own.'

'She wasn't all on her own when it happened,' says Johnnie comfortingly. 'And she seemed so happy. I think she'd gone right back in time and she believed that Jess was Juliet and that Al was alive too. It's Jess I'm really sorry for. What a thing to happen. I just hope she doesn't feel in any way

209

responsible.'

'I'll go and look for her.' Oliver gives Sophie a quick hug and goes out.

Sophie and Johnnie look at one another. His face is so sad that Sophie wants to weep again, but she doesn't. She's been here before, with Dickie and with Meg, and she knows that Johnnie's warm, generous, loving heart will be wrung again and he will grieve as deeply for his mother as he did for his father and his wife.

'Is there anything I can do for Rowena before Alan comes?' she asks.

He shakes his head, tears suddenly overflowing, and turns away so that she won't see them.

'Then I'll make some fresh tea,' she says. 'We never drink ours when it's getting Will back to school time.' And as she passes him to reach the kettle she touches him lightly on the shoulder.

'Bit tough on Gemma and Guy,' he mutters, blowing his nose. 'Rushing them all off like that. Terrible timing.'

'Rowena liked to make her presence felt,' says Sophie with a lightness she doesn't feel. 'I think she'd be rather pleased to know that her departure had caused a rumpus.'

He smiles, nods as if accepting her effort at raising his spirits, and she makes tea and they sit in silence waiting for the doctor.

*   *   *

Oliver approaches the sail loft. The door is open and he knocks, calls out, 'Jess?' and walks inside. The big room is in shadow but he sees her silhouette on the balcony outlined against the

210

dying light. He goes out and stands beside her. She stares across the river towards Cargreen, her arms wrapped around herself, her hands hidden. Below, on the soft pale mud, a flock of seagulls forage, strutting and squawking, and suddenly they take off, wheeling in one great cloud of beating wings, heading downriver towards the sea.

'It was awful,' Jess says suddenly. Her voice trembles. 'Terrible.'

She continues to stare across the river, and he leans with folded arms on the balustrade, not looking at her.

'Of course I hardly knew her,' says Jess rapidly, 'but even so. It was so quick.' She bites her lips and he feels her arm tense beside his own, as if she is clenching her fist. 'I just wish she hadn't muddled me up with Juliet. I think it killed her.'

'Perhaps it did,' he answers calmly. 'Something was going to. She was very ill. Johnnie said he thought she was happy, thinking that Al had come back to her with Juliet. She was ninety-two, Jess, with a very advanced heart condition and a few other things as well. It's not your fault.'

Jess takes a deep breath, nods. 'I know, but there was other stuff.'

He continues to lean beside her, looking down into the sedges. 'It's to do with the photograph, isn't it?'

She hesitates, nods briefly, clenches her hands again.

'Do you want to tell me about it?'

She shakes her head this time. 'No, not yet. It's not just about me, you see. I have to do something first.'

'OK, but don't be silly about it, will you? You've

211

had a very big shock. Come back to the house with me now and have something to drink and eat, and get warm.'

'OK. But don't say anything, will you? About the photograph?'

'I promise. Look, Kate will be back in Chapel Street tomorrow and Guy is going after lunch. If you wanted to go back for a few days I know she'd be very happy to have you there.'

She hesitates; thinks about it. 'It might be a good idea while they get everything sorted out here. I don't want to be in the way.' She turns and looks at him. 'Thanks, Oliver.'

'Come on, then,' he says, and she follows him out and closes the door behind her.

TAVISTOCK

Hardly has Kate waved Gemma and Guy off to London in the hired car than Cass drives up and parks outside the cottage in Chapel Street.

'Tom is driving me mad and I simply couldn't stand it another minute,' she says, following Kate into the living-room. 'But I didn't want to butt in on you and Guy. Oliver said that he and Gemma were going straight after lunch.'

She bends to make a fuss of Flossie, knowing she shouldn't have come quite so soon; she should have given Kate time to get over seeing Guy. At the same time she hates this stand-off between herself and Kate while Gemma and Guy get themselves sorted out.

'I think it'll work,' Oliver told her, when he

phoned yesterday, 'as long as nobody interferes.'

Meanwhile she feels jittery and unable to relax, and Gemma won't be back until tomorrow.

'They went about ten minutes ago,' Kate says. She too feels uncomfortable. It seems wrong, after fifty years of friendship, to be at odds with Cass. Yet she's still over-emotional, having spent this short time alone with Guy after nearly a year's separation, and she very slightly resents this unexpected visit, which is jarring her out of her mood.

'We haven't seen Guy,' says Cass—and she begins to laugh. 'I think that Gemma was terrified that Tom would go off half-cock and ruin everything, so first she hid in a hotel near Dartmouth and then here. Oh God, Kate, I so utterly hate this.'

She sits down at the table, pushing back her hair, which has faded into an ashy creaminess, smiling ruefully at Kate—and the ghosts are back again. Kate sees a much younger Cass; sitting just as she is now at that old table. This is how it's been in married quarters and naval hirings, cottages, the house in Whitchurch: Cass with a baby on her lap, toddlers playing round her feet, smiling over one or other of her misdemeanours. She remembers how they laughed at silly things together, raged at the unreasonableness of the navy—and how Cass wept after Charlotte died, filled with guilt, grief and the agony of loss.

'I hate it, too.' Kate sits opposite. She knows that Guy would not want her to tell Cass all his private thoughts and plans, so she decides to take another tack. 'I think Oliver has the right of it but we might have to sit it out a bit longer. It's great that they met

213

up with the Trehearnes, isn't it? Bad news about poor old Lady T, though. Gemma didn't know too much about it except that she was taken very ill just as they were finishing tea. Gemma and Guy simply gathered up the boys and cleared out quick.'

Cass takes the hint at once. If there are to be any important personal disclosures made about their children's future then they must come from Gemma. Well, that's fair enough.

'Oliver didn't tell me much,' she says. 'I know they were all going down to the Tamar for lunch but that's about as far as we got. Tom was furious that they didn't come to us. I hadn't heard about Lady T.'

To be honest, she doesn't care much about Lady T. The thing is, with Tom in this tiresome mood, she's begun to feel oddly lonely; this wretched question of the divorce, which lies between her and Kate, has made her realize how much she misses the old unconditional friendship. Nothing's ever been off limits between them before: children, husbands, lovers. Now they tiptoe round each other, each unable to be too honest in her criticism of the other's child lest the relationship should break under the strain. She wonders how Kate copes on her own with nobody to let off steam to when things go wrong, or to have a hug with when she wakes up in those bleak early hours with despair in her heart. Tom might be a bit of a pain at the moment but at least he is there and, to be fair, a great comfort when the chips are down. Of course, there is Bruno . . .

'How's Bruno?' she asks. 'Did you have a good weekend?'

'He's fine,' answers Kate. 'He's just begun the

research for another book.'

She wonders what thought process has led Cass to Bruno but at least she's sheered away from Guy and Gemma. Her heart lifts with a tiny surge of joy as she remembers what Guy said here in this room less than an hour earlier.

'I haven't seen Cass and Tom,' Guy told her. 'It would probably do more harm than good. I'm looking into coming home, Mum. I've decided I want to but it's not quite that easy.'

Her delight was so great she was unable to speak. She simply nodded, longing to propose all sorts of schemes and possibilities that could help bring it about, but wisely remaining silent. His rare smile and a hug that was barely more than a prolonged pat was her reward. There was certainly nothing about Guy to suggest that he was in touch with his feminine side and briefly she was seized with sympathy for Gemma.

Cass is watching her. 'I'm sorry, Kate,' she says, genuinely repentant. 'It was utterly selfish to arrive so soon after Guy went. It was just not knowing what was going on and I suddenly felt quite desperate. But it was too bad of me. It's been so long since you saw him and then you had—what?— an hour with him on your own?'

Kate relaxes; as usual Cass disarms her. 'It's fine. At least Gemma gave us the time alone. That was thoughtful of her. I wish he'd let us know he was coming home. Madness, coming all that way without a word to anyone. Oliver saved the day.'

'Yes.' Cass sits back in her chair. 'I just wish he and Tom didn't get across each other so much. I never thought that Tom would turn into such a grumpy old man. Mostly it's funny but just lately it's

215

become very wearing. I know he's thinking about Charlotte so much at the moment and then I feel so guilty and so miserable.'

'Why particularly about Charlotte just now?'

'Oh,' Cass shrugs, 'you know what it's like with Tom. Charlotte was always his favourite. She was so much like him, and she was so gentle and biddable with him. When she got older she began to be more independent. She needed to disapprove of me a bit. I think it can be like that with mothers and daughters, but she was always on Tom's side. Well, I didn't mind that. I thought it was rather sweet. The thing is now, though, Gemma's muddle has reminded him of that terrible time and brought back all the guilt and grief. It's never very far from the surface, one just learns to live with it, but now Gemma's problem has opened all those old wounds and they're very raw and painful. It wasn't just me who'd been having an affair, remember—he had too—but Charlotte would never have believed that. We were both guilty but because Tom doesn't really want to admit his own guilt it's easier to blow it all out in bad temper on Gemma and me.'

'I never realized,' Kate says after a moment, 'that it was as bad as this. I didn't see the connection with Charlotte.'

'Why should you? We've hardly talked, have we, because it's so horrid having this between us. As Gemma's mother I want to put the blame on Guy. As Guy's mother you want to blame Gemma. But we both know, deep down, it's not that simple. It makes it so difficult to talk about anything because it always comes back to this, doesn't it? And I can't talk to Tom because he's furious with Gemma and it's like walking on eggshells. Even Oliver is

216

being cagey because he's in Gemma's confidence. Of *course* I want Gemma and the boys back here rather than so far away but I'd honestly rather Guy was with them, Kate. I know he and I don't exactly hit it off but I also believe that Gemma loves him, and so do the boys.'

'I know,' says Kate. 'Of course, I know that. Look, the crucial thing is that neither Gemma nor Guy wants a divorce. That's got to be a good starting place. And, after all, Gemma and the boys are back for good, aren't they, so you can't lose now.'

'Yes, I can,' answers Cass sadly. 'Because if Guy doesn't come back things will never be quite the same between you and me. And I know that Gemma and the boys won't be happy either.'

'Divorce smashes things and affects so many people,' Kate says. 'I see that now. It's like war. Nobody really wins so there has to be a very good reason for it in the first place.'

'So what can we do?' asks Cass. 'They still love each other. There is no good reason in this case.'

Kate hesitates, unwilling to break Guy's confidence. Gemma must be the one to tell Cass their hopes and plans.

'We'll simply have to wait,' she says.

Cass looks at her; she remembers Oliver's words: 'I think it will work as long as nobody interferes,' and pulls herself together.

'OK,' she says cheerfully. 'Shall we have a drink?'

'It's barely three o'clock,' protests Kate.

'So? Is there a rule which says we can't have a drink at three o'clock?'

'And you're driving home.'

'You always did have these frightfully dreary fits

of conscience,' sighs Cass. 'Tea then. And then you can tell me all about Bruno.'

*   *   *

Hardly has she waved Cass off than Oliver drives up and parks outside.

'Do you feel as if you should set this place up as a refuge?' he asks. 'First Jess, then Guy, then Ma— not to mention me.'

'Don't tell me you've been hanging around waiting for her to go?'

'Not quite, but nearly. I simply cannot cope with Pa just at the minute so you must take pity on me. Seriously, the bad news is that Lady T is dead.'

'*Dead?*'

He nods, watching as she mechanically collects the tea things together as if she were in shock.

'But Gemma told me that she'd just been taken ill and Johnnie asked if they'd take Will back to school with the twins.'

'Well, it was another heart attack. She is dead, and it's possible that Jess might seek refuge from all the funeral arrangements.'

Kate sits down at the table. 'It's weird but I feel quite sad. She never much liked me and I was terrified of her but it's just . . .'

'Don't say, "It's the end of an era",' he says, 'or I shall wish I'd gone back to the Rectory. I knew at once just how Pa was going to go on about it. All the memories and the anecdotes and the dear old shipmates.'

Kate can't prevent herself from laughing. 'You are completely heartless.'

'No, I'm not,' he protests. 'I barely knew her. As

218

far as I know I met her for the first time a few days ago.'

She looks at him curiously. 'A few days ago?'

He looks back at her warily. 'Mmm. She was in bed. Guy and Jess and Johnnie had gone out sailing. Sophie took me up to say hello.'

'Really?' She is still watching him, half smiling, half frowning. 'How . . . odd of her.'

'Oh, I don't see why,' he says carelessly. 'I'm very nearly part of the family now, you know.'

'What a fast worker you are,' she observes. 'So you stayed with Sophie while the others went sailing?'

He beams at her. 'Do you have a problem with that?'

She laughs. 'Not a bit. I thought it was Jess you fancied.'

'So? I've never heard that it was against the rules to fancy two women at once.'

'You sound just like your mother. Do you want some tea?'

'That would be kind. Shall I make it? You still look a bit shell-shocked.'

'Yes, please, Ollie,' she says. 'And then come and tell me about Lady T and Jess and Sophie.'

She sits at the table thinking about Lady T and Johnnie, when she'd seen them in the Bedford and the old woman's expression when they'd talked about Juliet and Mike, and then again when she took Jess to lunch to meet them all and how Lady T stared at Jess with such intensity.

Oliver is back with two mugs of tea. 'The thing is that poor old Jess was with her when she died. It's been a huge shock for her. She thinks it's all bound up with her looking like Juliet and so Jess thinks she's partly responsible. It got Lady T a bit worked up about the past and with her weak heart it just pushed her over the top.'

'Oh God, poor Jess,' says Kate. 'I'm beginning to wish I'd never asked her down here.'

'Don't start feeling guilty. I think Jess is loving it on the Tamar, only she might feel that she's in the way just at the moment. I expect all the family will come home for the funeral.'

'Well, of course she can come back here. It's one of the reasons I got it all up and running, though I'm beginning to wish I hadn't bought this place either.'

'Oh, but why? It's a super little house.'

Kate sighs. 'I know it is, but now decisions have got to be made about all sorts of things. I hate making decisions.'

'Do you mean a decision about living here or in St Meriadoc? Does it have to be one or the other? Couldn't you have the best of both worlds? A cottage on the coast and one in the town?'

'It sounds good, doesn't it?' she agrees. 'The perfect answer. Don't think I haven't thought about it. The trouble is it doesn't always work like that. Quite the reverse, in fact. It can be a bit divisive.'

'You mean when you're at one end you feel you should be at the other and vice versa?'

'Something like that. I'd love to be laid-back about it but I know I'd be at St Meriadoc wondering if I ought to be looking after the garden here and when I'm here I'd be worrying about whether I'd left a tap running in St Meriadoc. And the very book I suddenly longed to read would always be in the other place. Oh, I know it sounds completely crazy but I know what I'm like.'

'You're loco, Kate. You know that?'

'Of course I know it. And, anyway, it seems rather silly for one person to have two houses.'

'The problem is which one you'd choose.'

'Exactly. This one at least is mine, and now that Gemma's back and the twins are just up the road at school it's so convenient. And Cass and Tom, too, not far away. And being able to walk into the town.'

'But? I feel that there's a "but" coming.'

'Crazy, isn't it? The last three years have been like a holiday. I've been really happy renting the cottage and being a part of St Meriadoc. After David died there was so much to sort out and wind up. So many decisions and things to come to terms with, like selling the house in Whitchurch, which was far too big for just me. And then I met Bruno through a mutual friend and his cottage was available, and it was as if a whole new life had begun. I suppose it's been rather like a dream and so it couldn't possibly last.'

'Why not?' Oliver asks almost crossly. 'Why do you have to look at it in that negative way? Why should it have to be a dream simply because you've been happy? Why can't happiness be reality for a change? You're still seeing your family and your old friends; you haven't simply turned your back on life. OK, so now you've bought another property, but it's an investment property, so make it work for you. Rent it out. You're only about an hour and a half from here, you'll still be close enough to be part of the scene.'

Kate thinks about what he is saying; it's all quite rational. She tries to pin down the flaw in it but it sounds too foolish to voice it.

'Your problem,' he tells her, reading her mind as

221

usual, 'is that you worry too much.'

'I suppose I feel I'd be rejecting them all, you see. I've got a wonderful chance to be close to them all again but I say "No, thanks". Something like that, anyway.'

'So why did you buy this cottage?'

'Giles was very anxious that I should buy again while the market was so low. I think he was worried about me. He pointed out that I might not always be able to rent the cottage in St Meriadoc or, even if I could, there might come a time when I needed to be less isolated, if I couldn't drive, for instance. This was such a sensible thing to do, he said, and everyone agreed with him. And anyway, I had really good vibes about it, too. Then Jess won David's Award and I suddenly thought that it would be great for her to come down and stay here for a bit. She was taking a year out and it seemed to be such a perfect answer. She had nowhere to go and wanted to come down, and I really believed it was all kind of meant.'

'A sign or a portent?'

She laughs. 'That's right. What I wasn't expecting was that she'd hit it off so spectacularly with the Trehearnes and want to be with them. I'm glad about it—don't think I'm not—but it's rather thrown me. It's great, isn't it, that they've taken to her? But how very sad for poor old Lady T to die just now. What a shock for Jess. The Sunday-out party came to a bit of an abrupt end, apparently.'

Oliver is silent; he is trying to think of some way of raising the subject of the photograph without breaking his promise to Jess.

'Guy was looking well,' he says. 'I think he's weakening, don't you? I think we'll have him back here before too long if only he can decide what he can do. He seemed to be very thick with Johnnie.'

Kate glances quickly at him. 'How d'you mean?'

Oliver shrugs. 'You know. Talking about boats and stuff. He's got a great set-up down there, hasn't he? I love it and I'm no sailor. I like old Johnnie and I've met Fred. So I know the whole gang now. Well, almost. There was Johnnie and Fred and Pa, wasn't there? And Al and Mike and some other guy. Do you know who he was?'

'What other guy?' Kate looks puzzled.

'I can't remember his name now. Johnnie said he was part of the old gang. I think he mentioned that he was invited to the reunion supper. Do you know who was going?'

Kate frowns, trying to remember. 'Johnnie did talk about some ex-submariners going,' she says. 'And then Tom was racking his memory for people who would have known Juliet and Mike. Oh, I know. I think they were going to invite the Mortlakes.'

'Mortlakes?'

'Stephen was a submariner.' Kate is silent for a moment, remembering that Cass had had a brief fling with Stephen Mortlake many years before. 'They live in Buckland Monachorum,' she says. 'I think Stephen was very much part of the gang when they were at Dartmouth.'

'Back in the day?' Oliver drinks some tea.

Kate smiles—and then sighs. 'Yes,' she says. 'Back in the day.'

*   *   *

Later, after Oliver has gone, Bruno phones.

223

'So what happened?' he asks. 'How is Guy? Is he back for good? I hope you realize I've been sitting here all day, wondering what's going on, completely unable to concentrate on my research for this wretched book?'

Kate begins to laugh. 'I wish you'd been here. First there was Guy with all sorts of ideas about sailing schools and goodness knows what. I haven't seen Guy so animated for years. Oh, it was so good to see him, Bruno. I'm not supposed to breathe a word yet but he's definitely coming home. He's got to go back and sort things out first but he's made up his mind. Then he and Gemma set off for London and Cass arrived seeking refuge from Tom and wanting to know what Guy's plans are. It's awful not being able to be open with her but Guy's such a private person and he hates anything going public until he's absolutely certain what he's doing.'

'Well, that's fair enough,' says Bruno. 'Especially in his situation, when there's been this question hanging over his marriage, and Gemma leaving him and taking the boys. He's not likely to want to have cosy chats with his in-laws just at the moment, is he?'

'That's what he said. He hasn't been to see Tom and Cass at all. Tom's not very pleased about it but Cass understands. I shall be so glad to get this over so that she and I can resume our old comfortable relationship. It feels all wrong to be at odds with Cass. Anyway, then Cass left and Oliver rolled up. I was telling him about my dilemma about where I should live.'

There is a little silence.

'And what did he say?' asks Bruno.

She thinks about her conversation with Oliver

224

and condenses it. 'He thinks I should stay in St Meriadoc and rent this place out.'

'Sensible fellow, Oliver,' says Bruno. 'And are you going to?'

'Well,' says Kate hurriedly, 'then, after Oliver left, Jess phoned to ask if she could come back to stay with me for a bit. Poor old Lady T had another heart attack and died yesterday, and Jess is in shock and says that she feels a little bit *de trop* with all the family coming back for the funeral. So of course I've said "yes".'

'Of course,' he agrees.

His voice is warm, full of understanding, and she is seized by a sense of gratitude and love for him.

'I'll be back soon, though,' she says quickly.

'You'd better be,' he says lightly.

*   *   *

When Oliver picks Gemma up from Plymouth station the next day he sees the change in her. She is luminous with happiness and wellbeing, and he grins slyly at her as she slides into the seat beside him.

'Well stocked up for the next few weeks?' he asks as he starts the engine and pulls out of the car park.

She gives a little snort of laughter and digs her elbows into his ribs. 'Shut up,' she says. 'None of your business.'

'So what is my business?'

'Well.' She gazes out at the city as they drive up North Hill towards Mutley Plain. 'You might like to invest in Guy's scheme for our future, of course.'

'Oh God,' he groans. 'I guessed it might come to that.'

Gemma continues to stare out of the window. She squeezes her hands between her knees and remembers Guy's injunction.

'On no account,' Guy said, 'ask Oliver for money. It's bad enough that he's paying the school fees. I know you'll have to tell him why I've decided to give this a go but make certain he knows that it's because of Johnnie's enthusiasm and his willingness to put his money where his mouth is. He believes in it; in me. I don't need any more of Oliver's charity.'

'Actually, it's a very good scheme,' she says now. 'Johnnie's very interested in it.'

'Johnnie? Yes, I could see that something was in the wind. This scheme is to do with boats, of course.'

'Well, of course. It's what Guy does. We've been to see someone in London who's advertising this kind of classic boat sailing experience. You take eight people out for two days or longer and show them what it's like to be on an old-fashioned sailing ship. I've got lots of brochures and stuff to show you.'

'How sweet of you.'

'Don't be like that. It sounds brilliant.'

'And would I be right in assuming that these dear old-fashioned sailing ships are actually state-of-the-art brand-new sailing ships, which cost a very great deal of money?'

There is a little silence. Gemma watches the passing traffic. Oliver pulls up to allow a woman with several small children to cross the road, and glances at his sister.

'How much?' he asks.

Gemma grimaces. 'A new boat costs about four hundred thousand,' she mutters, 'but we'd need half a million to get it all properly started.'

'I suppose if you say it quickly it doesn't sound so terrifying,' he muses, letting out the clutch and driving on.

'That's what it would take to realize Guy's ultimate dream,' she admits, 'but he knows he'll have to cut his cloth. We've got a hundred and eighty-five thousand invested from the sale of the cottage in Brent. Guy would never allow us to touch it because he always hoped that he'd be able to do something like this. He's been trying to persuade Mark to invest in it with him. He thought that if Mark and the bank each matched our share we'd have enough to get it started.'

'But Mark wouldn't play?'

'I think he just likes to keep Guy on a string and now that he's remarried I think it'll never happen.'

'So Guy has decided at last to come back here and give it a go?'

'He knows that the big classic ship option is a bit of a dream. He'll look for a second-hand one but if there's nothing around he'll settle for smaller boats,' she says. 'But this sounds so much fun and we could do it together during term-time, you see. Johnnie told him he could use a couple of his moorings and that he and Fred could help him out occasionally. He was really excited about it.'

'I believe you,' says Oliver.

'He's told Guy that he'd be prepared to invest several thousand in the scheme. Apparently he knows someone who does exactly this kind of thing around the Solent and he can see how well it could work down here. He said it's something he'd love to be involved in.'

Oliver raises his eyebrows. 'Old salts never die,'

227

he remarks. 'They just buy bigger boats.'

He doesn't hurry. The drive over Roborough Down and across the moor will give them the chance to talk in a relaxed and peaceful atmosphere. He's rather impressed that Guy has had such an impact on Johnnie so quickly. Obviously Guy made the most of his opportunity during that day he'd gone out sailing with Johnnie and Jess. He remembers them standing, heads together, at the rugby match and his respect for Guy increases.

'Well, at least Guy's made up his mind,' says Gemma. 'Coming back and being with us all again, and you taking him down to the Tamar and introducing him to them all has completely reinvigorated him. Especially meeting Johnnie and him offering Guy such positive encouragement. It's given him the confidence to go back and give a month's notice to Mark and then return here and try.'

'And how will Mark react?'

'He'll be cross because he's lost control but deep down he'll probably be relieved. I told you that his new wife doesn't like us being in the house while she and Mark live in the flat, and I think she'd like Mark to sell up the whole lot and retire. She's got a thing about travelling.'

'So what shall you tell the APs?'

'Guy says that we can tell them that he's going to come back and he wants to try to get things up and running as soon as he can.' She sighs. 'I rather dread telling Pa.'

'Because he'll be negative?'

Gemma nods. 'It's a big venture. And there will be other questions, about where we're going to live and so on. We can rent, of course, but I just know it'll be difficult.'

'If Johnnie's going for it then Pa will be impressed,' Oliver says. 'Ma will certainly be thrilled. And so am I.'

'Thanks,' she says gratefully. 'I've been so happy all the way down on the train, I can't tell you. But now, as we get closer to telling everyone, I feel my heart sinking. Do you think it'll work, Ol?'

'I can't answer that without a great deal more input. But it sounds as if Guy's put a lot of thought into it and he's not one of your chancer types, is he? Neither is old Johnnie.'

'Guy told me that I was on no account to ask you for any money,' admits Gemma. 'He thinks that it's bad enough that you're paying the school fees. For God's sake don't ever let him know I hinted about it. It's just I'd rather borrow from you than from the bank—assuming they'd lend it. You'd be kinder to us if things aren't going quite according to plan. But Guy was absolutely adamant that I mustn't ask you. So I haven't. OK?'

'But I shall still be allowed to look at the brochures?'

'Of course you will. I'm going to show them to Johnnie.'

'So if I decide that I want to be an investor then how would I approach Guy without involving you?'

Gemma gives him a blinding smile. 'You'd think of something,' she says confidently.

*   *   *

Mist lies thick along the river. It muffles the sound of the water as it creeps into small muddy channels, and mutes the crying of the sea birds as they retreat before the rising tide. In the thorny hedges, complicated cobwebs are swagged and weighted with moisture, trembling in the chill breeze that snakes upriver. Even the boats out on their moorings are invisible.

Jess drives cautiously in the twisting lane, keeping well into the verge, braking now and then as a sharp bend takes her unawares. The mist flows around the car so that she feels as though she is alone in this tiny capsule, travelling through white, damp, empty space.

She turns the wheel, stamping on the brakes, as the yellow glare of headlights flares in her eyes. Heart stampeding, she edges the car even closer into the twiggy, unforgiving hedge, hears the scratching of paint. The bigger vehicle sweeps past and vanishes into the wall of fog with a short sharp blast of the horn.

Jess sits quite still for a moment, her heart still bumping. Slowly, cautiously, she sets the car in motion and moves forward, gripping the steering wheel, shoulders tense. She realizes, with a little thrill of fear, that she might miss the left turn at the junction; she might simply drive straight across the lane and into the opposite hedge. She peers anxiously through the windscreen, looking for the single finger post that stands on the corner at the narrow junction of the two lanes.

She gives a little scream as a large dark shape crosses within a few feet of the bonnet of her car and she wrenches the steering wheel to the left so that the car bumps up onto the grassy bank. Trembling, she climbs out and walks forward over the grass, straining her ears for the least sound, her hands outstretched as though she were blind. Suddenly her left hand touches rough, splintery wood and, peering up, she sees the signpost. She is at the junction, and the lane is crossing directly in front of her.

She climbs back into the car, edges up beside the post with her window down, listening for the sounds of traffic as she turns into the lane that will take her up to the main Tavistock road. She takes a deep breath of relief, driving slowly and still hugging the hedgeline, but feeling happier now. The mist is thinning as the lane climbs out of the river valley to higher ground and she feels more confident. She is able to allow her mind to run more freely over the events of the past few days, since Rowena died.

'The last thing anybody wants,' Johnnie said, 'is that you should feel in any way that it was your fault. None of us could have imagined that she would get so excited about seeing you. Once Kate had told us that you'd won the Award and that you were Juliet's granddaughter she couldn't wait to meet you. If you ask me, you brought her a great deal of happiness. She was never happier than when she could be talking about Al, looking at the photographs, and remembering those happy days.'

He looked at Sophie for confirmation, for support, and she hastened to agree with him.

'And, anyway, we'd been warned that she was on borrowed time,' she said. 'She'd had a couple of those attacks, you know, before you arrived on the scene.'

'She looked so happy,' remembered Johnnie, 'with you kneeling beside her and I heard her talking about Al. I think it was all for the best. Please don't be upset, Jess.'

They were so sweet to her, but they didn't know the truth—though she suspected that Sophie was puzzled by certain events.

'There's no problem about you staying here,' Sophie said to her later when Johnnie was out. 'Really there isn't.'

'But I shall feel a bit of an intruder,' Jess said quickly. 'And you'll have a very full house.' The thought of being at such close quarters to Johnnie's daughters, knowing how she'd been with Rowena on the occasion of both of her latest attacks, was too awful to contemplate. 'Will you tell them that I was with her?'

Sophie shook her head. 'Johnnie feels it's better not to complicate it with the thing about Al. The girls don't really know much about all that past history and my guess is that Johnnie thinks it's more sensible to keep it simple. They were all expecting it, you know. It hasn't been a great shock. What will you do?'

'I'll go back to Kate. She's invited me and it will be good to have some more time with her. I'd like to come to the funeral, of course.'

'I hope you'll both come,' Sophie said.

Jess reaches the turning onto the Tavistock road and heads towards the town. The mist is clearing and she can see the moors away on the horizon, wreathed all about with drifting cloud. How long ago it seems since she first arrived to find Oliver waiting at the door and Flossie, tail wagging, at the gate. She drives into Chapel Street, where Kate and Flossie are waiting for her.

'I hope you don't mind me being early,' Jess says anxiously when she's hugged Kate and made a fuss of Flossie. 'Some of the family were arriving later this morning and I just felt a bit uncomfortable being there at such a personal time.'

'Of course I don't mind,' says Kate. 'It's great to have you back again. I was just being very lazy and sitting over my pot of breakfast tea. Why don't you take your stuff up and then come and join me?'

'I'd like that,' says Jess gratefully.

Upstairs she looks round her room with a sense of relief and recognition. Nothing will be demanded of her here and she feels some of the tension of the last week slipping away from her. Jess unpacks her bag, unwraps David's painting and places it carefully on its easel. She stands quite still, staring at it: the old stone bridge over the river, and the part of the bank beneath it where the group of foxgloves grow against the sun-warmed stone; the sunlight that glimmers on the water, which seems to flow and splash even as she looks at it. The deft, tender strokes that reproduce the foxgloves, the texture of the crumbling stone and the tiny springing cushions of moss that cling to it.

Bless you for everything. It's been perfect. Love D.

Jess takes a deep breath. She unzips the case that holds her laptop, slips out two photographs and goes back downstairs.

Kate is sitting at the big table in the living-room, reading a letter, drinking tea. Jess doesn't say a word but simply places the photographs beside her. Kate puts the cup carefully in its saucer and stares at the first photo. She is quite silent for a few moments and then she picks it up. The bride is beautiful, with flowers in her long shining hair. She wears a simple white dress with a high boned-lace collar and long lace sleeves. She gazes at the camera with a kind of pleased surprise. The groom,

233

in full dress uniform, proud and confident, stands protectively beside her with his hand on the hilt of his sword.

'How extraordinary,' she murmurs. 'Juliet and Mike.'

She continues to gaze at the photograph and Jess can tell that it is bringing other memories and images with it.

'Lady T gave it to me,' she says. It's not quite a lie; Jess feels certain that Rowena would have given it to her if she'd asked for it. 'I can't get over the likeness. I've never seen it before. Daddy didn't have much in the way of memorabilia and on the few occasions that I met Granny she never talked about the past.'

But now Kate is picking up the second photograph and exclaiming, laughing.

'Gosh, look, that's Tom. And is that Johnnie with him? Oh, and that's Mike, isn't it?'

Jess waits, standing behind Kate's chair, willing her to recognize the two men she has not yet been able to identify.

'And this,' says Kate pointing, 'is Stephen Mortlake.'

Jess leans forward eagerly. 'Stephen Mortlake?'

'He was a friend of Tom's. He's one of the old gang. I think he and his wife have been invited to the reunion thrash. It's a pity that it will have to be postponed for a while but I'm sure you'll meet him sooner or later. And this is Freddy Grenvile, Johnnie's cousin.'

'Yes,' says Jess. Her heart beats quickly and she sits down in the chair beside Kate's. 'It's so odd fitting the pieces together like this. So tell me about Stephen Mortlake. And Freddy Grenvile.'

234

Gemma sits in Costa in Brook Street drinking a latte and staring out of the window. She needs space to consider things: to think of Guy coming home and wonder whether his project will be successful. Telling the APs was just as tricky as she'd suspected it would be, and Oliver, who had dashed off to a meeting in London, was not at hand to support her. She'd done her best to explain the scheme but Pa would keep interrupting with negative comments, though Ma, as Ollie predicted, was delighted. It was only as a last resort that she'd descended to the ploy—also suggested by Ollie—of saying: 'Well, Johnnie Trehearne thinks it's a really good idea. Guy talked it through with him and he's suggested that we can use two of his moorings. He's even hinted that he'd like to invest in it.'

There was a complete silence. She could see that Ma was trying hard not to burst out laughing at the expression on Pa's face. He looked baffled, clearly wishing he could backtrack a bit now he knew that Johnnie viewed the scheme in such a positive light. She could see that he'd boxed himself into a corner—his irritation at the way she'd set about their problems was colouring his opinion of everything she did—but she wanted him to be pleased that Guy was coming home and that they'd be together.

'Guy would be able to explain it better than I can,' she said quickly, trying to let him off the hook. 'When he tells you about it you'll probably see it a bit differently. Have a look at these brochures we got in London and then you might get a clearer idea of it.'

She couldn't help remembering what Ollie told her in the pub about Charlotte, and their parents' grief and remorse, and suddenly she felt a huge need for Pa and Ma's complete approval and encouragement; longed to be able to make up just a little for the tragedy and for causing them such anxiety.

She'd watched them set off together this morning for old Lady T's funeral, looking suitably smartly sombre, and she'd borrowed Ma's car to come into Tavistock so that she could sit here alone, allowing herself the joy of thinking of Guy coming home and them both starting out on this exciting new venture. There would be difficulties, of course, and times when Guy would be stressed and silent and she'd have to jolly him along, but at least they'd be in it together.

'Don't say anything to the boys yet,' he warned her. 'Just in case it takes a bit longer than we think. I've got to explain to Dad and it's only fair to work out a month's notice. I can't leave him in the lurch. Try to think of where we could live. We'll have to rent. Have a look around Bere Alston. That would be ideal.'

Gemma sighs with impatience at the prospect of another month without him and glances round her. At the next table a good-looking man in his mid-thirties is sitting working at his laptop, his expression intent and preoccupied; beyond him, in the corner, two middle-aged women seem to be having some kind of business meeting with mobile phones at the ready and notes spread over the table. An exhausted-looking girl, with a baby in a pushchair, is trying to persuade her noisy toddler

236

that he wants to sit quietly and drink his milkshake instead of running about disturbing everyone.

Gemma finishes her latte and gathers her belongings together. The man at the next table glances up and catches her eye. There is that brief moment, the tiny flicker of recognition, in which each acknowledges that the other is an attractive person and accepts that this quick assessing glance might lead to something more; something fun and exciting.

Usually Gemma would allow herself to smile a little, wait for some casual comment to skewer the moment so that a light flirtation might be allowed to develop. Instead she thinks of Pa, and of Charlotte, and she picks up her bag and goes quickly out into the street.

*   *   *

Sitting at the back of the church, Kate feels the ghosts jostling again at her elbow. She knows that Jess is very on edge and they've agreed to slip in and sit right at the back and leave immediately afterwards.

'We don't have to go back to the house, do we?' Jess asked, clearly agitated, and Kate reassured her that she is very happy to keep a low profile.

'After all,' she told her, 'I didn't know the Trehearnes all that well and you've only just met them. It's Tom who is the real connection with the past.'

So here they are, sitting right at the back, watching people filing in with suitably solemn faces, including Cass and Tom, who are now sitting well forward. Kate stares at their backs while other

237

similar scenes unroll on the screen of her mind: Charlotte's funeral, and David's. Even as she remembers, she is aware of the tension of the girl sitting beside her and the way she glances intently at everyone who passes them.

Kate thinks about the photograph and wonders why it is so important. Natural, one might think, to be interested in your grandfather's youth, but Jess never knew her grandfather.

'He and Daddy really fell out big time,' she said. 'They simply didn't get on and that's why Daddy came back to England. He'd always wanted to join the army anyway, but I felt that it must have been very hard on Granny. We went back once or twice when I was a baby and a little girl but I can hardly remember it. Then, after Daddy died, Mum and I went out to Australia to visit some of her relations and we saw Granny again then. She was great fun but a bit kind of remote. Perhaps she couldn't bear to think about Daddy dying so young. Of course Mike had died by then, too, but she didn't want to talk about either of them.'

Kate finds it interesting that sometimes Jess calls Juliet 'Granny' but always refers to her grandfather as 'Mike'. Remembering the conversation they'd had about the photograph, Kate nudges Jess's arm.

'Stephen Mortlake,' she murmurs, and Jess looks up swiftly at the grey-haired man who follows his wife into a pew and sits down, looking around him. Cass, glancing back, sees him and gives him the tiniest of smiles.

Briefly Kate sees the ghosts of the young Cass and Stephen superimposed upon the black backs of the congregation—and then there is a little commotion and bustle and Rowena is with them,

238

being borne towards the altar followed by the family, and Kate stands with Jess beside her and opens her service sheet.

*   *   *

'I hate funerals,' Jess says, as they drive back to Tavistock. She leans forward, hugging her knees, not far from tears.

'That's because you were so young when someone really important to you died,' says Kate. 'It's a shock at that age to have to face the fact that we are not immortal.'

She wonders if this is true. She actually has no problems with funerals, hoping that whoever has died is now in a happier, more peaceful place. It's weddings she hates. Happy girls dressed in silly expensive clothes advancing towards nervous, hopeful men in uncomfortable suits, all believing that they are entering the world of Happy Ever After and making promises they cannot hope to keep.

'Don't do it,' she wants to shout. 'It's all a myth.'

She doesn't say this to Jess.

'It's terrible,' she says instead, 'to be made aware of the awful finality of death when you're only thirteen.'

To her horror, Jess begins to weep. She draws her feet up onto the edge of the seat, wraps her arms around her knees and hides her face in them. Sobs shake her body, and Kate wonders whether she should stop the car or whether it is better to drive on. Instinctively she carries on; she will take Jess up on to the moor in the hope that its immense majesty and sense of infinity will soothe and heal

239

her as it has healed her, Kate, in the past. They hurry through the town, out onto the Princetown road and pass Mount House School. At the cattle grid Kate turns left onto the little track beneath Cox Tor and reverses the car into a small unused quarry.

In the back of the car, Flossie begins to whine eagerly. Jess raises her head; her face is blotched and red and her eyes are swollen. She stares around her.

'Come on,' says Kate. 'Let's take Flossie for a walk up to the tor.'

Jess's eyebrows shoot up; she almost manages a smile. 'In these shoes?'

Kate looks down at herself, forgetting that they are more smartly dressed than usual.

'I've got some walking shoes under the seat,' she says, 'and gumboots in the back. We're about the same size. It'll do our heads good to look right out. It never fails to give a sense of perspective.'

They change their shoes, scramble up the side of the quarry, and set off towards the tor.

'Sorry about that,' mutters Jess. 'It takes me unawares. Silly, isn't it? Not at the funeral itself—I was OK with that—but afterwards I just suddenly thought about him, how he was, and I just couldn't bear it. I still miss him just as much as ever. And now . . .'

'Now?' prompts Kate gently when Jess falls silent.

Jess shakes her head; she crosses her arms, hugging herself, and stops to look around her. Flossie has raced ahead, scrambling among the scree and the ancient hut circles, following a trail. Kate stops too. She looks out to the west, towards

240

Cornwall and the sheltered, magical valley of St Meriadoc, and Bruno in his strange stone house on the cliff.

Jess has scrambled higher now and is looking away to the south, far beyond the granite jumble of Pew Tor and the slate roofs of Horrabridge, where a narrow shining ribbon snakes inland from the sea.

'Is that the Tamar?' she calls, gesturing with her arm. 'That river?'

Kate climbs up to join her and they stand together looking towards Plymouth.

'Yes, that's the Tamar,' says Kate. She watches the girl's face with its oddly wistful expression. 'You know, I think you've lost your heart to that river.'

Just for a moment Kate thinks that Jess is going to confide in her, to tell her the real secret, but instead she smiles and gives a little nod.

'I think I have,' she says.

TAMAR

After the funeral it seems as if everything goes into mourning for Rowena. The long spell of fine autumn weather changes: Atlantic fronts sweep in from the west, bruise-coloured clouds piling and toppling into downpours of rain. Rivers run high and fast, burst their banks, and smash small ancient bridges. In waterside communities, cottages are flooded and shops and cafés are under water; the local news is filled evening after evening with woeful stories of damaged stock and ruined carpets. Westerlies of gale force propensities sink small boats and fell trees, which crush cars beneath their

241

flailing boughs.

Then, suddenly, all is quiet again. The storms race away to the east and a waning moon, cast about with a shawl of stars, rises in the clear night sky. The temperature drops, hoar frost whitens bare twigs and fallen leaves, and puddles creak and splinter underfoot as ice begins to form. Unprecedented low temperatures for early December are forecast and there are hints of a white Christmas.

In the drawing-room, Johnnie switches off the television and looks at Sophie, who is sitting in a big armchair with her legs tucked beneath her, writing a letter. Her fine fair hair falls forward across her cheeks and she frowns slightly as she writes. He settles himself more comfortably in the corner of the sofa, reaching a hand to Popps, who is curled beside him. Popps is missing Rowena and is trading on it by demanding more attention and extra treats. Sophie is allowing her to get away with it because she feels that, in ministering to Popps, Johnnie is allowing himself his own form of grieving.

'She's missing Mother, poor old Popps. How she loved this little dog, didn't she, Sophes? She had such a soft spot for the dogs.' And he'd give Popps another little treat and stroke her head and murmur to her.

'Snow's forecast,' says Johnnie. 'Going to be another cold night. Black ice warning.' He chuckles. 'How Mother hated that expression. Black ice. "What does it *mean*?" she'd say. "How ridiculous!"' And he chuckles again with affection.

Sophie nods. The house seems oddly empty without Rowena's stringent, critical presence, and she is glad that Oliver will be over tomorrow—and

242

Jess is coming back, too.

'I wonder if it'll be a bit cold out in the sail loft for Jess,' Johnnie says, as if he reads Sophie's mind. 'Should she be in the house, d'you think?'

'I did mention it.' Sophie puts aside her letter. 'Especially after she's had that wretched cold since the funeral, but she really wants to be out there. I think she needs to be, somehow.'

Johnnie looks puzzled and Sophie casts about for some reason that Johnnie might be able to accept. She believes that Jess is coming to terms with something personal, something private, and that the sail loft is a good place for her to be while she's doing it.

'Her work,' she says. 'You know what creative people are like. They need their own space. She's trying to get a portfolio together while she's here. The sail loft must be a perfect place for that, wouldn't you say?'

'Yes, of course.' Johnnie agrees. 'I hadn't thought of that aspect of it. And she can come inside if the weather gets colder. Old Fred's back this week, too.'

He looks thoughtful and Sophie frowns.

'I still think it was rather odd of him, just taking off like that,' she says.

'He said something about meeting up with an old friend.' Johnnie shrugs evasively. 'You know Fred. Fairly typical.'

'I suppose so. Oh, and Oliver's coming over tomorrow.'

'Good.' Johnnie sits forward. 'I want to talk to him about this scheme of Guy's. Oliver's emailed me a few things. I really think it could work.'

'I hope so,' she says. 'It may well be a great thing

for all of us. It's something we can all be a part of, isn't it? You, me and Fred. Even Will, when he's around.'

'It would bring new life in,' Johnnie says. 'People coming and going and all sorts of offshoots like the RYA courses, which Fred and I are qualified to run, and skippering the boats on the day-runs. We could all take a turn at that. Lots to talk about, of course, but I feel very positive about it. I can't wait for Fred to come back so we can tell him about it.'

Sophie laughs. 'He'll be in his element. And it'll be so nice for Guy to have you both encouraging him. So long as the figures stack up.'

'Oliver's looking into all of that,' says Johnnie. 'He's got a head on his shoulders, that fellow. No wonder he's made a packet.'

Sophie feels a little thrill of pride. 'I haven't actually discussed it with him,' she says, unable to resist talking about him but not quite knowing what to say. 'He's an odd mix, isn't he?'

'Well, he's certainly sharp when it comes to business. He seems such a laid-back kind of chap as a rule and then you realize that under that amusing veneer is quite a tough nut.'

'I think he is,' she agrees. 'He was telling me that one of the things he's doing is providing the seed capital for a group of young scientists who have found a cheaper way to make solar panels. To quote Oliver: "It's green, they're great, and we shall all make money!" He's insisted that they form a limited company and he has a seat on the board. He says it's his job to provide the seed capital and the inventor's job to make things grow.'

'Sounds good to me.' Johnnie glances across at Sophie as he gently pulls Popps' ears, wondering whether to take a more personal direction. She catches his eye and smiles defensively, not ready yet for confidences.

'Time for Popps' last outs,' she says casually.

'I'll do it.' Johnnie takes the hint and encourages Popps down from the sofa, and they go out.

Sophie folds the sheets of her letter and tidies the drawing-room, piling the cushions together and putting the guard in front of the fire, and goes out to the kitchen. She guesses that Johnnie knows exactly what she is feeling but she can't bring herself to talk about those emotions just yet. She is still trying to form a plan that will enable her and Oliver to move forward without making any drastic changes to their lives. It is very difficult, with Oliver based in London, to allow the relationship to take the usual course of dating, and it would be so odd, now, to arrange to meet him at a restaurant, say, or even in a pub. It's as if they've already moved far beyond that—yet she hardly knows him. Now, with his connection to Guy's scheme and Johnnie's enthusiasm for the project, he's become part of the family and it's even more difficult to play it in a more normal way. She's glad that Johnnie hasn't questioned her or teased her; he approves of Oliver and he's on her side, and that's all that matters at the moment.

*   *   *

Johnnie strolls across the lawn. The air is icy and the moon's reflection swims clear and cold in the calm water of the river. Higher up the valley an owl hoots, a long wavering cry. He stands at the balustrade in the sea garden and stares towards the

245

sea. He thinks about other Trehearnes who have stood here, waiting and watching, and he puts out a hand to Circe, whose skirt is smooth and slippery to his touch.

Turning, he glances up at Rowena's window as if he expects to see her light shining out as usual.

'Goodnight, Mother,' he mutters and, calling to Popps, he goes back across the grass to the house.

*   *   *

When Sophie sees Oliver again she is seized with a most uncharacteristic fit of shyness.

'Hi,' she says, opening the back door to him, leading the way into the kitchen. 'Johnnie's in the Growlery getting on with the book but I was about to encourage him with coffee. Would you like some?'

He nods, and the amusement in his eyes suggests that he quite understands the reason for the shyness and isn't going to embarrass her by drawing attention to it.

'How is Johnnie?' he asks. 'Rowena's death can't exactly have been a shock but he must be feeling it.'

'He does. We both do,' she answers as she fills the kettle. 'She was such a major presence. It feels really weird without her around somewhere. I think he's working on the book to take his mind off it.'

'Guy's scheme will take his mind off it,' Oliver assures her. He puts a laptop case on the table. 'Johnnie and I have been exchanging emails but I think he forgets that I'm not a sailing man so I need some translation. But it's looking good and I like Johnnie's ideas of diversification. Old Unk, the chap who took me into his business, used to say that

246

to be successful you have to have a widget.'

'A widget?'

'Mmm. The crucial thing around which the business is built. In this case it'll be the boat itself, of course, but the more things we can think of to utilize the widget the better it'll be. Johnnie says that he and Fred are Instructor Members for the RYA, which he seems to think will be a positive asset. What exactly does it mean?'

Sophie's shyness has quite disappeared now. She leans with her back to the Aga rail and crosses her arms.

'It means that both of them are qualified to teach people to sail, which might be very useful to Guy, although I'm sure he'll want to become qualified, too.'

'Hang on. Qualified by whom? By this RYA?'

'Yes. It used to be called the Royal Yachting Association but they call themselves the RYA now. They're the body appointed by the Government to issue certificates of competence and teaching certificates. If you weren't such a landlubber you'd know that they're very highly respected and their certificates are recognized all over the world. Johnnie could use *Alice*, and Fred could use his boat, come to that. It's something they've often done as volunteers but at their ages they wouldn't want to take the responsibility of trying to make it work commercially. You and Guy running the show will give them the chance to become much more involved, won't it?'

'It sounds like it, but I'd have to check it all out properly. Insurance and so on. And Johnnie would be happy with all these people passing through? He's really thought about it?'

'He'd be in his element.' She turns round as the kettle begins to boil and pushes it to one side while she puts coffee in the percolator. 'He's at his best when the family comes to stay but, now that the children are older, visits have to be geared to the school holidays, so it's not like it used to be when they were little and everyone was coming and going a lot. I think with Rowena gone he's going to notice the draught and this would be a perfect solution.'

'And you?'

'Well, I'd love it, too,' she begins, and then hesitates. She's implying that she'll be staying here, that they won't be together, and she feels confused. She makes the coffee, tells herself not to be a fool, and turns to look directly at him. 'I want us to be together somehow,' she says firmly. 'At least, I think I do. But I still can't see how it is to be done.'

He comes round the table to her, puts his arms around her and kisses her. She holds on to him tightly and then relaxes.

'We'll sort it out,' he says lightly, letting her go, and at once she is full of happiness and relief. He seems to understand her so well, and she feels that she can trust him. She senses that he will allow their love to develop at its own pace, embracing the people around them and the events that are taking place. There will be no dramatics, no upheavals, and she is profoundly grateful. There's been a sense of sadness and emptiness since the funeral, but Oliver brings the prospect of change and purpose that is all a part of this exciting new love growing between them.

'Go and say hello to Johnnie,' she says, 'and tell him coffee's ready. And then you can show us how far you've got.'

'You'll stay with us, won't you?' asks Johnnie. 'While we're getting all this sorted out? Have you got a bic for Popps, Sophie? She's been such a good girl all morning.'

He pours the coffee, pushes a mug towards Oliver, and sits down at the table.

'Well, that would be very kind.' Oliver looks pleased. 'I'd like that.'

'I think we all would,' says Johnnie with a sly glance at Sophie, who is giving Popps a biscuit. 'Tom and Cass won't think we're poaching?'

'You're joking. My father has quite enough on his plate with Gemma staying with them.'

'But old Tom must be absolutely thrilled with this scheme, isn't he? Of course, he was never a great sailing man but, even so, if it gets Guy and his family back home again it's got to be good news.'

'I'm sure he'll be very pleased,' agrees Oliver, 'as long as the scheme is viable. It's got to pay its way.'

'It would be wonderful,' says Johnnie, 'getting another boat or two out on the river. People going to sea, learning to sail. Wouldn't it make a great postscript to my book? Another generation working the river. Young Will growing up and being a part of it. And Guy's boys, too. What could be better than to be part of such an enterprise?'

Oliver smiles at Johnnie's infectious enthusiasm and wishes Guy was there to witness it.

'It's sad,' he says politely, 'that your mother won't be here to see it all happening.'

Johnnie looks thoughtful. 'Probably just as well,' he says with devastating honesty. 'To be perfectly frank, my mother never quite trusted anybody's ideas but her own. We'd have had the devil of a job getting her to see the possibilities. She was very protective about the old place and I think she'd have been nervous about one or two aspects of our scheme. Not surprising at her age but, well, as it happens, it's worked out for the best. She liked things done her way but now it's time for change.'

'"The generations of living things pass in a short time,"' quotes Oliver idly, '"and like runners hand on the torch of life."'

'Yes,' says Johnnie, after a moment, 'that's exactly it. Who said that?'

'Lucretius,' says Oliver.

"Course it was,' says Johnnie. 'So what have you got to show us on that smart-looking laptop? Let's have some more coffee and get down to work.'

*　　　*　　　*

'It can work,' Oliver says to Sophie. Johnnie, having studied spreadsheets and specifications of various classic boats, has gone back to the Growlery taking Popps with him. 'I don't mean Guy's scheme. I mean us. We don't have to be conventional to make a relationship work.'

'I've been thinking about it,' admits Sophie. 'I even wondered whether we could have our own quarters in the sail loft, but Johnnie has plans for it being a kind of clubhouse for beginners to learn the rudiments of sailing before they actually take to the water.'

'A kind of perpetual *Swallows and Amazons*,' murmurs Oliver. 'I can just see it. Dear old Guy must think he's died and gone to heaven.'

250

'What luck that you brought him here,' agrees Sophie. 'It's certainly a marriage made in heaven.'

'D'you mean us?'

'No. Well, yes, in a way,' says Sophie, flustered. 'I just meant that putting Johnnie and Guy together was a miracle.'

'All thanks to Jess, really. She started it all.' Oliver thinks about the photograph. 'Something's bothering Jess, but I don't know what it is. Do you?'

Sophie shakes her head. 'I knew there was something going on right from the beginning when Johnnie saw Kate in the Bedford and she told him about Jess winning the Award and about her being Juliet and Mike's granddaughter. Rowena began to be really quite odd after that. Very preoccupied and secretive, and getting all those photographs together of the parties in the sea garden, and of the boys when they were young at Dartmouth. You remember I told you, Johnnie said he thought that Rowena was just enjoying the opportunity to talk about Al.'

'But you didn't believe that was true?'

'Not entirely. I thought it might be more to do with the fact that Al died in a drowning accident and I wondered if there might have been something going on. You know?'

'What sort of thing?'

'Well, it sounds a bit fanciful but look at it like this. Al and Mike are bosom pals and they both fancy Juliet but it's Mike who gets her. Supposing there's a bit more to it than that and they have a row about it when they're out sailing and Al goes over the side?'

Oliver raises his eyebrows. 'Goodness.'

'Well, it sounds very dramatic,' says Sophie

251

defensively, 'but I just know that there was something going on.'

'But if Rowena suspected that Mike killed her son, would she be particularly keen to meet Jess?'

'I can't quite see *any* reason why Rowena was so anxious to meet Jess,' says Sophie frankly. 'That's the whole point. She's a sweet kid—I like her—but I still say it's a bit odd. And now Rowena's dead.'

There's a silence.

'So do you wish Jess wasn't coming back?' asks Oliver.

'Good grief, no,' says Sophie. 'I told you, I really like her. And I feel terribly sorry for her. She was so thrilled to be here, where everything happened, and then Rowena had that attack and poor old Jess was really upset. And then, of course, she was there when Rowena died.'

'Yes. Actually, I was surprised that Jess was so keen to come back.'

'So was I. But I'm glad, too. Perhaps we'll find out what this mystery is.'

'You definitely believe that there's a mystery?'

'Yes,' says Sophie firmly. 'I do. I thought she might have said something to you.'

'I know less than nothing about it all,' says Oliver, remembering his promise. 'Apart from my old pa being a member of the group way back when. I'm not much help, I'm afraid. Perhaps, now that Rowena is dead, Jess might be a bit more forthcoming.'

'She might be. Anyway, let's forget all that for moment. I'm glad Johnnie's asked you to stay. Have you got any stuff with you?'

'I have. I drove down from London, left very early and came straight here, so my bag's in the car.'

'Very convenient. Let's go and sort out a room for you. Are you sure you'll be happy in this rather communal atmosphere? Jess will be in and out, and Fred, when he gets back.'

'I rather like it. My happiest time was when Unk and I were getting the business up and running. A friend of ours had written a very successful series of books for children called *Percy the Parrot*, which was made into an iconic TV programme. I had this idea of making a soft, cuddly Percy the Parrot toy and it just took off. There were T-shirts and mugs and all sorts of spin-offs. Even Unk was astounded by its success. His niece and her daughter and our designer, we all practically lived together, bouncing ideas off each other, making things buzz. As it grew and became successful we took on more and more staff and started to delegate, so that all that fun side of it became less and less necessary. The original team gradually split up after a few years and then Unk died. It had got too big, too impersonal, and that's when I got out.'

'I don't think this will be like that, will it?' asks Sophie anxiously.

'No, no,' he assures her. 'This is quite a different proposition. I can see young Will and Guy's boys coming into it and taking over when the time comes. We're definitely in for the long haul.'

'Sounds good to me,' says Sophie happily.

*   *   *

The temperature drops again; there is a brief light fall of snow.

Jess drives very carefully in the icy lanes though

253

she is still aware of the bright berries in the hedgerow and the sharp black thorns. She would like to get out and take some photographs but she is anxious to keep going lest more snow should fall and she should get stuck. Despite the anxieties that flutter in her mind, her instinct tells her that she is doing the right thing; that as a part of this story, it is her turn to take another step that will move her right into the heart of it.

She feels both terror and exhilaration and, as she drives around the curve in the lane and sees the river, dazzling in the brilliant sunshine with its two bridges slung across its shining width, her heart leaps up with joy. How strange and wonderful is this strong sense of home-coming. She turns right by the finger post at the little junction and drives down the steep hill, crosses the lane and begins the final descent to the river.

Johnnie comes to meet her, Popps bouncing and barking beside him, and he gives her a hug, his face alight with welcome.

'I'm glad you've come back to us,' he says. 'I thought you might be put off, you know.'

'Oh, no,' she says, smiling up at him. 'How could I be? Only it was awful, of course . . .'

She dithers, not wanting to sound too happy when Johnnie's mother is so recently dead, but so pleased to see this warm-hearted, kindly man.

'Awful,' he agrees. 'Terrible. But she was ill, Jess. We mustn't forget that. Now, come in. Sophie and Oliver have gone to do a big shop in Tavistock just in case the weather gets worse, but you'll be needing a cup of tea to warm you up. Sophie says that you'd still like to stay in the sail loft even though it's so cold. She's put an extra heater in for you.'

'But you must let me pay towards the heating and food costs,' Jess says firmly. 'It's bad enough me coming to stay, without asking you to pay for my upkeep. Honestly . . .'

'Nonsense,' he says at once. 'You're one of the family now, you know . . .'

And they argue amicably about it as they go into the warm kitchen.

'Mother hated it in here,' says Johnnie. 'She could never see why Sophie and the children all congregate here. It's nicest now when it gets the late-afternoon sun.' He pushes the kettle onto the hotplate and turns round to smile at her. 'What's that you've got?'

She's sliding the photographs out of her big bag and now she pushes them towards him.

'Rowena gave them to me,' she says. It's not true but it doesn't really matter. The moment has come: it is now or never. 'I love this one.'

She indicates the top one, the wedding photo, and he leans forward to look at it. His expression is cautious.

'Such a beautiful girl,' he murmurs. 'And you're so like her. I'm glad Mother gave it to you. She was fiercely possessive about these, you know.'

'Perhaps it was because she knew that I'd never really known Juliet and Mike,' answers Jess, watching him. 'I'd never seen any picture of them when they were young. Daddy didn't have anything. He and Mike really fell out, you know. They didn't get on at all.'

Johnnie frowns, still staring at the photograph. Jess moves it so that the other one is exposed.

'She gave me this one, too.'

255

The kettle begins to whistle but Johnnie doesn't move. He stares down at the group of young happy faces and his own face grows sad and anxious. He takes a deep breath and turns to make the tea.

'I know who you all are now,' Jess says. But he keeps his back to her. 'This is Al and this is Mike and this one is Stephen Mortlake. And this is you, isn't it?'

He turns at last and stares at the photograph. He nods. 'Yes, that's me.'

'And this is Tom and that one's Fred?'

He nods and she heaves a great sigh and picks the photos up.

'I needed to know, you see.'

'Yes,' he says. 'I can understand that. But do you mean to say that my mother knew the truth all the time?'

Jess smiles at him compassionately. 'She thought she did but she'd got the wrong man. She thought it was Al.'

He frowns, trying to puzzle it out. 'What did she say to you?'

'She showed me lots of photos of all of you when you were young but this was the one she was leading up to. She was very clever. She hoped that I might recognize someone.'

'Recognize someone? How could you? Well, Mike, perhaps. You might have seen photos of him as a young man, but how could you possibly have recognized anyone else?'

Jess looks at him, remembering. 'It was a terrific shock,' she says quietly, 'but her hunch was right. But by then I'd become suspicious, you see. She was so intense about it all; asking questions about Daddy. I didn't recognize any of you but there's one

256

face there that is so much like his at about that age that I gave a kind of gasp and then I knew I'd given the game away. She saw my shock and I deliberately misled her and pointed to a face I didn't know and said, "Who's that?"' She gives a little groan. 'It couldn't have been a worse choice.'

'It was Al,' he says.

She nods. 'She was absolutely jubilant. She was waiting for it and hoping for it, and the shock of it sent her into that terrible attack.'

'Oh my God!'

'I felt so guilty and ashamed. I was terrified of seeing her again and of what she would say. And when I did see her again that was all she wanted to hear me say: that Daddy was Al's son.'

'And you did?'

Again Jess nods. There are tears in her eyes. 'She looked so ill, but she was so happy. She thought I was Juliet, you see. She said, "It was Al's son, wasn't it?" and I just nodded and put my head down on her wrist so that she couldn't see my face, and then she died.'

Johnnie comes swiftly round the table and puts his arm round her. He presses his cheek against her head and she leans into him, weeping.

'Poor Jess,' he says. 'Poor little Jess.'

'I had to say something,' she sobs. 'You've all been so kind. I'm sorry.'

His arm tightens round her. 'It's not for you to be sorry,' he says. 'Will you give me just a very little time to sort things out, Jess? I promise you it's going to be fine.'

She puts up a hand to grasp his own, nodding, wiping her cheeks with the knuckles of her free hand. Popps suddenly begins to bark, bouncing out of her basket and running to the door, and Johnnie straightens up.

'Damn,' he says. 'That'll be Oliver and Sophie back. Are you OK?'

Jess nods, sliding the photos into her bag, slipping from her chair. 'I'll just go and tidy up,' she says, and disappears in the direction of the little cloakroom.

Johnnie goes back to his tea-making, takes some mugs down from the dresser. Sophie and Oliver come in, laden with bags.

'The forecast isn't good,' says Sophie cheerfully. 'We might get snowed in. Thank goodness Jess has arrived safely.'

'Just got here,' says Johnnie. 'I'm making some tea.'

'It's freezing,' says Oliver. 'And me with my London clothes.'

'There are plenty of spare jerseys,' says Sophie. 'Oh, hi, Jess. How are you?'

'I'm good,' says Jess, embracing Sophie and then Oliver. 'It's great to be back. I'm totally determined to try to get some work done.'

'In this weather?' Sophie shivers. 'Not many flowers around at this time of the year. Listen, are you sure you want to be in the sail loft? There are bedrooms going spare, you know.'

Jess glances quickly, anxiously, at Johnnie. 'I do, really,' she begins. 'I love it out there.'

'She'll be fine,' agrees Johnnie. 'Give her twenty-four hours, anyway. See how she copes.'

'OK then,' says Sophie. 'But don't blame me if you get snowed in.'

Jess and Johnnie exchange another glance. 'I won't,' she says. 'Thanks.'

258

After supper, they watch television and talk about the new scheme. Oliver and Johnnie work out an email to send to Guy, setting out some new ideas and suggestions.

'Remember,' warns Oliver, 'that he mustn't know that I'm too involved yet. He needs to be so keen and excited that he doesn't care where the funding will come from.'

'I should have thought he was at that stage long ago,' says Sophie.

'We must allow him his pride,' says Oliver.

Johnnie goes off to the Growlery to send the email and make some phone calls, and comes back in time to say goodnight to Jess.

He gives her a kiss and murmurs, 'Tomorrow morning, after breakfast,' in her ear. She smiles and nods.

Oliver and Sophie, with Popps, walk Jess to the sail loft and check that it's warm and that she has everything she needs. Sophie draws the curtains in the big room to keep it warm but, once they've gone, Jess draws them back. The moonlight drenches the room in a cold white light, which is chopped into fractured slivers in the black water. She stands for a moment, gazing on the magic of the night, and then goes quickly up the little staircase and into the warm cosiness of her bedroom.

*　　　*　　　*

Jess wakes to that strange but now-familiar

sensation that there are other people with her in the sail loft. She washes and dresses quickly, then goes out onto the gallery-landing, and down the stairs into the big room, and all the while she is aware of a presence: the echo of a light footstep on the shining wooden boards, muffled laughter suddenly quenched. She turns her head, listening, but she isn't frightened; she is filled with an odd kind of joyfulness as she makes her tea and carries it to the balcony window. She doesn't slide it open but stands sipping her tea, as she did once before, watching the mist drifting above the river.

As the sun rises so the hills opposite are washed in a brilliant rosy-gold light, which slides gradually down the little sloping fields and along black hedges, chasing the night shadows, until it touches the uneven slate roof-scape of Cargreen. A small rowing boat moves out from the darkness of the walls and slips across the water. As it approaches Jess can see the man at the oars, pulling strongly, glancing over his shoulder now and then so as to avoid the few boats still at anchor out in the channel. This time he doesn't stop. The dinghy comes on, ripples spreading across the water from the rhythmically dipping oars, until it disappears from view almost beneath her.

She takes a deep breath and turns back into the room, waiting. A shadow goes past the window and there is a light knock at the door: he is here at last. He comes towards her, looking at her intently, and she stares back at him, still holding her mug of tea tightly in both hands.

He smiles, as if he has made a great discovery, and taking her by one elbow leads her back to the big window, still gazing at her. She stares too, trying

260

to see her father's features in the face of this tall, broad-shouldered, much older man.

'When did you guess?' he asks. He is so excited, so pleased, that her remaining fears fall away and she laughs.

'I think it was when I first saw you,' she said, 'rowing out of the mist and climbing onto your boat. You waved to me.'

'But we saw each other before that,' he reminds her. 'That very first day you were walking along the river.'

'Yes,' she cries. 'Yes, I remember. You were on your boat and I waved to you.'

'You looked so like Juliet that I wanted to leap into the dinghy and row ashore to you.'

'Why didn't you?' she asks, her smile fading. 'I wish you had.'

He looks at her and there is sadness in his eyes. 'Juliet forbade any contact. She said nobody must ever guess. Even when I knew that your father had come back she held me to my promise. Oh my God, there's so much to explain, Jess. Jess.' He repeats her name. 'I never thought I'd meet you.'

'But what shall I call you?' she asks. 'This is so weird, isn't it? After all this time not knowing you I can't just suddenly call you "Grandpa" or "Granddad".'

'It sounds rather odd, doesn't it?' he agrees. 'Can't you simply call me Freddy?'

*　　　*　　　*

They sit together at the table, looking at the photographs while Jess repeats the story she told to Johnnie.

'Gradually I eliminated them all,' she says. 'Al, Mike, Stephen,'—she points to them in turn—'Johnnie, Tom, Freddy. You and Stephen were the last ones I identified. Kate told me, but somehow, deep down, I had a strong feeling that the one who looked so much like Daddy must be you. Seeing you out on the river, rowing in your dinghy. Somehow you were always just in the shadows, emerging from the mist, silhouetted against the sun, and I could never quite see you. You came and went when I wasn't around. I thought it must be you and yet it seemed that you were the least likely candidate.'

'Ah, but that was my strong suit, you see. I was always littlest, least and last. Young Fred, little Freddy. Nobody took me seriously. My mother was Dickie Trehearne's cousin. My father was killed at the end of the war and Dickie let us have the cottage in Cargreen and treated me as if I were another son, like Al and Johnnie. He was a lovely man. Johnnie's just like him. But Rowena always put me and my mother in the dependent relative category, you see; that's why it would have never occurred to her that the gorgeous Juliet would seriously prefer little Freddy to the glorious Al.'

'Did you know she guessed Juliet was having an affair?'

He shakes his head. 'I was away at sea when Mike met Juliet and got married. When I first saw her I was completely taken aback all standing. She was the most beautiful girl I'd ever seen. I simply couldn't hide my infatuation for her. To my surprise she responded to it. I never quite believed my luck.

'We began this mad affair. Mike was away at sea a lot, which helped, and Rowena invited Juliet here,

262

which was rather tricky because Al was around and we began to suspect we were being watched. She'd slip away and I'd row across and meet her. Sometimes here.' His glance flicks around the sail loft. 'It wasn't like this back then but she loved it here. We were crazily happy. And that was the problem. It was crazy. It was the whole mood, that summer, of magic. Those parties in the sea garden with the little lights glinting in the darkness and reflected in the river. The girls in long dresses and all of us in uniform or black tie. We had style, you know, back then. And then Juliet got pregnant. We knew it was mine. She'd had her period just after Mike went back to sea for six weeks so there was no doubt about it. We didn't know what to do. I wanted her to leave him but she was frightened. We were so young, you see, and she knew that her parents would be furious. Not to mention Mike . . .

'Well, then Al made his move. He'd been watching us, spying on us. He told Juliet that if she didn't sleep with him he'd tell Mike. She was very frightened then. She told him she was pregnant, hoping he'd believe it was Mike's, of course, and that she wasn't well and all sorts of things. He held it over her, though, and she broke it right off with me. She said she simply couldn't cope with it all and that I must promise never to admit anything to anyone. I was a fool to go along with it but Juliet was a strong character and Mike was coming home. Fool that I was, I gave in.'

'And what happened then?'

'Things carried on much as usual. With Mike back home Juliet was safe from Al. The four of us, Mike and Al and Johnnie and I, went sailing. A gale was brewing up. There was an accidental gybe and

263

somehow Al went over the side. We never found his body.'

Shocked, Jess stares at him in silence. 'Do you mean . . .? What are you saying?'

Freddy shrugs. 'Johnnie and I were below. Suddenly there was a lot of shouting and the boat gybed and when we got on deck Mike was bawling out that a squall had hit us and Al had gone over. He threw a lifebelt over the side and we did the man overboard drill but we never found him.'

'Oh my God. Do you think that Mike . . . well, hit him or pushed him over?'

'We're never going to know the answer to that one. Johnnie thinks that Al said something provocative to Mike about Juliet and Mike hit him. Johnnie always maintained, privately to me, that he heard raised voices *before* the boat gybed. But it was almost certainly an accident. Nobody could have done more than Mike did to find Al.'

'How terrible. Oh God. Poor Rowena.'

'Mike and Juliet went to Faslane and then Mike transferred to the Australian Navy. Juliet said that Mike never talked about that summer to begin with, but then they tried for another child and nothing happened. Eventually they had tests and it showed that Mike was sterile. On top of that Patrick, your father, was growing to look more and more like me. Juliet said that as he grew up it became almost intolerable. I begged her to leave Mike and come back to me with Pat but she told me that Mike still loved her and that she owed it to him to stay. She said it was better when Pat came to England, though she missed him terribly. And then he was killed.'

Jess stares at him wordlessly, tears filling her

264

eyes, and he stands up, pushing his chair aside, and holds out his arms to her. She gets up and stumbles into them, weeping.

'I miss him too,' she cries. 'I can't bear it,' and he holds her tightly and mutters against her hair, though she cannot hear the words. She feels the soft cotton of a handkerchief pressed against her cheek and takes it gratefully.

'Sorry,' she mumbles. 'Sorry. Only it's all been such a shock.'

'None of it's your fault,' says Freddy. 'Poor Jess. When Johnnie told me you'd turned up we agreed to play it very carefully. I kept a very low profile but the first thing I did was to phone Juliet. We always stayed in touch secretly, just so that I knew how Pat was, to begin with, and then, later on, you. Neither of us expected that you'd turn up quite like this. We had to assume that you were happy and well cared for but when you came here looking for your past I was determined that Juliet should lift the ban she'd imposed. She agreed to talk. I flew out to the States and she came from Oz and we met up in Los Angeles. She's got friends there. It was the first time we'd seen each other for more than forty years.'

Jess stares up at him in amazement. 'You met her? You met Juliet?'

He shrugs. 'The time had come. No Mike to worry about now. Pat gone. It was time to think about you. To sort things out. I didn't think that it would be too much of a shock for you. After all, you never knew Mike very well and it wasn't going to affect Pat, so I got a bit bolshie about it. I tried to persuade her to come back with me so that we could tell you together, but she wouldn't. She says

265

it's too late for us, and I agree with that, but that she hopes to see you again before too long.'

'You did that for me?'

He smiles at her rather ruefully. 'I suspect I wouldn't have been a very good father, sweetheart, but I'd like to give our relationship a damned good shot. I have Juliet's permission to tell you everything. That's what I went for. And I got it.'

'I don't know what to say.'

'Johnnie's thrilled to bits.'

'He knew all the time?'

'Oh, yes. Johnnie knew everything. After the first shock he thought it would be a wonderful opportunity to set things right at last. But then he began to get a bit anxious about Rowena. He said she was behaving very oddly. He had no idea she knew anything about it, you see.'

'She'd guessed that Juliet had had an affair, and that the baby wasn't Mike's, but she assumed it was Al's child.'

'Johnnie told me that when he phoned last night after you'd talked. It was a complete shock that she knew anything at all. It's been a very difficult few weeks, sweetheart, but Johnnie's just so happy about it. He hates subterfuge and lying, but we agreed that I should keep well out of the way at first. I watched you at a distance.'

'It's been so odd,' she says shakily. 'When I first came it was like I belonged, you see.'

'And you do, sweetheart. It's your home. My family have been here for generations. You've come home, Jess.'

When Johnnie arrives they are sitting together drinking tea, still talking. Jess gets up and goes to him.

'You're my cousin,' she says. 'Freddy's told me. Isn't it wonderful?'

'Yes,' he says, hugging her. 'It's wonderful.'

'We've made a plan,' says Freddy. 'I'm going to take her over to the cottage now and bring her back this evening on the tide. You've been selected from a host of applicants to tell Sophie.'

'And Oliver,' adds Jess quickly.

'Thanks,' says Johnnie drily.

Freddy grins at him. 'We must go while there's still enough water. Come on, Jess. Put on something warm, it's freezing out there.'

They all go down to the dinghy, Jess climbs down into the boat and sits in the stern. Freddy follows her, sitting down midships and shipping the oars. Johnnie drops the painter into the boat and pushes them off.

As Freddy rows, Jess watches him searching for things that will link him with her father. She recognizes the way his hazel eyes crinkle up before he smiles and she sees that the iron-grey hair would have been that same dark brown. He is strong, still vigorous, and she feels a sense of pride in him: this is her grandfather.

'Don't think,' he says, between strokes, 'that I don't want you to stay with me. I hope you will, but it's only fair that you see the cottage first. And anyway, I think I'll have a bit of tidying up to do.'

Jess is glad that he hasn't offered. The sail loft, between the big house and Freddy's cottage, is neutral territory. Just for now it's her own space in which to come to terms with the unexpected happenings of the last few weeks.

'I'm glad you're a sailor, though,' he is saying, and he smiles at her; his son's smile.

267

She feels a strong desire to burst into tears but she smiles back at him, and turns to wave to Johnnie.

Johnnie continues to watch them for a moment, raising a hand in response to Jess's wave, and then turns back towards the house, rehearsing the story in his head.

*　　*　　*

'I knew there was a mystery,' says Sophie, her cheeks pink with excitement. 'I just knew it. And you've kept it a secret all these years.'

Breakfast still isn't over. The shock has made them all hungry and Johnnie has fried a second helping of bacon while Sophie makes more toast.

'There wasn't much to tell until Jess turned up,' Johnnie says. 'Juliet kept in touch in a very low-key way with Fred but he wasn't allowed to write to her in case Mike saw the letters. When Pat came to England Fred begged to be allowed to see him but Juliet was absolutely adamant. Poor old Fred used to tear himself into pieces as to whether he should simply go against her wishes but, at the same time, he had no idea whether it was worse for Pat to go on believing that his father—Mike, that is—didn't love him or to discover that his mother had been . . .'

He hesitates over the word and shovels more bacon onto Oliver's plate.

'Not a good place for poor old Fred,' agrees Oliver. 'And the longer it went on, I expect, the more difficult it became.'

'And the trouble with that kind of mad affair,' adds Sophie thoughtfully, 'is that it's generally based on simple lust, and Juliet probably wondered what it would be like if she actually threw caution to the winds and came back to Fred.'

'We'll bow to your experience in the "simple lust" department,' says Oliver, 'and assume that poor Juliet was between a rock and a hard place.'

'There's much to be said for that theory,' says Johnnie, ignoring Sophie's side-swipe at Oliver's swiftly ducked head. 'Fred was the youngest of us all, even younger than Juliet, and you wouldn't have seen any sign of gravitas in him back then that might have helped Juliet to make the decision to leave Mike. Freddy was in his final year at Dartmouth and Mike was already third hand on *Optimist*.'

'How awful it must have been for her,' says Sophie, suddenly serious. 'Pregnant with another man's child, having to keep it a secret, and then going so far away from home. Poor Juliet.'

'But before that happened,' says Oliver, 'Al died.'

Johnnie looks at him quickly. Oliver finishes his bacon and pushes his plate to one side.

'Sophie was right about there being a mystery,' he says, 'but the point is that Rowena seemed to be tied up in the middle of the mystery.'

'Yes, that's right,' agrees Sophie. 'It was Rowena who made me suspicious in the first place before Jess arrived.'

Johnnie is silent. He puts down his knife and fork and pours some more coffee.

'I had no idea at the time that Mother suspected that Juliet was having an affair,' he says at last. 'Remember, it was one short summer fling, that's all. I knew because Fred and I were so close. More

269

like brothers than Al and I had ever been. We swam and sailed together, went fishing. All our lives we'd been inseparable. Johnnie and Fred. Freddy and John. My father and Fred's mother were cousins and there had always been a close connection. Living across the river from each other, same schools, Dartmouth.

'When Fred told me about him and Juliet I was very envious. Well, you've seen the photographs, you've seen Jess—what young man wouldn't be? But even then I guessed that dear old Freddy was very slightly out of his depth. There was magic all around that long hot summer and he was enchanted. It was all a midsummer's night dream and he was Bottom to Juliet's Titania. When he found out she was pregnant he was horrified and then elated. "She'll have to leave him now," he said to me, but he was reckoning without Juliet's streak of common sense. The dream was beginning to fade and Oberon was on his way home. Mike had specialized and he was now a submariner. Fred was still at Dartmouth. I think Juliet panicked and self-preservation came to the fore. Luckily she was just about in the time frame for Mike to believe the child was his—and anyway, he had no reason to doubt it . . .'

'Until Al told him?'

Johnnie nods at Oliver. 'That's very quick of you. Al had guessed at the affair. He'd spied on them, and now he saw his chance. He'd always fancied Juliet.' He sighs. 'He was the golden boy and he wasn't used to coming second. He threatened her, said that unless she slept with him he'd tell Mike the truth.'

Sophie stares at him in horror. 'Oh God. What

happened?'

'Juliet attempted to reason with him, said she was pregnant and tried to stall him, but there was a bullying streak to Al and I can imagine that she was frightened of him. She told Fred it was all over, that they simply couldn't risk being found out by anyone else. He was desperate but he did as he was told.

'Mike came home from sea and we all went out sailing together, the four of us. Me and Fred. Al and Mike. It was something we did a lot. We'd been racing out in the Western Approaches and were on the way home. Fred and I were below. Al and Mike were on watch.' For a moment he is silent, remembering the raised voices, the boat's sudden gybe. 'Al was steering. The boat gybed and he went over the side.'

Oliver waits but Sophie rushes in.

'Are you saying it wasn't an accident?'

Johnnie rubs his hands across his face. He's thought about it a thousand times. 'How can we know? The wind was really getting up. Mike said a squall hit the boat. It took Al by surprise and the boom knocked him over the side. And that's when Mike began to shout for help. But I heard the voices, you see. I heard angry voices *before* the squall hit the boat. I'll tell you how I think it was, but this is just between us. We were running before the wind and I think that Al would have been steering. Well, suppose Al taunted Mike about Juliet? Suppose a row started and Mike swung a punch at him? Al always liked to stand up to steer. He would have overbalanced, fallen backwards and swung the tiller to port. Result: an accidental gybe. The boom could have knocked Al over the side. Mike would have felt guilty, horrified, which

271

is exactly how he behaved. When Fred and I got up on deck, Mike had flung the lifebelt over the side and was beginning the man overboard routine. We searched all night but we never found him.'

'How ghastly,' says Sophie. 'How utterly awful for you all.'

'And now you believe that your mother knew all the time?' asks Oliver.

Johnnie gives a little groan. 'The trouble is,' he says, 'when you know something to be the truth, you never imagine anyone else seeing it differently. It never occurred to me that she believed that Al and Juliet were lovers. One thing it explains, though, is why Mother was very ready to accept Mike's story about the accident. You'd have expected her to rage about Al's death, to question us all, and blame everyone but Al. But she was very quiet, very guarded. If she believed that Al and Juliet had been having an affair she wouldn't have wanted to expose him; to force Mike to any kind of admissions that might prove embarrassing. But it never occurred to me that my mother had guessed about the affair until we knew Jess was coming and Mother began to behave so oddly. Even then I didn't put two and two together. It was Jess who told me that my mother believed that Patrick was Al's son and that she was his granddaughter. But now my guess is that Mother knew at the time about the affair but she'd assumed that it was Al who was Juliet's lover, not Fred. She'd never have suspected little Fred of being Juliet's lover. Al made no secret of his lust for Juliet and it probably irked my mother that Juliet had chosen Mike over Al. She probably saw much more than I ever suspected. So much of it happened here, in the sea garden, that summer. I'm beginning to think that, over the years, she'd built up a little dossier of facts to support her fragile theory that Juliet had had Al's son. No wonder she was so excited when Jess appeared on the scene. She hoped, at last, that she'd be proved right. It would have been so important to her, you see. She made that little test for Jess with the photograph, hoping that Jess might identify Al through some likeness to her father. Poor Jess, trying to come to terms with her own shock at seeing the photo and trying to protect herself and Fred, quite by accident allowed her to believe it to be true. Mother was so elated that she had an attack and then she died before the real truth could come to light.'

'How extraordinary that Jess should by chance point to Al,' says Sophie. 'Good God! What a muddle.'

'Thank heavens she didn't point to *me*,' says Johnnie. 'Imagine the explaining I'd have had to do!'

Both Sophie and Oliver begin to laugh at his horrified expression.

'And at least poor Rowena died thinking that Jess was Al's granddaughter and that his genes were being passed on. That would have meant a great deal to her,' says Sophie.

'It could have been much worse,' says Oliver. 'From what you've told me about Rowena, if she'd lived she'd have probably demanded some kind of restitution on Jess's behalf.'

'You mean that she should be living here instead of me?' Johnnie nods. 'Then the truth would have had to come out and poor Mother would have been devastated. It was bad enough for Al to be displaced by Mike—but by little Fred? Oh dear.'

273

'And Jess is coping with all this?' Sophie asks. 'I mean, what a shock for her. She comes down to look for her roots and finds them with a vengeance. Thank goodness Freddy is so pleased. And to think of him going out to America to meet up with Juliet. That's just so amazing.'

'Freddy never forgave himself for giving up so easily on Pat. As soon as I told him that Jess was coming to visit us he began thinking of a way to persuade Juliet to break her silence. I wonder, now, whether Juliet suspected that Al had said something to Mother and that she might know the truth, or some of it. Anyway, with the three major players no longer with us she clearly believed that she could break the silence and give Jess and Fred the opportunity to get to know each other.'

They sit in silence, each thinking about this little piece of history; the story that is still unfolding.

'You'll tell the girls?' asks Sophie.

'Of course,' says Johnnie. 'An expurgated version. They'll be delighted. They adore old Fred.'

'And Will and Jess are cousins,' says Sophie contentedly. 'Several times removed, but cousins. He'll be ecstatic.'

'Thanks, Johnnie,' Oliver says, 'for including me in on this. I feel very honoured to be taken into your confidence.'

'Oh, well.' Johnnie pushes back his chair and stands up. 'You're part of the family now.' He looks from Oliver to Sophie and back to Oliver. 'Aren't you?'

'He's on probation,' says Sophie primly.

'Yes, indeed,' agrees Oliver thoughtfully. 'It sounds like I might have rather a lot to live up to.'

'Well, let's have none of that creeping about

274

corridors at night,' says Johnnie. 'I can't stand that sort of thing. Bumping into people when I'm going for a pee. I went through all that when the girls were young. If you're going to do it, then just get on with it.'

'But not when Will or the children are here,' says Sophie firmly. 'Then Oliver stays in his own quarters until we're sure that . . .' She hesitates.

'Until we're sure that this is not one of those affairs that are based on simple lust,' Oliver prompts her. 'What fun it's going to be, finding out.'

'I'm glad to hear you say so,' says Johnnie. 'I like to think of people enjoying themselves like we did. When we were . . . well, you know . . .'

'Back in the day?' suggests Oliver.

Johnnie beams at him. 'Back in the day,' he says.

TAVISTOCK

There is another heavier fall of snow. Coloured lights gleam and twinkle in shop windows; the pannier market is thronged with happy shoppers; in the Bedford the fire is alight in the bar, and the Christmas tree is decorated.

Kate sits at the corner table with Flossie at her feet. Gemma comes back from the bar, where she's been ordering coffee.

'So,' says Kate. 'This all sounds amazing. Guy coming home for Christmas, Johnnie all set to help you make things go.'

Gemma sits down, takes a deep breath. 'I'm not sure I can take it all in. Everything's happened

275

so quickly. To begin with, like I said, Mark went ballistic and then told Guy he didn't want him around. Guy says that secretly Mark's pleased to get out of the whole thing. He just wants to sell the business and settle down with the new wife. Apparently, she has great plans to go travelling. Guy feels guilty, of course, but there've been a few more rows so I think he'll just be glad to finish the packing and get the next flight out. Luckily, because the place was furnished, there's not much packing to be done.'

'But how will you live?'

Gemma makes a face. 'With great difficulty. Oliver is going to get the business set up, Guy's found a second-hand boat and we start advertising sailing holidays and training weekends to begin in the spring. Guy's got to go on a few courses but that's not a problem.'

'Thank God for Oliver.'

'I know. I have to say without his support I wouldn't be feeling quite so gung-ho about it all.'

'And Guy has accepted that Oliver is going to be a shareholder or whatever you call it?'

The coffee arrives and Gemma sits back while the tray is put on the table. Kate begins to sort out cups and saucers.

'It's been slightly tricky,' admits Gemma, accepting her coffee. 'In a way it's lucky that it's had to be done by telephone and emails. Guy has simply had to come to terms with it quickly instead of doing that arguing and walking out and coming back thing that can waste so much time. But it's Johnnie who's really swung it. He's just carried on by assuming that Guy would be only too pleased that his brother-in-law is so excited by the scheme

276

and wants in.'

'Poor Guy,' says Kate. 'You mean he knows he's being set up but because it's to his advantage there's nothing he can do about it.'

Gemma glances at her anxiously. 'I know. It's tricky, and I really don't want Guy to feel that Oliver's patronizing him but I don't see how else we can get it going, do you?'

'Of course not. This is Guy's dream and if Oliver can help him realize it then he's simply going to have to swallow his pride.'

'After all,' says Gemma quickly, 'it'll make money. Everyone is sure of that, including Oliver.'

'Oh, I believe you. Oliver is very canny when it comes to money. It's given me huge confidence to know that he's investing in it.'

'He says that he's been looking for an investment, and this is a really good business idea, but he wants to have some control over Guy in case he gets too carried away. You won't tell Guy that, will you? Anyway, we're investing a hundred and fifty thousand from the sale of the cottage in Brent and Ollie is matching that. He's asked Johnnie to buy a few thousand shares so that he holds the balance of power if ever there's a stand-off between Guy and Oliver. Ollie says that it would be wrong for him to be the majority shareholder so he's putting in the rest as a loan. Guy would rather borrow it from the bank but I'm glad it's coming from Ollie. Less to worry about.'

'I quite agree,' says Kate fervently. 'I can't see Ollie foreclosing on you or forcing you into bankruptcy, or whatever, if it went wrong.'

'Well, that's it. I know Johnnie feels that way, too. It's going to be very hard work and huge fun.'

She speaks with great determination and Kate looks at her affectionately. She can imagine that Gemma knows just how difficult the months ahead will be. This dream of Guy's will come with a price tag that includes a great deal of stress and anxiety. Suddenly she is very pleased to know that Gemma will be working with him, encouraging him, sharing her strength and optimism with him. Guy will need all these things before the dream can become a reality.

'I can't tell you how pleased I am to hear you say that,' Kate says warmly. 'And it's wonderful to think that you'll all be here, back home again.'

'It *is* wonderful.' Gemma drinks some coffee. 'The twins are off their heads with joy. The only thing I'm afraid of now is that the weather prevents Guy from coming home. Flights are being delayed and goodness knows what. Well, that and finding somewhere to live. I can't expect Guy to settle down happily at the Rectory for very long. He wants something in Bere Alston, if we can get it, but there's nothing going for rent at the moment. Johnnie says we can go down there until we find something, and there's some sense in that while we get the business set up, I suppose, but it's a bit awkward, living with other people, whether they're family or friends. Anyway, he's coming up for lunch at the Rectory tomorrow, bringing Oliver and Jess in that four-track of his. Oliver says he can't get his car up the lane but he doesn't sound too upset about it.'

'Johnnie's dropping Jess off with me,' says Kate. 'She wants to do some Christmas shopping and then he's picking her up after tea.'

'And talking about Christmas,' says Gemma,

278

'you'll be coming to the Rectory, won't you? Ma said to be absolutely sure to nail you. It'll be great with Guy home, and the twins. You must be really glad now that you bought the cottage in Chapel Street. After three years of hardly seeing you and the APs we'll all be settled around Tavistock. Gosh, it's going to be good.'

Kate finishes her coffee and pours another one. 'Yes,' she says, 'I'm sure it will be.'

'Oh, and when I told him I was meeting you, Oliver said to remind you that home is where the heart is. Does that mean anything to you?'

Before she can answer, Tom appears. He looks around for them, then comes over and bends to kiss Kate.

'I don't want to break up the party but we ought to get back, Gemma. It's started to snow again. Will you be OK, Kate?'

Kate looks at Tom's face, at the network of lines and his grey hair, remembering Cass saying, 'I never thought he'd turn out to be such a grumpy old man.'

'Of course I will,' she answers. 'It's only a few steps away. It must have been a bit scary coming round by the ford.'

Tom grimaces. 'Thank God for four-wheel drive. Wouldn't have risked it otherwise. Cass says you're welcome any time, Kate. She doesn't want you stuck in Tavistock unable to get to us for Christmas.'

'That's sweet of her. Bit early, though, isn't it? Nearly two weeks to go yet.'

'The twins break up on Thursday,' Gemma says. 'You'll come to the end-of-term service, Kate?'

'Yes, please,' says Kate. 'I wouldn't want to miss

that.'

She remembers those end-of-term services at St Eustachius', whose grey tower she can see between the bare branches of the trees across the road. Parents meeting up with their children in the porch; the matrons, Gert and Foggy, with Mr Wortham. Giles and Guy in their cord shorts and high-neck jerseys, bobbing excitedly in the pew beside her; sweet singing in the choir.

'We'll take a rain check then,' Tom is saying. 'Or a snow check.' He laughs at his little joke. 'If you want to come back with us after the service, Kate, just say the word.'

She smiles at him gratefully. 'Thanks, Tom,' she says. 'But don't you think it'd be a bit of a crush: the boys and Flossie; two school trunks; you, me, Cass and Gemma?'

'Oh, we'll manage,' he says. 'Come on, Gemma. Got everything?'

'Thanks for the coffee,' Kate says. 'Let me know when Guy's due home, assuming he's going to tell anyone this time.'

She sits for a moment when they've gone, thinking about Bruno and wondering what he is doing: working in his study, in the kitchen preparing something for his lunch, walking with Nellie on the cliffs. The bar is beginning to fill up. A tall, elegant woman comes in with a little white dog, which she settles on a towel on one of the chairs before she goes to order coffee. An elderly couple exclaim with pleasure at the sight of the fire and settle themselves at the table beside it. Kate thinks about Tom and Cass, wondering if he will ever persuade Cass to leave the Rectory, and how the return of Gemma and the twins will affect them. She's seen in Tom's face the ravages of grief and remorse, and she thinks about Charlotte, always gentle with the smaller children, such a loving little girl.

Outside the window the snow whirls and dances. Kate finishes her coffee. She gets up, puts on her coat, and she and Flossie go out into the snow.

*   *   *

That evening she telephones Bruno.

'So how is it?' he asks. 'We're practically cut off. Rafe's managing to drive up the lane to the main road with the old Land Rover so he's getting supplies in. It's just so unheard of down here by the sea. Thank goodness we have an unending supply of logs. Are you appreciating the virtues of living in the town?'

She listens to his voice, missing him, thinking of the magical valley filled with snow.

'I'm not sure,' she says. 'It must be very beautiful down there at St Meriadoc.'

He is silent and she knows he is wondering what he should say to her: trying to second-guess her needs and motives. They have been so careful to give each other space, to make no demands.

'Have you decided,' he asks now, 'what you'll do for Christmas? You're definitely not going to Giles and Tessa?'

'No,' she says. 'After all, I've been to them for the last two years, and I think they might like a little break. They all came over last week and we exchanged presents and they've asked me for the New Year. I was hoping to do a pre-Christmas-run quickie but I'm not sure I'll get down to their cove now if it goes on like this.'

'And Cass? She's invited you. And Guy will be home, and the twins.'

'I know,' she says. 'What about you?'

'Well, I shall be here,' he says cheerfully. 'Stuck on my rock, as usual. And it would be very good to have you here with me but I know how you feel about your family. How's Flossie?'

Kate knows that he's trying not to influence her; that he will never come between her and her sons and their families.

'Flossie is fine,' she says. 'She doesn't like the snow much. How about Nellie?'

She imagines the scene: Bruno on the sofa by the fire, legs stretched out, ankles crossed. Nellie will be curled up beside him, nose on tail.

'Nellie is loving it,' he says. 'We went up on the cliff earlier and she positively pranced along. She puts her nose down in the snow and then throws her head up and tosses it about rather like a water buffalo in a river. She's never seen snow before.'

Kate laughs. 'I'd like to see that,' she says.

'Well,' he says, 'there's no reason why you shouldn't. The main roads are still open and Rafe's got the Land Rover. You only have to say the word.'

'I know,' she says. 'I just wish I knew what the word is, Bruno.'

'The word is "love",' he says lightly. 'I shall be here, Kate. Just don't be anxious or feel guilty. Let me know what you're going to do. But the weather isn't going to get better, by the sounds of it. I hope Guy manages to get back in time.'

'Yes,' she says. 'So do I. Jess is coming tomorrow. Then I shall know a bit more.'

'About what?'

'About whether I continue to live here, or rent it out. She might help my decision-making process. After all, I did offer her the cottage as a bolt hole for a while, though she seems to have settled in very happily down on the Tamar. And yet I had such a strong instinct that the cottage was important. Everyone is assuming I shall stay here, of course, now that Guy's coming home and they'll be somewhere close at hand. Anyway, we'll see.'

'It's easier if other people make your decisions for you,' he says, 'but not so life-affirming as making them for yourself.'

*   *   *

As soon as she sees Jess Kate knows that something extraordinary has happened. She can barely get through the door before she starts into her story. As the names tumble out—Juliet and Mike, Al and Freddy—Kate grows more and more bewildered.

'Hang on,' she says. 'Remember it was a long time ago, those parties in the sea garden. You don't mean Freddy Grenvile?'

'He's my grandfather,' says Jess, halfway between tears and laughter. 'My grandfather, Kate. Can you believe it?'

And she explains it all over again, more carefully, and Kate is struck by the strange story; how it began, how it has been played out, and how it is being moved on now by Jess.

'Just think,' Jess is saying, 'if I hadn't won the Award I'd never have known.'

'All these little links,' says Kate, marvelling, 'all interconnecting. And now you've got a huge new family.'

Jess heaves a sigh of huge happiness. 'Some of them will be home for Christmas, if they can make it.'

'So you won't be going to Brussels for Christmas?'

Jess shakes her head. 'I'd already told Mum that I might be spending Christmas in this part of the world or with friends in Bristol. She's fine with that. They have a very social Christmas. I haven't told her about Freddy yet. I want to do that face to face, not that she'll mind much. After all, we never really knew Mike, and it's not her side of the family. Still, I don't want to do it on the phone. And I love Freddy's cottage, Kate. Wait till you see it. It's so sweet and looks straight across the river to the sea garden. And you won't believe this but he does beautiful little sketches. Mostly different kinds of boats, nothing big, but I'm sure I've got my love of drawing from him. He's getting a bedroom ready for me in case I need it but I'm staying in the sail loft just for now. Will can be there with me when he breaks up on Thursday. His parents and little sisters are coming over from Geneva.'

'Well, that answers my question about whether you'll be needing this cottage.'

'I don't think I will but I'm so grateful. If you hadn't offered it I might never have come down here.'

'Well, it's the most amazing thing. So you're right in the story now.'

'I am, aren't I? I wanted to be a part of it and now I really belong. I felt it all along. It was really weird. When you talked about the sea garden and the parties and stuff I could really, like, see it. And the sail loft, I can kind of feel Juliet there with me. I know it sounds crazy but it's true.'

'So you'll be staying on for a while?'

Jess nods. 'And I want to get down to some serious work. I haven't done anything much, though I've got a little idea about something.'

'Oh?' Kate raises her eyebrows.

'Mmm.' Jess grins at her. 'But I'm not saying anything yet. Wait and see.'

*   *   *

'Freddy?' Tom says incredulously for the third time. 'Young Fred? I mean, can you credit it, Cass?'

Johnnie and Oliver have gone back to the Tamar, collecting Jess from Chapel Street on the way. Oliver has packed a bagful of casual clothes and Cass has given him his Christmas present.

'Lucky I did my wrapping early,' said Cass, giving it to him when they were on their own for a moment.

'You don't mind, do you, Ma?' he asked, giving her a hug. 'Look, the truth is that Sophie and I have got a bit of a thing going so I've decided to stay, since they've asked me.'

'Sophie?' Cass was pleased. 'Well, of course you must stay. It's hardly as if you're miles away. It's only this wretched weather making everything so difficult.'

'That's why I grabbed this chance in Johnnie's Discovery. I can't get my car up the drive. I'll see you again as soon as I can get out. Gemma and I Skyped Guy while Johnnie was telling you the family secret and he's catching a flight out on Friday.'

'Thanks for helping them out, lovey.' She kissed

him. 'And have a happy Christmas.'

'I shall. How's Pa taking the news about the lovely Juliet?'

Cass made a face. 'Ructions later,' she said.

And now Tom is pouring himself a drink and saying disbelievingly, 'Freddy, of all people.'

Cass stops herself from saying provocatively, 'You mean when it could have been you?' and says instead, 'But Freddy was a very attractive man.'

'Man!' Tom snorts contemptuously. 'He was barely shaving.'

'You weren't that old yourself.'

'I was older than Fred,' he protests. 'Everyone was older than Fred. Anyway, what d'you mean, "attractive"? He was thin and gangly.'

'He was tall and elegant,' Cass corrects him. 'He still is. I've always rather fancied Freddy. Great legs. Anyway, what does it matter? Clearly Juliet fancied him, too. That's the point.'

Tom shakes his head, swallows down some wine.

'And it's lovely for Jess,' says Cass. 'And the other news is that Oliver and Sophie have got a thing going between them. That's why he's spending Christmas there.'

Tom gapes at her. 'Oliver and *Sophie*?' He thinks of the attractive, fair girl, athletic and strong: one of Betjeman's tennis girls. First Juliet and now Sophie; he groans aloud with envy and Cass begins to laugh.

'Cheer up,' she says. 'I think it was very nice of Johnnie to come and tell us himself. Pour me a drink and stop behaving like a prat.'

'Who's behaving like a prat?' asks Gemma, coming in. She puts an arm round Tom's shoulder. 'What's going on?'

'Nothing,' says Tom shortly. 'Only, apparently,

that Oliver and Sophie are about to become an item.'

'Oh, great,' says Gemma. 'Guy noticed that something was going on. I really like Sophie and I suppose it's about time Oliver committed to someone. I shall be jealous but at least she'll be a part of the team. Listen, Guy should be with us by Saturday if this weather doesn't get worse. It's a pity that he'll miss the end-of-term service but it's just so great that he'll be home for Christmas, isn't it?'

'It's wonderful,' agrees Cass. 'Shall we drink to it?'

*   *   *

At the end-of-term service, the church is packed. The snow lends a very special effect; children's faces glow with the knowledge of trunks and tuck boxes packed and waiting, with the prospect of going home, and of Christmas presents. The atmosphere is charged with joy and the organ prelude sounds even more beautiful than it usually does.

How odd it is, Kate thinks, to be sitting with Gemma and Cass and Tom, whilst Oliver sits across the aisle with Sophie and Johnnie and Jess. Will's blond head bobs beside Jess's dark red-brown one as she bends to hear his whisper.

Kate smiles down at Ben—Julian is in the choir—who beams up at her, and more ghosts appear at his shoulder: Guy and Giles at nine years old, suppressing their excitement, turning to see who is coming down the aisle. On Ben's other side Gemma sits staring forward, her hands clasped on her lap. Just for this moment she is preoccupied;

287

thinking about her family and their future, wondering where they will live and how Guy's dream will work out in reality. She looks slightly vulnerable, thinner; she's lost weight in these last few months. She turns her head, smiles quickly as Ben whispers to her, alert to his touch and his needs, putting her own fears to one side.

As Kate watches Gemma an idea crystallizes in her mind and in that moment she makes her decision. As she does so, her anxieties fall away and she is filled with peace. Oliver glances over his shoulder, catches her eye and winks at her, and she remembers his message: 'Home is where the heart is.' Cass sees him and turns to smile at Kate.

'It's going to be such fun,' Cass said earlier, as they gathered in the porch. 'I wish you were coming back with us this afternoon, Kate. You're just being stubborn.'

'No, I'm not.' Kate shook her head firmly. 'Come on, Cass, it's still ten days to Christmas.'

'Well, Tom's worried about the weather.' She peers about her, looking for him. 'I hope he's managed to park the car. They're forecasting a white Christmas, you know. I don't think the white stuff's just going to go away.'

'Well, I'll have to take my chance.'

'Are you OK?' Cass looked more closely at her old friend. 'It's all good now, isn't it? Guy coming home, Oliver backing this enterprise of theirs. Thank goodness you've bought the cottage so that you'll be close to us all again. It'll be like old times. I thought you were thrilled to bits that Guy is sorted?'

'I am,' Kate said. 'You know I am. It's just been a bit odd lately.' She gave an amused, dismissive

288

snort. 'I think I'm going a bit mad. I've been seeing the ghosts of Christmases past.'

'Oh, lovey,' said Cass, looking suddenly sombre, 'we all do that. Poor little Charlotte, Kate. There isn't a day when I don't think about her, wonder what she would have been like. Whether her children would have been here today with Ben and Jules.' She clutched Kate's arm. 'I have quite a battle with my demons. I have to remind myself about what my old dad used to say: "Don't let the buggers get you down." I still miss him.'

'So do I,' said Kate sadly. 'How I loved him. Oh God, Cass. All these ghosts.'

And then Jess suddenly appeared beside them, beaming, delighted to see them, and the ghosts vanished in the face of her vitality.

'I've got something for you,' she said to Kate, drawing her a little to one side. 'My way of saying thank you for making all this happen. It's not a Christmas present. It's more important than that. If you hadn't invited me, and said I could use the cottage, and then taken me down to the Tamar I wouldn't have known about any of this. How can I really hope to say a sufficient thank you for all of that? Anyway, I hope you like it. And, listen, I was thinking on the way here that you could come down for Christmas and share the sail loft with me and Will.'

Kate burst out laughing. 'Now that's an offer I can almost not refuse, but no, darling. Thank you very much, though.'

'Johnnie's fine with it,' said Jess. 'And Sophie. But I told them I thought you'd rather be with your own family. Anyway, here's your pressie, and thanks again, Kate.'

289

She passed over a small package, and Kate took it, hefted it, raised her eyebrows at the weight of it.

'Very mysterious,' she said. 'Thank you, Jess. We'll get together for a jolly in the New Year.'

And now, sitting in the church, Jess turns to smile at her and Kate smiles back and is filled with happiness and gratitude for this new flourishing of friendship and love that travels both backwards to the past and other loved ones, and forward into the future. She wishes David could have met Jess.

The organ music changes from Bach to the opening chords of 'Once in Royal David's City' and there is a sudden expectant hush. The choir moves forward from the back of the church, the congregation rises to its feet, and Kate picks up her hymn sheet for the first carol.

*　　　*　　　*

The parcel remains on the big table until Kate has changed back into her jeans and some Ugg boots and wrapped herself in a cashmere shawl. She makes some tea and, still shivering, takes the mug along to the living-room. It's been a tricky walk home through the deep, frozen snow, slipping and sliding along, clutching the little parcel.

She puts the mug down on the table and, still standing, begins to pull at the Sellotape, which holds the thick brown paper in place. Having ripped the paper across she sees a box, handmade out of corrugated cardboard. She removes more Sellotape and the box falls apart to reveal a watercolour painting in a delicately carved wooden frame.

Kate picks it up quickly, staring at the painting. A stretch of gleaming water at dusk and, on its far

290

bank, a lawn upon which figures are just visible in the fading sunset: light brush-strokes—the sweep of pale chiffon and a swirl of scarlet silk—indicate slender girls, whilst darker shapes, with flashes of white shirt-fronts, show tall, elegant men. Tiny coloured lights are sprinkled over the scene and reflected in the water. The stone balustrade is sketched in, and here is a larger, bulkier figure, immobile and remote: Circe, gazing downriver. It is the sea garden.

Sitting down, Kate tilts the little painting; she marvels at the way the twilight glow on the water has been captured, the suggestion of movement amongst the shadowy figures, the sense of magic. Now, looking more closely, she sees that there is some writing across the corner of the narrow grey mount: 'Bless you for everything. It's been perfect. Love J.'

Tears well up and overflow. She wonders if Jess knows how hard it's been to part with that other little painting which, by such odd ways, came into her own possession. It seemed right, somehow, to pass it on to Jess as a sign for the future. Now, Jess has responded to it.

Kate balances the frame against a blue ceramic pot of hyacinth bulbs and looks at it again. She guesses that Jess has sketched the scene from Freddy's cottage across the Tamar and then peopled it with those ghosts of the past about whom she has been told. She has stepped into the story and made it her own, and now she will become a part of it; a link in the chain that connects its past with its future.

Kate raises her mug in a toast to Jess's future and to her own. She drinks her tea and reaches for the telephone. Bruno answers very quickly.

'Was it a good service?' he asks. 'A strong aroma of incense, old hymn books and small boy?'

She laughs. 'Small girl, too, these days,' she says. 'And hymn sheets.'

'Ah,' says Bruno. 'Well, it's a long time since I was at school. I wondered whether you might go back with Cass and Tom. More snow is forecast this weekend.'

'I know it is,' she says.

She lifts the painting and studies it. She thinks of Cass and Tom, preparing the Rectory for Christmas, and of Jess and Will in the sail loft down on the Tamar, of Guy and Gemma and the twins.

'Have you made your decision, Kate?' asks Bruno.

'Yes,' she answers. 'I've made my decision. Tell Rafe to get the Land Rover out, Bruno. I'm coming home tomorrow.'

TAMAR

Snow falls heavily on the night before Johnnie's birthday but the day dawns clear and bright. The sun rises, washing the frozen white fields with crimson and scarlet, spilling its light into the wooded valley. The lanes are blocked, airports in turmoil.

'It's going to be just us,' Sophie says at breakfast, after Johnnie has gone out with Popps. 'Fred will bring his little motor boat across but nobody else will get through. With the tide as it is, he won't make it until just in time for tea. Never mind, we'll have to make the best of it.'

'But we could still have Grando's tea party in the sea garden, couldn't we?' wheedles Will, eating bacon and eggs with relish. 'He'd really like that.'

Jess looks at Sophie wistfully. 'It would be rather fun.'

Sophie hesitates, concerned with the wellbeing of the oldest and the youngest of the family.

'I know the temperatures are sub-zero,' says Oliver, 'but this sunshine will warm up the summerhouse. We could put heaters in . . .'

'And string up the coloured lights like we do in the summer,' says Will eagerly.

'Why not?' Sophie gives in. 'I suppose it could get quite cosy in the summerhouse with the sun shining in all day, though it'll be nearly dark by tea-time.'

'But that's what will make it such fun,' says Will. 'That's why we need the lights.'

'OK then. Tea in the summerhouse and then, when we've cut the cake and he's opened his presents, we can have Buck's Fizz to drink Grando's health.'

'Cool,' says Will contentedly.

He's in that exalted state of mind that promises that nothing can be denied him. Jess is his cousin and an artist—he's googled her and been really impressed by what he reads—and he and she have turned the sail loft into a real den. She's teaching him to sketch and paint, and he's done a really good little picture of the *Alice* for Grando's birthday. He beams with the pure pleasure of it all and wipes his eggy plate with a piece of toast.

'And you,' Sophie says to Oliver, 'have been selected from a host of applicants to put up the lights.'

293

'I always get the good jobs,' says Oliver, resigned, reaching for his coffee. 'Are they like Christmas tree lights? Do they go neatly into the box in perfect working order on Twelfth Night, only to reappear the next Christmas Eve tangled and inexplicably bust?'

'There's miles of them,' Will tells him gleefully. 'Grando always says it's like sorting out a bag of knitting.'

'Well, thanks for that,' says Oliver. 'Do I get volunteers?'

Jess and Will both put their hands up and then grin at each other. Johnnie comes in with Popps.

'It's freezing,' he tells them, his scarf still wound around his neck. 'Exhilarating, though. There's been more snow in the night and poor old Popps fell into a drift. I think she deserves a bic, Will. I know I've already had breakfast, Sophie, but I'll have another cup of coffee if there's any going. Warm me up a bit.'

Will slips off his chair to minister to the expectant Popps, who waits imperiously for attention, and Sophie pours Johnnie some coffee.

'Did I tell you that I had a text from Kate yesterday quite late to say that she's safe at St Meriadoc?' says Oliver.

'Just in time, I should say,' says Johnnie. 'I think it's very good of her to give her cottage over to Guy and Gemma. Solves lots of problems.'

'I'm not certain that Kate's heart was ever truly in it,' Oliver says. 'She really bought it because she felt she should get back into the housing market but I never could quite see Kate living in the town. Ma will be disappointed but it's certainly a bonus for Gemma and Guy and the boys.'

'And it's such a lovely little cottage,' says Jess. 'Gemma must be so pleased.'

'She's ecstatic,' says Oliver. 'It's lifted a great worry from her. She was so anxious about where they would all go, and this means they can start straight off all together as a little family without having to be dependent on anyone else. Kate had even put bunk beds in the smallest bedroom so that any of the children could come to stay with her. It's ideal for the twins.'

'Ben and Julian are coming down after Christmas,' Will tells them. 'I told them we can take the Heron out. We can, can't we, Grando?'

'Can't see why not,' Johnnie answers. He picks up his birthday cards and looks at them again, smiling at one, looking more closely at another.

'There would be more if only the post could get through,' says Sophie regretfully.

Will goes to stand at Johnnie's elbow to look at the cards with him. It's true there aren't many cards and he feels sorry for Grando. He smiles up at him and his grandfather smiles back at him.

'Presents at tea-time,' says Will encouragingly.

*   *   *

'I'll shovel the snow off the grass around the summerhouse and make a path of sorts across to the back door,' Oliver offers. 'Have you got a good shovel?'

'We'll still have to wear our wellies to the party,' says Sophie. 'We must've had another three inches in the night. I hope Louisa manages to get home. They've given up on a flight and are catching the Eurostar. They've got snow tyres on their car, she says, so she's hoping they'll get down safely.'

'I feel slightly daunted at the prospect of meeting them all,' says Oliver.

'Jess will distract them,' Sophie tells him. 'I've explained as best I can to Louisa. Will simply thinks that Jess's father was related to Fred. I haven't gone into details but I think that's enough for now, don't you?'

'More than enough.' Oliver pulls on someone's warm coat. 'Thank goodness you have all these spare clothes and boots.'

'Well, it's crazy carrying heavy clothes half across the world each time they all come to and fro. There's always something to put on and enough boots to fit most feet. Put this hat on. You lose most of your body-heat through your head. Did you know that? Don't look at it like that.'

'This is a beanie,' Oliver says. 'You realize if Will sees me in this thing I shall lose all my street cred?'

'Oh, stop fussing and put it on. Come on, I'll show you where the shovel lives.'

'I think I love you,' Oliver says, following her out into the winter sunshine, easing on the tight-fitting hat.

'Mmm,' she says, taking his arm. 'Me, too. But don't let it go to your head.'

'Wearing this thing,' he says, 'there wouldn't be room for it.'

*　　　*　　　*

By four o'clock the sun is setting behind the hills and long blue shadows stretch across the whitened grass. Already the sea garden is *en fête*: the lights twinkle in the frosty air and Circe wears a necklace

296

of holly and ivy. The summerhouse, lit by oil lamps, glows invitingly and on one end of the table Sophie has put the jug of Buck's Fizz within a circle of delicate, fluted glasses.

Johnnie stands beside Circe, sampling the Buck's Fizz. The tide is rising and, as he watches the long-legged avocets scooping and probing for food on the mudflats, he sees a small motorboat set out from beneath the walls of Cargreen: Freddy on his way to the birthday party. Leaning with his back to the balustrade, Johnnie is aware of other shadowy figures in the sea garden: Al and Mike standing together, sharing a wicked joke, Juliet moving gracefully in her long chiffon dress, and Rowena, half-hidden by the corner of the summerhouse, watching them.

Suddenly, from the house, a procession emerges, led by Popps. Sophie comes next, carrying a tray laden with the tea things, followed by Jess and Will, entrusted with plates and forks, and lastly by Oliver carrying the cake. They are all wearing fleeces and gumboots and woolly hats.

Johnnie smiles at the sight of them, and the ghosts slip back into the shadows. Now Sophie has begun to sing 'For He's a Jolly Good Fellow' and the others are joining in. Raising his glass in a salute to the past, he sets out across the snow to meet them.

297